The Doctor Is In

The Doctor Is In

Carl Weber

With

Brenda Hampton

www.urbanbooks.net

Urban Books, LLC
300 Farmingdale Road, NY-Route 109
Farmingdale, NY 11735

The Doctor Is In

ISBN 13: 978-1-62286-628-1
ISBN 10: 1-62286-628-2

First Mass Market Printing January 2018
First Hardcover Printing October 2016
Printed in the United States of America

10 9 8 7 6 5 4 3 2 1

Distributed by Kensington Publishing Corp.
Submit orders to:
Customer Service
400 Hahn Road
Westminster, MD 21157-4627
Phone: 1-800-733-3000
Fax: 1-800-659-2436

Dedication

To all our fans!

Prologue

September 15, 1993

After waiting in the sweltering heat for a bus, the seven-year-old girl and her mother, Sabrina, finally walked into their two-bedroom apartment. Sabrina released her daughter's hand then wiped the sheen of sweat from her aching forehead. She was tired, having just gotten off work then picking up her daughter from school.

"Go put your book bag in your room and tidy it up for me, okay?" Sabrina said, smiling at her daughter, whom she loved more than anything in the world. "Mama is going to fix you some mac and cheese and bake one of your favorites, a chocolate cake."

The little girl was overjoyed. She loved chocolate cake, especially the ones her mother made. Sabrina bent down, tapping her cheek where she wanted her daughter to give her a kiss. Her daughter happily smacked Sabrina's cheek with a big ol' kiss then marched toward her bedroom to do as her mother had told her.

As she turned the corner, she bumped into her father, standing in his dirty drawers, smelling like he had bathed in Hennessy. His scruffy beard resembled a broke-down Santa Claus, and it was evident that he hadn't shaved in months. A mean mug was tightened on his face, and the nappy beads of hair on his chest made him look like a monster to the child. She tilted her head back to look up at her father who, through her eyes, was a giant. She waited on him to say something nice to her, but the greeting she got from him was nothing like the way her mother had greeted her at school that day. Sabrina had tightly embraced her daughter, asked how her day was, and told her she loved her. Her father, on the other hand, spewed, "Where is that bitch at? Did she come in here with you?"

Bitch was the name her father, Joshua, had given her mother. The little girl had become very accustomed to hearing that word around their home. All she knew was her mother didn't like the name, and her parents always got into heated arguments when her father referred to her as a bitch. Today would be no exception.

The girl pointed toward the kitchen, referencing her mother as the person she knew her to be.

"Mommy is in the kitchen making me a cake. You can have some too, Daddy."

Joshua grunted then charged toward the kitchen to confront Sabrina. The girl tiptoed behind him but stopped at the doorway to hide behind the wall. She peeked around it to see what her father was so angry about.

Sabrina sat at the table, stirring cake batter. She looked up when she saw Joshua march into the kitchen with his face scrunched.

"What did you do with the fucking money I gave you to pay the electric bill?" he barked.

Sabrina stopped stirring the batter to address her angry husband, who was trying his best to pick a fight with her. She figured he was still upset about last night, when she had refused to have sex with him because his ass needed a shower, and she wasn't about to keep laying on her back for a nasty, abusive motherfucker who didn't have a job and didn't respect her. His petty drug-dealing money hadn't paid their overwhelming bills in a long time. Everything was behind. Sabrina had been working twelve-hour shifts sometimes, in order for them to stay afloat. In addition to that, her new man had been keeping her busy. He treated her like a queen. So, she didn't have time for Joshua and his mess. Basically, she wanted a divorce.

"I used the money to buy our daughter some clothes and tennis shoes. You've seen the way she's been looking. The kids at school make fun of her, and I want them to stop. We can pay the electric bill in a few days when *I* get paid. What's the big deal?"

"The big deal is, that asshole who works for the electric company showed up today to cut that shit off. I had to dig into my stash and give him something so he wouldn't turn off the electricity. What I don't understand is, when did you start making decisions around here about what gets paid and what doesn't? I decide how to spend our money, and that li'l bitch in there already got enough clothes and shoes. Who gives a fuck about kids making fun of her? She needs to learn how to beat their asses. I bet that'll stop 'em from saying anything to her."

Sabrina disagreed, but she remained silent, getting up from the table to pour the cake batter into a baking pan. Joshua hated to be ignored by her, so he continued his harassment.

"It's funny how you can ignore me, but I bet you don't ignore that nigga you've been giving my pussy to. You were with him last night, weren't you? That's why you didn't want to make love to me."

Sabrina had heard enough. She wished that Joshua would take his drunk ass somewhere and go sit down, but like always, that wasn't going to happen. He wasn't going to chill until he got certain things off his chest, or until he felt satisfied from beating Sabrina's ass.

"For your information, you and I haven't made love in a loooong time, and I haven't been with Stoney in months," she lied. "But if I were with him, how can you blame me? You're fussing about bills, yet you barely pay them around here. If you had to go into your stash for the electric bill, that's good! Dig in it some more so we can get out of this rut. You aren't doing—" Sabrina stopped abruptly and turned around to ignore him again. She didn't want to insult Joshua or damage his ego, which would only escalate the situation.

Joshua walked up behind her and placed a tight grip on the back of Sabrina's neck. The girl looked on with tears in her eyes. She feared what was about to happen next. Her father would do what he did best, and her mother would come out of it looking like a different woman, with a disfigured, bruised face.

"Don't bite your tongue, bitch! Speak up and tell me what you were about to say. What's on your mind? Open your got-damn mouth and say it. Then again, keep it shut before I bust yo' ass clean in it."

Joshua's spit sprayed on the side of Sabrina's face as he yelled at her. She wiped it away, afraid to say another word. Her narrowed eyes, however, spoke volumes for her. She wanted to kill her husband. She had had enough. He deserved to die, and she told herself that this would be the last time he ever put his hands on her.

With the tight grip still on Sabrina's neck, Joshua shoved her head forward, banging it against the edge of a cabinet. Sabrina felt blood trickling down the side of her face. The nasty gash on her forehead made her dizzy, but not dizzy enough where she couldn't reach out and grab a sharp knife from the dish rack on the counter. She swung around to face Joshua with the sharp weapon in her hand.

"Back the hell up now, Joshua! Get your ass out of here. We're not doing this today! I've had enough of your bullshit!"

The girl had seen enough too. She figured things were about to turn ugly. She wanted this to stop. With tears cascading down her face, she ran into the kitchen, still carrying her backpack from school. She stood right in front of her mother, trying to protect her.

"Stop it, Daddy! Stop being so mean to Mommy!"

Sabrina's focus was distracted as she tried to move her daughter out of the way so she wouldn't get hurt. That was when Joshua snatched the knife from her hand. He shoved his daughter out of the way, causing her to skid across the floor. Almost instantaneously, she witnessed her father snatch her mother into his arms and press the sharp blade close to her neck.

Tears welled at the rims of Sabrina's eyes, then they began pouring over. She narrowed them again, to show her repulsion for Joshua. In return, he showed his hatred for her.

"This is for betraying me, bitch. I win; you lose."

Joshua slid the blade across Sabrina's throat, slicing it so fast that when his daughter blinked, she missed it. All she saw was her mother's body crashing to the floor. She ran over to Sabrina, sobbing as she placed her hands on the gaping hole in her mother's neck. That's what she had learned in her first-aid class: adding pressure would stop the bleeding. Unfortunately, it was too late. Sabrina was gone. She had stopped breathing, and the little girl could see that her mother wasn't coming back.

"Mommy, noooo!" she shouted as she tried to lift her from the floor. "No, Mommy, come back."

The girl turned to glare at her father. He stood still, as if cement had been poured over him. No doubt, he was in shock. Even he couldn't believe what he had just done.

"I . . . I'm sorry, baby girl. I didn't mean to do—"

Joshua paused, dropped the bloody knife that he had been squeezing in his hand, and then ran off. Seconds later, his daughter heard the front door shut. She crawled on her hands and knees, making her way over to the phone. She dialed 911, and when the dispatcher answered, the girl begged for someone to come and save her mother.

When the police and ambulance arrived, they found the girl lying next to Sabrina with her arms around her. Sabrina's daughter kicked and screamed as they cautiously pulled her away. She knew she would never see her loving mother again.

Chapter 1

Current day: May 6, 2015

Dr. Kasen Phillips sat tentatively at his desk, listening to Mr. Jones speak. Kasen's heart went out to his terminally ill patient, who was dying of cancer, but the doctor refused to let his emotions spill over. On the inside, he was broken. He hated to see Mr. Jones, whom he considered a friend, suffer like this.

Mr. Jones didn't look fifty-four years old anymore. With sunken cheeks, swollen eyes, and pale, flaky skin, Mr. Jones looked every bit of seventy or eighty years old. Just from looking at him, Kasen's stomach felt as if it were tied in a knot, and his throat ached badly. Several times, he blinked to clear his watery eyes. His hands were clenched together while he gave his patient all of the attention he needed.

"To be honest with you, Doc . . ." Mr. Jones scratched his bald head then licked across his dry lips. "I have no idea how much longer I'll be around. Nonetheless, I wanted to come here and thank you for all of your help. You've been good to me, and your counseling helped me change things. I can only wish that I had been granted additional time to reverse more of the mistakes I've made with my wife, but it looks as if I won't be given that opportunity."

Kasen swallowed then cleared his aching throat. "Whatever you do, make every single day count. I appreciate you for coming here, but go to your family. They need you. Our friendship has meant a lot to me, and I'm not writing you off just yet. You're a strong man. I truly believe that you still have a substantial amount of fight left in you."

Mr. Jones smiled, but deep down, he knew his life was about to abruptly end. "Your words are kind, Doc, but look at me. I have no more fight left. This cancer done kicked my ass and shut me down. If I had known this a year ago, I would have taken extreme measures to change my life around. The best I can do is encourage you to live for today, not tomorrow. Whatever you deem wrong, make it right. Whatever you want to do, don't hesitate to do it. And whomever you want to be with, settle down and do right by her."

As Kasen watched Mr. Jones struggle to stand, he rushed out of his chair to assist him. Mr. Jones shooed him away.

"I'm good," he said. "Where I'm going, I'll be okay, but please continue to pray for me."

Kasen reached out to Mr. Jones, wrapping his arms around him. "I have and will continue to do so. Take care, my friend. I will see you soon."

"If your future travels consist of Heaven, then yes, you will see me one day."

Mr. Jones chuckled as he backed away from Kasen, limping his way to the door. Kasen gazed at him with sympathy in his eyes. He only wished that they were about to go play golf like they used to, or indulge in lengthy conversations while having a drink or two at the bar; but from the looks of it, Kasen suspected that it was probably the last time he would ever see Mr. Jones.

After Mr. Jones closed the door, Kasen returned to his chair, exhausted. He wiped his hands down his handsome face, thinking hard about Mr. Jones's advice: Live for today, not for tomorrow. Those words alone caused him to reflect on his relationship with Raine. She meant the world to him, but Kasen had been procrastinating when it came to fully committing to their relationship. He wasn't ready, but the more he thought about Mr. Jones's situation, the more he realized that he didn't want to lose Raine. Their relationship was more than just a fuck-thing, and Raine had made it clear to him that she deserved better.

At one point, she had threatened to leave him if he didn't make some kind of commitment to her. That was when they moved in together. That move allowed Kasen a little more time to prepare for what he thought Raine ultimately wanted, which was marriage. One day it would happen. Kasen was sure of that, but he hadn't expected his patient's situation to help speed things along. He definitely considered Raine the full package, and only a foolish man would let her slip away. He realized now that it was time to make a move. A big move. A move that would let Raine know he was on the same page as she was.

It wasn't that Kasen had been involved with other women. He hadn't been in quite some time. He had cheated on Raine only one time during their three-year relationship, and after that, never again. Lessons were learned; he didn't like the idea of hurting her. Fortunately, they had managed to work it out. Kasen promised Raine that, going forward, she would be his one and only. He had remained true to that promise, although Kasen was still a flirt. Now, he was a looker who didn't touch. He smiled at women who smiled at him, but he was very aware of his limitations.

So, why not get married? he thought while sitting behind the desk with his index finger pressed against his temple. He was in deep thought about seriously making Raine his wife. It was time. Now or never, before it was too late.

There was a soft knock at the door. Kasen snapped out of his trance to see his receptionist, Voncile Harper, strutting into his office. She was more than attractive, with short layered hair that was cropped in the back, and cat-like hazel eyes that lured in many men. Her mellow-brown skin appeared soft as satin, her five foot six height was just right, and her shapely legs rivaled those of any model. Kasen appreciated women who went the extra mile to look good, and Voncile certainly went above and beyond to look her best every day. When Kasen had hired her two years earlier, he took her skills into prime consideration, but he also knew that her good looks and bubbly personality would do his business good.

As she sauntered closer to Kasen's desk, his eyes scanned her from head to toe. The tight navy blue skirt she wore hugged her slim curves and gripped her heart-shaped ass. Kasen took one last look at the cleavage that was visible through her sheer blouse, but when she cleared her throat, his eyes shifted to hers.

"In deep thought again," she teased. "Every time I come in here, you seem preoccupied."

"I can't help it. In case you haven't noticed, I do take in a lot of information from my patients. I'm always thinking about things they've said to me, and about what I can do to truly help them."

Voncile extended her hand to give Kasen a manila folder. "I totally understand that. And after seeing Mr. Jones leave, I assumed you needed a few minutes to regroup. Your one o'clock appointment cancelled. You don't have another appointment scheduled until three this afternoon. If you want to get out of here for a while and go get some fresh air, I have you covered."

Kasen did indeed need some fresh air after that intense session. This was also the perfect opportunity for him to stop at the jewelers to pick out a ring for Raine. Envisioning her reaction made him feel slightly better, and by the end of the day, he hoped, things would be looking up.

Kasen looked up at Voncile. "You know, you're right. Mr. Jones's situation has taken a toll on me today, so I'm going to take your advice and go get some fresh air. Can I get anything for you while I'm out?"

"Well, I was gonna say that what I would like only my boyfriend can give me, but since we called it quits the other day, that's not likely to happen. So, I guess you can bring me back a salted caramel shake."

Kasen stood up and took his jacket off the back of the chair. "I'm sorry to hear about your boyfriend," he said.

Voncile shrugged. "No big deal. We weren't together that long anyway, and I can do better than him," she said with a flirtatious smile.

He chuckled. They often teased each other around the office. If he was being honest with himself, there was some sexual tension there, but he had never pursued it.

Voncile often wondered why he didn't make a move. She certainly had thrown enough hints his way. She knew that Kasen was involved with Raine, but she always hoped the relationship would run its course so she could step into position by Kasen's side. Obviously this wasn't the right time, because he changed the subject like he hadn't even noticed she was trying to flirt.

"So, a caramel shake today, huh? You usually order chocolate," he said.

"No, not today. I'm in the mood for something a little different. That happens from time to time."

Aren't you ready for something different too, Kasen? Don't you want to dump that boring chick and sample what I have to offer? she thought, wishing she had the nerve to speak the words out loud.

Kasen nodded. "I get it. In fact, I'm making some changes in my life too," he said.

"What do you mean?" she asked, totally unprepared for what she was about to hear.

"Well," he started, slipping into his tailored jacket, "my talk with Mr. Jones really put some things in perspective for me this morning. I've been thinking for a while about taking my relationship with Raine to the next level, and, well, today's the day."

She looked at him with a puzzled expression. Something inside her knew where this was going, but she didn't want to believe it could be true. "Huh?" she said, unable to form a sentence at the moment.

"I'm going to propose," he said happily.

The words were like a punch to Voncile's gut. Her legs suddenly felt like they were made of jelly, and her heart took off like an out of control racehorse. She struggled to keep her composure.

"Voncile, are you okay?" he asked when he noticed the odd expression on her face.

She tried to straighten her face to look more neutral. "Oh, yeah," she said, trying to sound calm. "My blood sugar is probably a little low or something. I guess I shouldn't have skipped breakfast."

He frowned at her excuse. He had been a therapist long enough to know when someone was avoiding the truth. "Blood sugar, huh? Why don't you have a seat for a minute," he suggested.

She inched backward and slumped into the chair where his patients usually sat. Kasen leaned against his desk.

"What's really going on?" he asked.

"Um, I don't know," she answered. "I'm just surprised. I mean, I didn't think your relationship was that serious. You barely talk about her, and when she comes here to visit, it looks like the two of you barely click. Are you sure you're ready to tie the knot? As a friend, I think you really need to think this through more carefully."

Kasen was a little taken aback by her assessment of his relationship. "We don't click?" He shook his head. "I disagree. I don't like to put my personal life on display in the office, so maybe it appears like we don't click, but trust me, Raine and I have been together for a long time, and this is the logical next step for us."

Voncile felt an anxiety attack coming on. It wasn't supposed to go down like this. Was she really too late to make Kasen her man? She had seen the way he looked at her in the office, and she knew he wanted her. She had always thought it was just a matter of time before they were a couple. This marriage thing sure messed up her plans. She took several deep breaths to calm herself.

"If you say you're ready, Kasen, then by all means, go for it. Congrats," she said, hoping she didn't sound too phony.

Kasen could see that something was wrong with Voncile. Trying to get a sense of where the negativity stemmed from, he walked up and stood directly in front of her. Putting a hand under her chin, he lifted her face to look into her eyes.

Voncile momentarily took in the view before her. Everything about Kasen was perfect—from his muscular frame to his tailored suit that fit him so well. The scent of his masculine cologne set her on fire. Normally she loved to gaze into his tranquilizing light brown eyes. In the moment, though, she avoided them so he wouldn't see the jealousy that rested in her eyes. In her opinion, no woman, especially one who gave off such cold vibes like Raine, deserved to have a wealthy, established, and handsome man like Kasen all to herself.

"Listen," Kasen said, "I don't know what's going on here, but is there something you need to talk to me about?" He was thinking that maybe the breakup with her boyfriend was affecting her more deeply than she was ready to admit.

It was moments like this when Voncile truly believed that Kasen cared deeply for her. He was such a gentleman, taking her feelings into account in a way most men didn't. No man had ever made her smile and laugh as much as he did. She treasured the time they spent together at work and hoped that someday they'd be spending lots of quality time together outside of the office. If she didn't get herself together quick, though, she might scare him so much that he would let her go. She certainly wasn't willing to take that risk, so she stuffed down the tears that were threatening to burst forth from her eyes and tried to put a smile on her face.

"I am very happy for you, Kasen," she said as she stood up. "And please know that all I want is the best for you. Your news just took me by surprise. I didn't mean to come off so negative. Marriage is just so serious. You have a lot to offer Raine. I hope she's able to give you all that you need in return."

Kasen stepped back to the edge of his desk, sitting against it. He hadn't expected this kind of a reaction from Voncile. If anything, he would have expected this from his boy Omar, a self-professed lifelong bachelor.

"Of course I know marriage is serious. But it can also be a beautiful thing. My parents have been together since they were twenty years old, and they're still happily married. They work hard at it, and I'm ready to do the same thing with Raine."

"But why so suddenly?" Voncile asked.

"It's not really that fast," he answered. "We've been together for years. But I don't know, I guess seeing Mr. Jones like that today reminded me just how precious life is. I don't want to waste my life being indecisive. God forbid I get sick like Mr. Jones. I don't want to look back and have any regrets. I love her and she loves me, so why not just go ahead and do it, you know?"

Voncile felt like she was ready to explode. She wanted to break down in tears, or else go crazy and break something, but she blinked away her tears then stood with open arms.

"Congrats," she said with a forced smile. "As long as you're happy, that's all that matters. Now, go get your woman her ring, and do not forget to bring back my salted caramel shake. If you forget, I'll never forgive you."

They both laughed, but this was no laughing matter for Voncile. She regretted not telling Kasen how she felt, but she also knew that one day the opportunity would present itself. She would not give up her dream; she would just put it on hold while she worked out a new plan.

Kasen looked at his watch, ready to make a move to the jewelry store. "I'm out," he said. "Wish me luck. I should be back around two, with or without your melted shake."

She flashed another fake smile. "Whatever, boss," she said as he left the office.

As soon as she heard the elevator doors closing and she knew she was alone, she picked up a chair and threw it against the wall to release some of her pent up anger.

"Damn!" she shouted out loud. "Please, please, please don't do this. I hope that bitch has enough sense to say no."

The chair had left a sizable dent in the wall, which she was sure Kasen would question later. She put the chair back where it belonged, hoping she could come up with a reasonable excuse before he returned. In the meantime, she had a phone call to make.

She shut the door to his office and then snatched up the phone on her desk.

"Hey, hey, mmm, I need your help," Voncile said when her friend picked up the phone.

"Depends on what you need."

"I need you to kill somebody. Can you handle that?"

The woman on the other end laughed. "Of course I can. Tell me when, where, and how you want it done. I'll take care of it, especially if the price is right."

"The price is always right. Meet me later. We'll talk more about it then."

Voncile laid the phone back on the receiver feeling a whole lot better. Maybe that darn proposal wasn't such a bad thing after all.

Chapter 2

Kasen sat uneasily on a sofa in Raine's spacious office. She had left for lunch over an hour ago but was expected to return shortly. Raine had no idea Kasen was in her office waiting for her, nor would she be prepared for what he was about to do. This was sudden. But the timing, according to Kasen, felt right. He also felt that Raine needed some good news. She was overwhelmed with the many troubled children who attended the school district where she worked. They both had full plates, but Kasen's plan was for him to propose, for Raine to say yes, and then the two of them could celebrate this evening when they got home.

Kasen was hyped about his plan, but a little tense because he wasn't sure how Raine would respond. While he knew she loved him, he also figured that there was a chance, however small, that Raine could say that she wasn't ready to be a wife, or to give her all to one man. She had been the one to insist on more of a commitment when he moved in with her, but since then, it wasn't like they really discussed their future beyond that move. What if he was wrong to assume that she wanted to take that next step?

This new doubt that had crept in weighed heavily on Kasen's mind as he paced the floor for a while and then plopped back down on the sofa. A sheen of sweat formed on his forehead, and his once-crisp white shirt was now stuck to his skin. He removed his jacket, hoping to loosen up a bit and feel at ease. This was a very intense moment for Kasen. He couldn't help but wonder if all men felt this way when they were about to propose.

"Chill," he mumbled under his breath. "Relax and calm down."

That was what he attempted to do, but before he knew it, he was back on his feet, pacing back and forth again. His thoughts switched to the tiny black box in his pocket. As soon as he had laid eyes on the three-carat diamond ring at the jewelry store, he knew it was the one for Raine. She had superb taste, and he knew she would love it. Just the thought of her opening the box and locking her eyes on the ring made him crack a smile. He felt himself relaxing ever so slightly.

He took a deep breath and walked over to the window. From the third floor, Kasen watched the children playing kickball on the school playground. Several teachers stood nearby, watching their classes. Two police cars were parked at the end of the street, reminding Kasen that Raine worked in a dangerous neighborhood. It was something that had always bothered him, but he knew there was nothing he could say or do to get her away from this place. She loved helping children, and even though her salary as a grade school counselor wasn't great, Raine found her job to be very rewarding. Kasen understood, because he loved helping his patients too. He just wished that Raine would look for a better district to work in, so he didn't have to worry about her driving to and from this rough neighborhood every day.

Raine didn't deny that the area was sketchy. She had been robbed before, almost stabbed once while trying to break up a fight, and she caught a substantial amount of flak from parents who felt as if their bad-ass children had done no wrong. Yet in spite of all that, Raine made it clear that she was exactly where she needed to be. He couldn't argue with that, and just like on many issues between them, he had learned to keep his mouth shut in order to keep Raine happy. She was a bright and accomplished woman, and she was definitely strong willed. He didn't want to be the kind of guy who squashed that confidence. Kasen always wanted her to feel like an equal in their relationship, so if he knew she felt strongly about something, he often went along with it to keep the peace.

Kasen spotted Raine's burgundy Saturn as she attempted to squeeze between two cars parked on the street.

"Don't do it," Kasen warned out loud. "Find somewhere else to park before you hit that—" He paused, shaking his head when he saw Raine's car bump the one in front of it.

He watched her exiting her car, and while she examined the vehicles for any damage, he examined her. His eyes were fixed on his beautiful woman, who made his package swell every time he saw her. Her hips swayed from left to right, and as she bent over to examine the cars, dirty thoughts invaded Kasen's mind.

He couldn't help but to think about their lovemaking session from the night before. It was on point, as usual, and Kasen was ready for round two. He hoped that Raine would be in the mood, before or after his proposal. He moistened his thick lips with his tongue and stroked the fine hair on his goatee. Many women considered

Dr. Phillips to be one fine motherfucker, and with his smooth chocolate skin, a six foot two chiseled frame and mysterious brown eyes, not many could deny it. Raine was well aware of the prize she'd been gifted, but Kasen was the one who felt real lucky today.

He watched Raine as she opted for another place to park her car. Once the car was settled in a more sensible spot, she locked it and then sashayed across the street in her peep-toe high heels and a mustard-colored dress that cut right above her knees. Her square silver-framed glasses, her makeup free face, and her loosely pinned-up hair made her look like a sexy librarian. Kasen was so proud of his woman's good looks.

As he watched her enter the building, he rushed back over to the sofa with a wide smile on his face. He slipped the ring box in to his pocket so Raine wouldn't see it when she walked in.

Showtime, he thought, rubbing his hands together excitedly.

Minutes later, the door swung open and Raine breezed in. When she spotted Kasen on the sofa, she stopped in her tracks. Her man was always handsome, but this day he had a glow about him. Something was different. He looked overly happy to see her.

"Surprise, surprise," Raine said, making her way over to him. He stood and pulled her in for an embrace.

"Mmmm, you always smell so good," she said. "What brings you by? If you brought lunch, sorry, I already ate."

Kasen gave her a light pat on the ass. "Baby, I can bring you breakfast, lunch, and dinner whenever you want it, but that's not why I'm here today." He stepped back slightly to take in all her beauty. She was so damn beautiful.

Their eyes connected, and then Raine's face crumpled into a frown. "Are . . . are you okay?" Raine asked with a slight frown on her face. "All of a sudden, you seem a little off."

Kasen snapped out of his trance. "No, no, I'm good. Just happy right now. Feeling real good and happy about us, that's all."

His words made Raine smile. She leaned in for a kiss that turned into a wet and juicy one she hadn't expected. Kasen's strong arms tightened around her waist. She could feel his package, slowly but surely, rising to the occasion.

"Wow," she said, backing away from Kasen. She wiped a finger across her wet lips then cleared her throat. "I think I'd better go lock the door. The temperature in here is starting to rise."

"It's on full blast, baby. I agree that locking the door may be a good idea."

Raine walked to the door eagerly. She was always in the mood to make love to Kasen. Since both of their schedules were so busy, they took any opportunity they could to indulge in sex.

With sexiness in her stride, she approached Kasen as he started to unbutton his shirt. She placed her hand on his chiseled chest, running her palm along his rock-hard pecs.

"Let me get that for you," she said, assisting with the buttons on his shirt. "And while we're doing this, would you like me on the sofa, at my desk, in the closet . . .? Where exactly would you like to serve me?"

"Hmmm, let's see. The last time it was on the sofa. Time before that, on your desk. Let's shoot for the closet today. It's roomy and real dark in there. I love looking into your pretty eyes, but I'd hate to see them when I put this hurting on you."

Raine giggled then removed her glasses. "Hurt me, baby, please. But make it quick, because I do have a lot of work to do."

She reached for his tie, tugging gently on it like a leash as she directed him over to the closet. Inside were several boxes, school supplies on a shelf, and a broken wooden desk that needed the seat to be screwed on tighter. Raine turned off the light, and in a matter of seconds, she was in her bra and panties.

Kasen stood naked. Curious about the length his steel had grown to, Raine reached out to examine it. She knew he was too well-endowed to fit it all in her mouth, but she was always willing to venture there first. Kasen had other ideas, though, and this time, he took charge. He snatched her into his arms then proceeded to kiss her deeply. During the intense lip-lock, he removed her bra, tossing it over his shoulder. He then fell to his knees, and after easing her panties to the side, he dipped his curled tongue into her honeypot while she was still standing.

She gasped then released a deep breath. Her legs trembled, and after almost losing her balance, she backed up to the wall for support. Kasen lifted one of her legs, resting it over his broad shoulder. He resumed his intimate conversation with her candyland and painted every single inch of her walls with his tongue.

Raine moaned loudly, lightly scratching at his back with her long nails. Saliva started to drip from the corner of her wide open mouth, while on the other end, the sweetness of her juices stirred in his.

"Wha . . . what in the hell did I do to deserve this!" she murmured. "Kasen, baby, what are you doing to me?"

Just so he could answer, Kasen slithered his tongue out of her moist haven. He planted delicate kisses on her thighs before offering a response.

"Nothing special, but in a few seconds, the doctor will be in—all the way in—so prepare yourself."

Raine loved the idea of that, and after he stood tall, she removed her panties and wrapped her legs around him. His hard muscle cracked her secret code, unlocking it like no other man had ever done before. Raine was on a serious high, and so was Kasen. She was by far the best lover he'd ever had. They each had some pretty serious bedroom skills, and in this one stolen moment, they utilized them to the best of their ability.

"I love you," Kasen confessed as he tackled her goodness from behind. She was bent over the desk, holding on for dear life as their bodies rocked together.

"I love you too. And I'm about to show you just how much I doooo!"

The closet echoed with the sounds of enthusiasm expressed from both of them as they came simultaneously. Light sweat glistened on their bodies as their breathing slowed in sync.

They took a few minutes to regroup, and then when the festivities were all done, they settled together on the sofa, fully clothed again. Their hands were clenched together, smiles on full display.

"I don't know what to say about you, Mister, but I'm glad you decided to stop by and bring me lunch."

"If you thought lunch was good," he answered, "wait until you get a taste of dinner."

Raine wet her lips before leaning in to steal a kiss. "Now I'm eager for this day to get a move on so I can get home to you tonight."

They cuddled next to each other for a few quiet minutes before Kasen spoke up again. "You know, I came here for another reason, but every time you're in my presence, I get sidetracked."

She laughed. "Is that a good thing or a bad thing?"

"All good, baby. Definitely all good."

Any nervousness he'd been feeling was gone now. As he gazed into Raine's eyes, he was ready to make his move.

"I have never loved any woman the way I love you," he started.

"I know, baby, and I love you too," she said, giving him a quick kiss.

"But this is different, Raine," he said. "Something happened today, baby, and it was my wakeup call. I had to come see you just so I could tell you what I was feeling inside"—He eased off the sofa and got on one knee in front of Raine— "and to ask you this."

Out came the black suede box, flashing right before Raine's eyes. She looked at it and then shifted her eyes to Kasen. There was a sharp silence before she burst into laughter.

"Oookay. Stop playing, would you?" She covered her mouth to contain her laughter. As soon as she noticed that Kasen wasn't laughing, she rested her hand in her lap and attempted to look at him with a straight face. Still, she suspected this was a joke.

"You need to quit," she continued. "Why would you play with me about something so serious?"

Kasen never would have expected this. Was she really laughing at his proposal? "As you can clearly see," he said as he opened the box so she could see the glistening diamond ring, "this is no joke. I really want you to be my wife." His voice took on a quality that was a little more stern than he would have hoped for a romantic marriage proposal, but his pride was wounded by her reaction.

Raine stared at the diamond for almost a full minute. In fact, she stayed quiet for so long that Kasen started to feel uneasy and got up off his knee. He sat next to her on the sofa.

"Baby," he said, "this is no joke." He removed the ring from the box. "Give me your finger and try this on."

Raine watched as Kasen slid the ring on her finger then kissed the back of her hand. She spread her fingers, gazing at the sparkling stone. *It is real*, she thought. *I'll be damned, this ring is real!* She slowly lifted her head, looking at Kasen with wide eyes. Now she felt bad for having laughed at him.

"Uh, allow me a minute or two to think about what I need to say right now," she said. This caused a frown to appear on Kasen's face.

"Raine," he said, his voice full of tension, "what the hell is going on? Don't you know how much I love you? Why would you think I was joking about this?"

She sighed, feeling a little guilty for her lack of enthusiasm. She didn't want to hurt his feelings. "Baby, look. I love you too. You know I do. It's just that we have soooo much going on right now, and marriage would just, just take us to a level that I don't believe either of us is ready for. I love you with every fiber of my being, but I—no, we—need more time to think this through. Don't you think?"

Kasen's feelings were beyond bruised. He didn't want her to see the hurt in his eyes, so he stepped around her and walked over to her desk. He swallowed an oversized lump in his throat.

He turned to her and said, "Personally, I don't think the timing could be more right. We've been together for three years. I seriously thought this was what you wanted. Before we moved in together you told me that you wouldn't wait too long for me to make my move, and now that I've made it, you turn around and slap me in the face. What's changed all of a sudden?"

Raine stood biting her nails. She really didn't know what to say to make this conversation more comfortable for either of them. The fact was that she wasn't ready to become Kasen's wife. Her career wasn't exactly where she wanted it to be, and that bothered her. Kasen had provided for her in ways that she thought no man would ever do, but she was a woman who wanted to feel like she could take care of herself if it came down to it. With her making only thirty-five thousand dollars a year compared to his two hundred thousand, she wasn't there yet—not by a long shot. It mattered to her, because she wanted to contribute to their lives in a major way. Lying on her back and having his baby wasn't enough. She wanted more out of her life.

She could see the hurt in his eyes, but she didn't even know where to start to explain how she felt. This discussion needed to resume at home, when they would have more time to talk it out and get a better understanding of where their lives were headed.

Raine stepped forward and eased her arms around his waist. She laid her head against his shoulder, feeling how tense he was. "Kasen, I am so madly in love with you. I hope you know that. All I request is that we take some time to think about everything, and then we can talk this through tonight. You know, you did kind of spring this on me out of nowhere," she said, trying to sound lighthearted.

When he didn't laugh or say anything in response, she continued.

"I don't want to rush into anything, and I apologize if I've hurt your feelings. Just . . . just don't be mad, okay? We'll work this out, and one day I'll have the pleasure of being your wife. Does it matter if that's today or somewhere down the road?"

It certainly mattered to Kasen. His ego was crushed, and he was so upset that he was prepared to end it right then and there. Something wasn't adding up. She had been the one pushing him to move in, she was the one who had been playing Russian roulette by stopping her birth control pills, and now all of a sudden she sounded like she didn't want to commit to a life with him. All he wanted from Raine was a simple yes, but she had turned this romantic afternoon into a painful and confusing one.

He pivoted to face her. "I really don't want to spend hours and hours discussing this, but I do need something from you right now. That would be a yes or a no. I know you have some doubts. Hell, I do too. But why wait? We have the kind of relationship many people can only dream of having. . . . Unless there is something you're not telling me. Are you hiding something that I should know about?"

Raine moved her head slowly from side to side. "No, baby. Trust me, I have no secrets. I just want us to be sure before I give you an answer. I want to say yes, but—"

"Then say it. Stop all this nonsense about wanting to be sure and just say it. Will you marry me?"

Raine realized in that moment that the last thing she wanted was to disappoint the man she loved. Regardless of her uncertainty,

Kasen's feelings mattered to her, and she knew just how to repair the hurt she had caused.

"Yes," she said softly. "Yes, I will marry you. Any day, any time, and anywhere."

A bright smile reappeared on Kasen's face. Even though things hadn't gone as smoothly as he would have liked, she had still said yes. Raine was going to be his wife. He embraced her and planted a big kiss on her forehead.

"I'm going to make you one of the happiest women in the world," he said.

"I know you will," she said, but her enthusiasm still didn't match his, and Kasen sensed it immediately.

He raised her chin so he could look into her eyes. "Listen," he said. "I know this is a lot all at once. But we are good together—and good for each other. Everything is going to be fine, and once you get over your nerves, I'm sure you're going to feel the same way."

She nodded and gave him a small smile.

"I'll see you this evening, and I promise we can talk about this some more. It is my hope that after our discussion, your yes will be confirmed," Kasen said, wiping away a small tear that had formed in the corner of Raine's eye.

She shook her head as if she was trying to reassure him. "I'm confirming it now," she said, and they sealed the deal with a kiss.

***

When Kasen returned to his office, Voncile was right there waiting for him. She noticed right away that Kasen wasn't nearly as enthused as he had been before he'd left earlier.

"So, what's the verdict?" she asked, following Kasen into his office. Inside, she was screaming, *Please tell me she said no!*

He swung around to face her. "Good, not great, but I don't want to talk about it right now. My appointment should be here shortly, and I need to make a few phone calls before Mr. Louis arrives. Please shut my door. I don't want any interruptions until he gets here."

Voncile was taken aback by Kasen's demeanor. She was dying to know what had happened. In her opinion, nothing was good, or great, about the mood he was in. She headed toward the door.

"Uh, Voncile," he said, and she stopped, turning around to look at him from the doorway. "What happened here?" he asked, gesturing toward the dent in the wall made by her chair-throwing tantrum.

Voncile squinted at it, hoping she looked perplexed and not guilty. "Huh. I noticed that the other day too. Figured one of your patients threw a tantrum in here, but I didn't bother to ask."

Kasen touched the dent, tilting his head like he was thinking about which one of his patients might have done it. Voncile was on pins and needles, waiting for him to realize that if a patient had done it during a session, he damn sure would have remembered it. Instead, he just shrugged after a few seconds and walked back to his desk. He was acting really weird, but at the moment, Voncile was too relieved to be worried about what was going on with him. She exited his office with a grin on her face.

Chapter 3

"What? She laughed at you? Man, come on. I like Raine a lot, but I've always warned you about her sneaky ways. Something is up with her. You need to dig deep tonight and find out what is really going on before you walk down the aisle having some serious regrets."

After his awkward proposal to Raine, Kasen had felt a need to reach out to his best friend. Omar was stunned to learn that Kasen had proposed, and his two cents full of negativity weren't exactly what Kasen wanted to hear, even if part of him agreed with his friend's assessment of the situation.

"Yeah, I know, man. She didn't exactly act the way you would expect a woman to act when you put a big-ass diamond ring on her finger. I was so out of it after her reaction that I didn't really know what to say, but I plan to get to the bottom of it tonight."

"You're a better man than me, brother," Omar said. "I would've jetted. Hell, I probably would have slapped the shit out of her, too, for laughing—but that's just me."

"You know I don't get down like that," Kasen said. "And when all is said and done, I do love her. You're right about the laughing, though. I don't know what the hell she thought was so funny. I mean, here I was pouring my heart out, and she thought it was a joke. You couldn't have paid me to believe that she would act that way. I always thought she wanted to get married. Did I really misread her so badly?"

"Uh-uh, man. You're a good therapist, and you know how to read your patients well. Maybe this is different because it's someone you love."

"You mean like I was blinded?" Kasen asked.

"I don't know. Not blinded, but, you know, maybe willing to overlook some things that you wouldn't have if she was a patient. That's why I'm saying you need to dig deep with her and don't let anything get by you. Gaze into her eyes, and really read between the lines of whatever she's saying. Hell, play some mind games with her if you need to, but whatever you do, find out exactly where she's coming from."

Kasen sat quietly for a minute, thinking about all the possible reasons Raine might have acted the way she did. Maybe she was just nervous because it was so sudden, he thought. After all, he hadn't really given her any indication that he was thinking about proposing. Or maybe he'd messed up by not making the whole scenario more romantic. He'd seen her watching those sappy bridal shows on TV before, where every last detail is planned out so the bride can feel like a princess. His proposal had turned out more like a booty call with a ring ceremony at the end. Just as he was about to start beating himself up for proposing the wrong way, Omar came out with a totally different point of view.

"Personally, I think you're too good for her. You should've hooked up with that fine bitch in your office—but on second thought, stay away from her. I'm claiming her for myself. She's looking better and better every time I come there. Sometimes I go to your office and pretend I need to see you, just to get another look at that phat ass."

"I'm sure you do," Kasen said, chuckling at his friend's bad-boy behavior. "But clean up your words, man. Women don't appreciate being called bitches. And yes, Voncile is undeniably a beautiful woman. She's just not for me."

"Exactly," Omar said. "That bi—I mean that *lady* is for me. So put in a good word for me, will you?"

Kasen shook his head. "Once a player, always a player, huh?"

"Yup," Omar said proudly.

"You're a fool, but I will put in a good word for you," Kasen said. "Meanwhile, I have to go. Need to wrap up a few things before my patient arrives. I'll give you a call tomorrow to let you know how the night unfolds."

"Can't wait to hear all about it. And don't forget to tell the beautiful one I'm interested. She already knows I am, but she be playing hard to get."

"If it's meant to be, it will be. We'll talk soon, and thanks for listening." He hung up the phone.

Kasen heard a knock on his door. "Come in," he said, thinking it was Mr. Louis, his next patient. He looked up to see Voncile stepping into his office. "What's up?" he asked.

"I have a slight headache. Wondered if I could leave an hour early to go home and get some rest."

"Of course you can. Go home and get some rest," Kasen said.

"Thanks," she said, and then added in what Kasen thought was a rather flirtatious tone, "You know, maybe my headache is because I'm hungry. *Somebody* forgot to bring me back the salted caramel shake he promised to get."

"Oh, shoot. I'm sorry, Voncile. I—"

She raised her hand to stop him. "No need to apologize. I was just kidding. You looked like you had a lot on your mind when you came in," she pressed.

Kasen's face crumpled into a frown, letting her know she was right. "Yeah, I guess I was kind of preoccupied." He tried to recover quickly, putting on a fake smile. "I promise to make it up to you tomorrow. Lunch is on me. Anything you want, I'm buying. We'll lock up the office and go together. How does that sound?"

Voncile was beaming. Her smile was wide and toothy, the kind of smile he wished he had seen on Raine's face earlier. "Sounds good," she said happily. "I'll see you tomorrow. And don't stay too late. I know Raine will be at home waiting for you, especially after your good news today."

"Yeah, well, that's another story, but I promise not to stay late." He pivoted the subject in a hurry, needing to get his mind off of the botched proposal. "Speaking of news, what happened with you and your boyfriend?"

"I am so done with him," she said, not giving any more details. "I'm single for now."

"Okay," he said, a little surprised that she was smiling. She didn't seem to be upset in the slightest. "Well, I have a friend, a close friend, who's interested in you."

Now the smile fell off her face. "Let me guess," she said, frowning. "Omar, right?"

Kasen understood her reaction to a certain extent, because Omar could come on a little too strong when he was interested in a woman. But that was still his boy, and he wanted the best for him. He had faith that his friend could tone it down with the macho player stuff if he needed to. "He's a really nice guy, Voncile. I think you should at least go out on one date with him. I guarantee you that you'll have fun."

She scrunched up her nose like something smelled bad. "No, thank you. He already asked me out on a date. It's not that he's bad looking or anything like that, but I just can't see myself with a man like him."

"Meaning?" Kasen asked, feeling protective of his friend. He knew Omar could be a little heavy-handed with his approach, but Voncile's reaction was a little too dramatic as far as he was concerned.

"Meaning I'm simply not interested. And please don't ask me again. This whole thing feels a little pushy," she said.

That stopped him in his tracks. He still didn't know why her reaction was so strong against Omar, but he definitely didn't want to cross any kind of lines and offend her. She was his employee, after all, and potential sexual harassment claims were not a joke. "Sorry. I won't ask again," he said, raising his hands defensively. "I'll let him know that you're not interested. Now, go home and take care of that headache. See you tomorrow, and be prepared to eat well."

That reminder of their lunch date was all it took for Voncile's mood to lift.

"Oh, I'll be prepared," she said happily. "You have a good night, now."

Voncile left the office looking practically giddy—not like someone with a bad headache— but Kasen still had a lot on his mind. Voncile had wished him a good night, but in truth, he had no idea how the night would go. Kasen sat there feeling as if some things in his relationship with Raine were about to change. His intentions were to make the best of it that night, but he wasn't going to hold back on Raine like he had done earlier. He wanted her to know the disrespect he felt, and if she wasn't on board with the marriage thing, he needed specifics as to why.

Kasen's appointment with Mr. Louis was another successful one. Mr. Louis had a fetish for wearing women's clothing, and for the past three weeks, Kasen had assisted him with getting in touch with his deepest feelings. Kasen suspected that Mr. Louis was leaning toward becoming a woman, even if he hadn't admitted it to himself yet. It was amazing to Kasen how many more patients were coming to him to discuss gender issues ever since Bruce Jenner had announced he was becoming Caitlyn.

"I know that by being completely honest with you, I can begin to be real with myself," Mr. Louis said. "This is just so hard, Doc, and I'm afraid to break out of this shell I'm in and let everyone see the real me."

"In due time I hope you will feel more comfortable. When you're ready, you won't have to fight this anymore. I think you will be surprised by how comfortable you'll feel, as hiding who you really are only prolongs your misery and prohibits you from being the person you know you are deep inside. But until you feel ready to open up to your friends and family, I'm here for you."

Mr. Louis patted his chest and released a deep breath. "Thank you," he whispered with tears in his eyes. "You have no idea how good it feels to speak to someone who truly understands my situation."

Kasen was masterful at his job. He knew how to make people feel that he really cared, but it wasn't an act for him. He truly did care about his patients and their problems. Now it was time for him to pack up for the day and head home to deal with his own issues.

In his car, he tried to call Raine to let her know he was on the way. He tried not to read too much into the fact that she didn't answer either the house phone or her cell. He even allowed himself a momentary fantasy that she was naked in the tub, waiting for him to come in so she could surprise him with some bomb-ass make-up sex.

Forty-five minutes later, Kasen parked his BMW in the four-car garage of the immaculate house he shared with Raine. It had set him back a pretty penny, but to come home to this every day felt worth it. The modern four-bedroom house with plenty of windows to let in a beautiful, natural light sat on an acre of well-manicured land. Kasen liked his privacy, so he had chosen a house that was far away from the city. It was decorated with contemporary furniture, shiny marble floors, and plenty of gadgets that made the entire place unique.

He checked to make sure the alarm was off, then he touched one button to turn on every light on the lower level. Before going up the floating staircase, he used a remote to flick on the mounted fireplace. The music was next, and with the same remote, he pressed a button that spilled sweet melodies throughout the house.

"Raine," he shouted as he walked up the steps. "Baby, are you here?"

There was no answer. Maybe she hadn't made it home yet, he thought. He removed his jacket as he passed through the double doors of the master suite. The second his feet touch the plush white carpet, he could tell that something was wrong. The bed covers were a mess, the decorative pillows were scattered around on the floor, and a broken glass lay on the carpet next to a big red wine stain.

He suddenly felt very disoriented. Raine was usually so meticulous. She would never leave the bedroom in disarray like this, and a stain on her white carpet? That would have freaked her out. Something was very wrong, he realized, and this feeling was confirmed in a hurry when he glanced over toward the dresser where Raine kept her clothes. Every drawer was pulled open, and as he stepped closer to it, he realized that every single drawer was empty. He whirled around and headed toward her walk-in closet with dread growing in the pit of his stomach. His worst fear was confirmed when he opened the door and saw nothing but the hangers where her clothes used to be.

He raced into the bathroom, worried that he might actually throw up, and that was when he spotted the worst thing of all. The ring he had given Raine that afternoon was in the bathroom, sitting in the water at the bottom of the toilet bowl.

"What the fuck?" he shouted, reaching in to retrieve the ring without hesitation. He wiped his hands on a towel and headed out of the bathroom, pacing wildly as he tried to put the pieces of this scene together in his mind. He just could not comprehend the thought that Raine might have packed up and left—until he spotted the letter on his nightstand and read the proof she had left him.

Kasen,

I'm sorry I had to do this, but you need to know that I have no regrets for leaving like this. After today, I realized that I couldn't go on like this. I couldn't continue to look into your eyes, make love to you every day, and pretend that our relationship was solid. The truth is, I refuse to spend the rest of my life with a man who I believe has been unfaithful to me. I have proof that you have been, and your whorish ways have caused me, in return, to be unfaithful to you. I never thought that I could love another, but the new man in my life has opened my eyes. He has truly been there for me, and today I decided to choose him over you. I didn't want to be here when you got home, simply because I knew you would try to talk me out of leaving. But please know that my decision is final. This is a done deal, and you'll be wasting your time if you ever come looking for me. The ring is one that I always dreamed of having, but under the circumstances, please do what you wish with it. Feel free to give it to one of your lovers, or place it on the finger of a woman who will accept you for the way you are. I am one woman who won't, so good-bye, Doctor. Have a nice life.

Raine

Kasen did his best to read the letter through the tears that were forming at the rims of his eyes. It was difficult for him to swallow the huge lump that felt lodged in his throat. He knew that their relationship wasn't perfect, but it wasn't anywhere near the way that Raine had described it in the letter. The last time he had cheated on her was a few years ago, not long after they had met. It wasn't anything serious. He'd met a chick at a bar, had sex with her that night, and that was it. She wound up stalking him for a couple of weeks, and then the chick found out who Raine was and told her about it. Kasen had some serious explaining to do, but when all was said and done, Raine had forgiven him. At least he thought she had.

Now he realized that she had probably never trusted him after that incident. How else could she think that he had numerous other chicks on the side now? It was utterly ridiculous, in his mind. Sure, she complained that he flirted too much, and she was probably right about that. How could he not, when his job provided easy access to so many lonely and vulnerable women? Sometimes, when he was acting in a way their partners weren't, listening to all their problems and paying them compliments, they responded with adoration in their eyes. On a few occasions Kasen had let his ego get the best of him and flirted with a female patient, but he was quick to check himself before things became unprofessional. Raine complained that he went above and beyond to please his patients, especially women, but Kasen assured her that he had learned his lesson after the first time and he would never hurt her like that again. Apparently his assurances had not been enough.

As he read the letter again, his tears were replaced with a rising fury. It dawned on him that she could be using this claim that he was cheating as an excuse. Maybe she didn't even really believe he was cheating, he thought, but instead she made that shit up so she could step out with another dude.

Letting out a roar, Kasen tore the letter in two and threw it on the bed, then paced around the room, throwing wild punches in the air. "Fuck!" he shouted, spit spraying from his mouth. "How in the fuck can she do me like this?"

After a while, he ran out of steam and flopped down onto the bed, panting and sweating. He picked up his phone, prepared to call Raine and spew every bad name in the book, but when he punched her number into his phone, it went straight to voice mail. He tried it three more times, and every time, the same thing happened.

What the fuck? he thought. *Did she block my number now?*

He pitched his phone into the wall, causing the screen to crack. When he bent down to pick up the phone, he caught sight of the background screen, which was a photo of him and Raine from a few months ago, when they had taken an awesome trip to Las Vegas. He dropped to one knee, feeling like all the wind had been knocked out of him. How had they gone from those happy moments to this chaos in such a short time? He just could not wrap his head around it. His watery eyes fluttered, and as his tears picked up speed, he shut his eyes, covering them with a shaky hand.

"Daaaamn," he cried out. "What did I do? I can't believe this is happening. Why me?" Kasen was broken. His heart felt as if it had been ripped from his chest.

As he sat on the floor of his bedroom, still in shock, he began to reflect on everything that had happened that day. Now Raine's reaction to his proposal started to make sense. Of course she wasn't happy about the ring. She'd probably been thinking about the other guy the whole time she was standing there with Kasen's ring on her finger.

He felt like a fool. Why would she have played him like that? Why couldn't she have just been honest with him and told him she didn't want to get married? Didn't she owe him that much honesty after all they'd been through together? Shit, if she had any kind of integrity, she would have told him a long time ago that she thought he was cheating. For a second, he imagined a conversation where she accused him of cheating and he was able to convince her that it wasn't true;

and then their relationship could have been saved. But he was smart enough to realize that it was just a fantasy—a stupid daydream that could never come true with a heartless, cheating bitch like Raine. That was what she had become in his eyes, now that his ego and his pride had been decimated. He didn't use the word *bitch* often, but in this case, it fit her perfectly. He had given her his heart, opened up his home to her, and without a second thought, she had replaced him with another man. That, to him, was unforgiveable. It would be a cold day in the devil's lonely hell before he ever let her back into his life.

Chapter 4

The next morning, Kasen found himself sprawled naked on the living room floor, with an empty bottle of vodka next to him, along with a photo album full of pictures of him and Raine. He remembered getting ready to take a shower the night before, but he figured it was safe to assume that he'd never made it.

As he got up off the floor and entered the bedroom, he could still smell Raine's perfume. Was he imagining the scent, or had her presence really permeated every corner of his room, or better yet, every corner of his life? One glance at the wine stain on the carpet reminded him that even if the scent of her perfume remained, she was definitely gone. From the looks of the mess she left behind, she had left in quite a hurry. He wondered what could have been going through her mind as she raced around there gathering her things. Then he remembered the words of her cruel letter and decided he didn't give a

shit what she had been thinking. All that mattered was that she had ripped his heart out.

The last thing Kasen wanted to do was go
to work, but he never liked to cancel on his
patients, so he went into the bathroom to get
dressed. Besides, work might keep his mind
off of everything that had happened. He took a
quick shower, put on a pair of loose slacks and
a wrinkled button-down shirt that did nothing
for his stallion-like frame, and ran a brush
over his waves. Staring at his reflection in the
bathroom mirror, all he could do was hope that
no one would comment on his puffy eyes or
his unshaven face, because he didn't have the
energy to do anything about them right now. It
took everything he had just to mentally prepare
for the long day ahead of him.

Kasen arrived at his office at ten o'clock sharp,
and Voncile noticed right away that he appeared
totally out of it. Voncile had never witnessed him
looking so disheveled and distraught. She called
his name, halting his steps before he opened the
door to his office.

"I don't mean to pry, but are you okay? You
look awful."

"No, I'm not okay, and thanks for the compliment."

"I didn't mean to say that. What I meant to say is you look *different*. Sorry if I offended you," she said.

"It's not a big deal, Voncile," he said with very little energy in his voice.

His zombie-like demeanor worried Voncile a little, but he obviously didn't want her to pry, so she changed the subject. "So, Dr. Fields called to say that he was sending a young lady your way this morning. He said she's in dire need of your assistance. I wasn't sure if you wanted me to pencil her in, but he stopped by to give me her number, as well as her file. Are you able to meet with her?"

Dr. Fields and Kasen were always recommending patients to each other, often when one doctor felt the other might be better for a particular patient. Kasen knew Dr. Fields wouldn't send a patient his way unless she really needed help, so he didn't want to disappoint his colleague or this potential new patient in need of help.

"Sure. Go ahead and call her. What's her name?"

Voncile retrieved the file from the top of her desk and handed it to Kasen. "Her name is Patrice Davenport. Dr. Fields said good luck with this one." Voncile resisted the urge to roll her eyes, but Kasen still heard the cynicism in her voice.

He glanced at the patient file, skimming the first page, which stated that Patrice had left her first appointment with Dr. Fields after just five minutes. Apparently, she didn't feel they connected. This woman sounded like a handful for sure, but Kasen was a little disturbed by the attitude Voncile was displaying. He preferred to approach every one of his new patients with an unbiased opinion. He wasn't quite sure what was up with Voncile, but after what he had been through the previous night, he didn't have the energy to confront her about it, so he chose to let it slide.

"Thanks. Call her and see if she can come right away. I'll be in my office," he said and walked away without waiting for a response.

Kasen entered his office still feeling completely out of it. He walked sluggishly to his desk and plopped in the chair. He tried to read the rest of the file that Voncile had handed him, but within minutes, his mind drifted back to his own issues. With Raine on his mind, he massaged his forehead and closed his eyes, thinking about yesterday. He thought about their encounter inside the closet of her office.

All of his senses immediately went to that place. He could imagine the sweet taste of her nectar, and the soft, juicy feeling of her walls gripping him tightly. He imagined the sound of her moans as he slid deeper inside. As much as he wanted to forget about her, his mind would not let him. He laid his head on the desk and squeezed his eyes shut tightly, trying to block out the images of her naked beauty. How could someone so beautiful be capable of causing so much pain?

A knock on the door startled him, and he lifted his head from the desk, wiping away the saliva that had pooled in the corner of his mouth. As he jumped up from the chair, he caught sight of the clock and realized he'd fallen asleep in this position. What felt like only a few minutes had actually been an hour. He plucked at his wrinkled shirt and smoothed the front of his rumpled pants.

"Come in," he called out, thinking it would be Voncile who came in.

Instead, he caught sight of Patrice Davenport as she entered, causing his eyes to grow wide.

"Are you sure it's okay for me to come in?" she asked. "I didn't see anyone at the front desk, so I knocked on the first door I saw."

Kasen's eyes scanned the super-sexy woman who damn near brought him back to life. Her sandy-brown hair was brushed into a sleek ponytail, and her slanted eyes drew him in like a magnet. She rocked a soft blue criss-cross halter dress that displayed a healthy portion of her firm breasts. Her makeup was on like a work of fine art, and her mocha skin looked as if it had been dipped in baby oil. For a few merciful minutes, Kasen's thoughts of Raine were washed away.

He was almost speechless, but managed to invite the gorgeous woman to have a seat.

"Anywhere?" she asked, shifting her eyes from the chair to the chaise.

"Wherever you'd like."

Kasen studied her as she sashayed to the chair in front of his desk. His eyes were glued to her, until she was planted in the seat. She crossed her legs, causing her dress to slide to the side and reveal her cellulite-free, toned thighs.

Kasen extended his hand to hers. "Dr. Kasen Phillips," he said. "I understand you didn't have a successful experience with Dr. Fields, but I hope you feel okay speaking to me this morning."

Patrice shrugged then licked across her full lips to moisten them. "I'm perfectly fine with speaking to anyone who can help me. I just didn't get that vibe from Dr. Fields, you know?"

Kasen nodded. "Dr. Fields is a very competent doctor, but sometimes it just happens that a doctor and patient don't click. It's not anyone's fault; it just is. Hopefully you and I can develop the kind of connection that you're looking for in a therapist. Why don't you start by telling me what you're here for?"

"I'm kind of in a rut," she started. "I'll be the first to admit that I need some major help."

Kasen eased back, situating himself comfortably in the chair as he clasped his hands together. "Recognizing that you need help is the first step, and I'm here to listen, not to judge. I won't push, and all I ask is that you be honest and as open as you can about your situation. Doing so will enable me to offer you the best advice possible."

"I intend to be honest," she said, fidgeting with her hands. She glanced down at Kasen's desk and saw the file with her name on it. "I guess you already know my story from Dr. Fields, huh?" she asked.

"Actually, I just received this file a little while ago and I haven't had a chance to review it," Kasen said. He wasn't about to tell her he had fallen asleep as soon as he started reading her file. For all he knew, he had drooled all over the pages as he slept. "So you can start anywhere you like, Patrice. By the way, is it okay if I call you Patrice?"

"Patrice is fine." She smirked. "Can I call you Dr. Sexy?"

Kasen was taken aback but tried to hide it. He didn't really like it when his patients acted this way, but he had learned to deal with it. The first time he had asked a patient not to do it, she suffered a horrible attack of anxiety because she felt so embarrassed and guilty for overstepping the doctor/patient boundaries. Now he just let it go. Whatever made his patients comfortable, he was down with it, as long as the name wasn't offensive.

"Sure. Why not? Now let's get started," he said.

Patrice jumped right into some pretty deep waters. "I think I'm addicted to sex. I feel out of control. I mean, my friends say this is normal, but why do I feel so guilty? I'm not married, so I can sleep with whoever I want, but the problem is I just can't seem to get enough. All I think about is sex, sex, and more sex. At this point, I'm willing to do anything to get laid."

Kasen listened attentively as Patrice told him of her numerous sex partners. In one week alone, she'd had six different partners and multiple ménage à trois. To her, dick was like food; she couldn't live without it. Size didn't matter, race didn't matter, and neither did a man's marital status.

"I mean, I've had it all from A to Z," she confessed. "And in the moment, I feel like I'm high on drugs. I love being the only woman in the room, and the more men there, the better."

This wasn't the first time Kasen had spoken to a sex addict. He knew all too well that many of their problems stemmed from not loving themselves. Even though Patrice came across as a confident woman, he suspected there was something profound going on beneath the surface.

Kasen spent the next several minutes trying to get her to dig deep and revisit certain instances from her past. As soon as Patrice started to speak about her past, her eyes filled with tears. She became overwhelmed with emotion, refusing to carry on with the session.

"I . . . I thought I was ready to talk about this, but I can't. I'll come back again when I'm ready." She stood and rushed toward the door.

"Patrice, please wait," Kasen called after her, but she ignored him and left.

Kasen felt terrible. He had managed to keep thoughts of Raine out of his head during their session, but he was still worried about his ability to treat his patients in the midst of his own crisis. Were his own issues going to make him a less effective therapist? Kasen had never had to worry about this before. He'd always been so good at getting to the heart of his patients' issues and helping them reach conclusions that healed their hurting souls. Now that he was hurting too, he was afraid it would affect his professional ability. He hoped that Patrice would come back soon and that he would be able to give her what she needed to feel better about herself—for her sake and for his.

Fortunately for Kasen, the rest of his day felt a little more like a typical day. His next appointment was with an older man who was obsessed with playing video games. His two o'clock was a woman who didn't want to leave her abusive boyfriend, and his four o'clock appointment was with a compulsive gambler. In each session, Kasen found he was able to listen and offer advice without letting his mind drift to thoughts of Raine. He felt good about it, but also exhausted from the effort it took. By six, Kasen was ready to call it a day.

He stood by Voncile's desk, holding his briefcase in his hand. "How much longer are you going to be?" he asked.

"Not long at all, but I do need to get out of here and go get me something to eat. A certain someone promised me lunch today, but just like my shake, I guess he forgot again."

Kasen slapped his palm on his forehead. "Oh, shoot. I did forget. Please forgive me. I just have a lot of things on my mind, but I promise to make it up to you."

"You promised the same thing yesterday," she answered, sounding a little snippy for a second, but she caught herself quickly and cleaned up her tone. "Don't worry. All is forgiven. I can tell that you're kind of out it." She reached out and put a hand on his arm. "Whatever is bothering you, please know that I'm here if you ever want to talk."

Kasen wasn't ready to tell anyone what had happened between him and Raine. For one, he was kind of embarrassed. It would be difficult for him to explain how things just simply fell apart, especially since he didn't totally understand it himself. He knew that sooner or later he would have to share the news with his friends and family. He could only imagine what his parents would say about the breakup. As for Voncile, she was a nice person, but certainly not the first one he would share his terrible news with.

"That's nice of you to offer," he said, "but I'm not really ready to talk about it yet."

There was an awkward silence between them for a minute, so Kasen tried to ease it by saying,

"Anyway, as for the promises I keep breaking, you have to tell me how I can make it up to you."

Voncile flashed a smile. "Well, since you asked, how about dinner? I promise I won't question you about anything, although you can feel free to talk to me about anything. I promise not to judge you—and unlike you, I do keep my word," she teased.

Kasen laughed. The truth was, if he went home he'd probably start wallowing in self-pity anyway. Voncile's company might do him some good.

"Sure. Why not?" he said, accepting her offer. "I need to go to the post office and drop off a few packages first, though, so how about I meet you across the street in about thirty minutes."

"I'll be waiting."

Voncile was ecstatic. *Yes! Yes! Yes!* She silently screamed while watching him exit. An intimate dinner with him was right on time.

She had thirty minutes to waste before their dinner date, so she did something she often did when he wasn't around: She went into his office. Walking over to his chair, she rubbed her hands all over the leather, imagining it was his shoulders she was massaging. The Clive Christian cologne he wore infused the entire office. She inhaled, thinking dirty thoughts of him fucking her on top of his desk. *If he only knew how many times I've had an orgasm in his office,* she thought wickedly as she fingered herself into a climax.

As she cleaned herself up in the bathroom, Voncile thought about Kasen's strange demeanor. She wished Kasen had felt comfortable enough to talk to her about why he was so off his game today, but she had an inkling what was bothering him, and it made her super happy. Voncile knew that her time to be with Kasen was coming. Her mission now was to make Kasen forget all about Raine. If it were left up to Voncile, it would be a cold day in hell before that slick bitch had a chance to marry Kasen.

After half an hour, Voncile went across the street and entered the busy restaurant, searching for Kasen. He was already there and had taken a seat at a table near the bar, where he was speaking to someone on his cell phone. She eased her way through the crowded restaurant, bumping shoulders with a few people and eavesdropping on a couple who seemed to be arguing rather than eating. The whole place was too noisy for Voncile, who really wanted to spend a quiet and cozy evening with Kasen, but when he displayed his pearly whites after seeing her coming his way, she was good. She didn't care where she was with him, just as long as they were together.

Kasen held up one finger as Voncile approached the table.

"I'll tell you more about it later," he said over the phone. "You're not going to believe how it all went down. Then again, maybe I should have listened to you from the beginning."

Kasen paused to listen then laughed and said, "I hear you, my brotha. I truly hear you. But I have to go. We'll continue this conversation later for sure." He paused again then ended the call a moment later.

"Sorry about that," he said, standing to pull back a chair for Voncile. "That was Omar. It's always difficult getting him off the phone."

"I'm sure it is, especially when you have a lot of juicy gossip to share with him," she said, hoping he might open up a little bit so she could see where his mind was.

Unfortunately for her, Kasen didn't take the bait. He sat back in the chair and picked up the menu. "I'm really not that hungry, so I'll just have a chicken wrap or something. Feel free to order whatever you'd like."

Voncile scanned the menu quickly then said, "I guess I'll have the bacon cheeseburger, a Cobb salad, fish and chips, and the pasta platter. For dessert, I'm thinking about salted caramel cheesecake and a slice of chocolate cake. Does that sound good or what?" She was hoping to lighten his mood.

"What it sounds like is you're pregnant," Kasen joked.

"No, not pregnant, just hungry. Besides, there is no way in hell that I'm pregnant. Women who have sex get pregnant, and, uh, that wouldn't be me."

Kasen laughed and shook his head. "You mean to tell me that your boyfriend done left you high and dry? I thought you were serious about the last guy."

"Dating, yes. Serious, no. We did have sex one measly little time, but I'm too embarrassed to tell you what happened with that."

Kasen pushed. He enjoyed their open conversation, and he needed a good laugh. "I'm all ears."

"I bet you are, but I'm not going to tell you, because you may want to charge me for your services. Your fees are too high, and I'll be the first to admit that I can't afford to pay you."

"My services are free after five," he said, "so let me hear it."

Voncile flagged down a waiter to order a drink. Before this conversation went any further, she needed to get a little alcohol in her system. "I'll have rum with a little Coke," she said to the waiter who came to the table. "And if you don't mind, we're ready to order."

Voncile ordered a T-bone steak, and Kasen ordered a chicken wrap, along with a shot of Hennessy.

"Okay. Now, where were we?" Voncile asked when the waiter left the table to get their drinks.

Kasen was eager to hear Voncile's story. "Stop teasing me," he said. "Tell me what happened between the two of you."

"You mean what didn't happen. I was hyped; I was ready. I was sooo excited about being intimate with him." She took a deep breath then blew it out in a huff. "I can't believe I'm telling you this, but when he pulled it out, I wanted to cry. I was like, 'Okay, girl, just work with it and do your best.' But after two long strokes, it was over. Then that fool had the nerve to lay there like he had done something."

Kasen was laughing out loud. He almost felt bad for the guy, even though he'd never met him.

"And that was the last time I ever saw him," Voncile said to finish her story.

"Two strokes? Come on, Voncile. You're lying. You can do better than that."

She shook her head adamantly. "I thought he could too, but obviously not. I am telling you the truth, and when I tell you I shed tears that night, I'm not lying."

"So now you're telling me you cried? Cried for what?"

"Because I was highly disappointed. I had never experienced anything so horrible, and don't you dare sit there and act like men can't have bad penises."

"How in the hell am I supposed to know?" Kasen laughed, and so did Voncile. "It's just that the two stroke thing seems far-fetched, and I can't envision you crying just because the sex was bad."

Voncile playfully rolled her eyes. "Well, I did, and two strokes were all I got. Trust me, I counted."

"That's bad. Real bad. But if that did happen, it's a compliment to you. Your stuff must be so good that the man couldn't control himself," Kasen joked.

"Not good, but spectacular. And even you ever want to try it for yourself, just let me know."

Voncile laughed to play down her bluntness, but she wanted to see how Kasen would respond. They kidded around with each other from time to time, but neither one of them had ever put a clear offer on the table.

He definitely paused for a minute, so she knew he'd heard her and understood it was not a joke. But unlike in her many fantasies, he didn't take her up on the offer. Instead, he looked up at the waiter, who was delivering their drinks to the table, like he was grateful for the interruption.

"Thanks, man. Perfect timing," he said as he took the Hennessy from him and downed it in one gulp.

There was an awkward moment between them as Voncile's proposition hung in the air between them. The offer had filled Kasen's head with images of the two of them, naked in his office, but he wasn't about to tell her that. She was a beautiful woman—he had always found her attractive—but he didn't want to take advantage of her. He appreciated the close friendship they'd had, and as tempting as it might be, using her to soothe some of his pain for the night wasn't what he wanted to do. For her part, Voncile figured she had laid the groundwork by putting the offer out there, but she wasn't about to start begging. So, to escape the awkwardness they were feeling, they made small talk until the waiter delivered their food.

"Oh my God," Voncile said, looking at the juicy steak he placed in front of her. "This thing is huge. You've got to help me eat this, Kasen. I had no idea it would be this big."

"Well, if you insist," Kasen said. "Pour on some of that A.1. sauce and gimme a bite."

Voncile happily did as he asked, slicing a piece of steak and reaching across the table to feed it to him. Her eyes remained focused on his thick lips as he ate the steak. She wanted to jump across the table and taste those lips. The way his mouth moved, she could tell he was proficient at eating the hotbox. She didn't mean to stare, but damn, did he have to chew like that? Her pussy thumped from watching him, and in an effort to calm it down, she crossed her legs—tight.

"Now, that was good," he said. "If you can't eat all of that, be sure to pass it to me."

It took all of her self-control not to tell him what she really wanted to share with him. Instead, she continued to feed him more steak, showing him how good she could be to him if given the opportunity.

"Stop spoiling me," Kasen said with a full belly. He was slightly tipsy, too, and extremely tired.

"I don't mind spoiling you," she said seductively. "Whatever you want, all you have to do is ask for it."

Voncile felt good about sending another hint, but Kasen didn't bite. He yawned and stretched his arms in the air.

"What I want is some sleep. I'd better go ahead and get out of here before I fall asleep in the car. Let's get the check and then I'll walk you to your car."

"I'll be fine," she answered, trying to hide her disappointment. "I think I'm going to stay for a while and have another drink."

"Okay," he said, standing up from the table. "Well, you have a good night then. I'll see you tomorrow at the office."

She smiled at him, even though she was disappointed that he was really leaving. As much as she wanted things to happen right away, she knew that it was better to be patient. She didn't want to scare him away by coming on too strong, especially since she already had other plans in place to get her to her ultimate goal. "Thanks for hanging out with me tonight," she said.

"Anytime. This was fun. I'll see you tomorrow."

Kasen opened his wallet, dropping a hundred-dollar bill on the table. He gave Voncile a tight hug before making his way to the exit. Even though he had left, she wanted to jump for joy. She predicted that this was just the beginning of many more interesting nights to come.

Chapter 5

Voncile sat at the table by herself for a while, thinking about how things had gone that night. Kasen might have pretended he wasn't interested in her offer, but she could see in his eyes that he really wanted her. Her biggest hurdle, she knew, would be to get his mind off of that waste of space he called a girlfriend.

Voncile had hated Raine from the first time she met her. She walked into the office like she owned the place, and when Voncile tried to make friendly small talk with her, Raine barely even looked in her direction. When she did bother to speak to Voncile, her tone was always sharp and condescending, like she thought she was so much better than Kasen's secretary. Basically, she treated Voncile like she was a nobody.

The way she treated Voncile was just a part of the problem, of course. The worst part, the most nasty part, was the way she strutted into Kasen's office like some kind of princess when it was obvious she was really coming to get laid.

Sometimes Voncile would stand by the office door to listen in. She could hear the moaning and groaning, the "I love yous" and the sound of Raine slurping on Kasen's package. It was very unprofessional to carry on that way, although Voncile never blamed Kasen. He was a man, and no man had the strength to resist when a woman was offering to get down on her knees and swallow him whole. As far as Voncile was concerned, Raine was totally to blame for the disgusting behavior. That stupid ho was just doing it to make sure she kept this wealthy doctor in her pocket.

In Voncile's eyes, Kasen was always innocent. She felt that he could do no wrong, mostly because of the way he treated her. He was always kind, sweet, and respectful. When she first started working for him, she was blown away by how gorgeous he was, but as soon as she got to know him and realized what a caring person he was, that was when she fell head over heels. Sure, she dated other men, but that was really only to pass the time until she could win Kasen over to her team. That would take some time, but she was willing to be patient. She only felt the need to rush things along once she heard that he was thinking of proposing to Raine. That was when she put together a plan that included

Patrice Davenport, who was waiting for her now in the parking garage.

Voncile got up from the table and left the restaurant, crossing the street to meet up with Patrice. This was the real reason she had waited to be sure Kasen was long gone before she went to her car. The last thing she wanted was for him to see her meeting with the woman he thought was just a new patient in his practice. In truth, Voncile had hired her friend Patrice to pose as a patient and try to keep Kasen distracted. She figured that the more ways she could utilize to get his mind off of Raine, the better. She was determined to do almost anything to make him forget about a woman who was nowhere near good enough for him. She was sure that once that worthless woman was out of his mind, he would be free to finally act on the lustful feelings Voncile knew he'd always had for her.

Voncile got in her car, shutting the door behind her. She was a little on edge from the sexual tension of her date with Kasen, so she reached for a cigarette in her purse. She lit the cigarette, taking several puffs and blowing smoke rings into the air. A knock on the passenger's side window startled her, but she relaxed when she looked over and saw Patrice standing there. She unlocked the door so Patrice could get in the car.

"Please put that away," Patrice griped, fanning away the thick smoke. "I'm about to choke."

"You haven't been in here long enough to choke," Voncile answered, but she opened a window anyway to let the smoke out. "There. Happy? Now tell me how your visit with the doctor was today."

Patrice smirked. "First of all, why didn't you tell me he was so damn hot?"

Voncile snapped her head to the side, catching an attitude. "Let me repeat myself," she said with a stern voice. "I'm not paying you to hook up with Kasen. I'm paying you to keep him occupied. Under no circumstances are you to have sex with him, understand? If you feel as if you can't control yourself, then I will find someone else who is willing to follow the rules. Let me know now if you're in or out." She took another deep drag of her cigarette, purposely blowing the smoke in Patrice's direction.

Patrice rolled her eyes. "Look, don't get your panties all in a bunch, okay? I didn't say I had any plans to fuck the guy. I just meant that he's easy on the eyes, and this is going to be a lot of fun spending time with him." Then, because she couldn't resist jabbing at Voncile, who was obviously in love with this guy, she added, "So much fun that you may not have to pay me. I may have to pay you for hooking me up with him."

Voncile started to curse her out. "Bitch, don't make me—"

Patrice began to laugh, cutting her off. "Don't be so feisty, Voncile. I was only kidding. I am well aware that this is business. Speaking of which, I need my first payment."

Voncile stubbed out the cigarette into the ashtray, then reached into the glove compartment to retrieve an envelope for Patrice.

With a grin on her face, Patrice sniffed the envelope. "I love the smell of money. It always excites me." She opened the envelope, flipping through several hundred-dollar bills. "Thank you. I really needed this. You are always right on time, and I love working with you."

"Same here," Voncile replied. "I'll let you know when I need you again. Maybe early next week."

"Just let me know and I will be there," Patrice said before leaving the car.

This wasn't the first time Voncile and Patrice had worked together to get something they wanted. They had known each other since high school, and there was a trail of schemes, plots, and criminal activity that could send the two of them to jail for a long time. Luckily, neither one was worried about being exposed by the other. Even though they argued from time to time, they had developed a good working relationship, and they trusted each other.

Voncile drove home to her two-story, three-bedroom house. She parked near the white picket fence and went up onto the porch, standing beside the porch swing as she searched for the key in her purse. She noticed that the grass was in need of a cut, and she would have to call the landscaper to find out where the hell he had been. If only she had a man in her life, he could take care of things like that, she thought.

Inside, the entire house was as neat as a pin. No dust. No clutter. No noise. The hardwood floors were polished to perfection, and the traditional décor had cost Voncile a fortune. She left her purse and keys on the coffee table in the living room and climbed the stairs up to the second floor, thinking about the day she would finally be walking up those stairs with Kasen. She couldn't wait for him to share a bed with her, and she looked forward to opening her legs, allowing Kasen to dive right in.

Voncile's guest rooms were usually empty, but one of them had been occupied for the past day by someone she would rather not have as a guest. Some things were just necessary, though, to reach her ultimate goal, so she would put up with this guest, at least for a while. The door to the guest room squeaked as she pushed it open. Inside the stuffy, windowless room, she saw Raine and the sight made her want to laugh out loud. Little Miss Perfect was totally helpless now, with her mouth gagged and her hands tied behind her back. She was also hideous, dressed in a raggedy cotton pajama top that cut right above her knees, with her hair matted, nappy, and tangled. Smudged mascara stained her face where tears had run from her swollen eyes.

Raine was still in total shock that she had been snatched up from Kasen's place and brought here. Voncile had lied, telling her that there was an emergency and something horrific had happened to Kasen. The next thing Raine knew, she had been knocked over the head, and when she woke up, she was in this room. She didn't understand why, until she was forced to write a letter to Kasen, telling him that he was a cheater and she was leaving him for another man. Nothing in the letter was true, but here she was, and there was nothing that she could do about it.

With a wicked smile on her face, Voncile walked up to Raine. She lifted her chin, forcing Raine to look at her. "What is that horrible smell in here?" Voncile asked, wincing. "Did you shit on yourself? If you had to use the bathroom, that's all you had to say. Damn, stinky woman."

Raine moaned, knowing that Voncile couldn't understand her with a piece of cloth tied around her mouth. She kept turning her head in circles, hoping that Voncile would remove the cloth so she could speak.

"You know what?" Voncile said. "I really don't want to hear anything you have to say right now. Let me go take a shower, get me a bite to eat, and then I'll be back so we can chat. Okay?"

Raine nodded like a bobblehead doll. She was trying her best to cooperate with Voncile in the hopes that she would rethink this whole thing and let her go. She never would have guessed that Voncile was this evil. This crazy woman was nothing like the woman Raine had seen at Kasen's office. Kasen had nothing but nice things to say about Voncile, and even though Raine didn't know her personally, she had still viewed her as a decent person—or at least a normal one. Raine had even felt that Voncile was beneficial to Kasen and his practice, so this situation left her totally in awe. She hadn't stopped crying all day.

She wondered if or when Kasen would start looking for her. The phony letter had told him not to bother, so all she could do was hope he would ignore what the letter said. Their relationship was strong and loving. He had to know that she wouldn't just walk away from him, she thought, but then she realized that her behavior the day before might have actually given him reason to doubt her.

She was worried now that her uncomfortable response to his proposal might actually be enough for him to believe all the things Voncile had made her write in the letter. The truth was that she had just wanted a little more time to talk though her trust issues before she committed herself fully to the idea of marriage. Also, she had been keeping a secret from Kasen for a while, and she didn't want to get married before she cleared the air about Omar.

Omar had been trying to push up on Raine for years, and she had never told Kasen about it. That was his best friend, and she figured as long as she kept Omar in check, there was no need to hurt Kasen's feelings by telling him. But Omar had become more aggressive lately. He begged her to be with him, and when that didn't work, he started making threats. He also kept insisting that Kasen was being unfaithful to her, and said he had photographic proof of Kasen's ongoing affairs. Raine was smart enough to be skeptical, but a small part of her wondered if it could be true, so she held off telling Kasen about it until she was sure Omar was lying.

When Kasen had proposed, she was taken by surprise, and she felt a little stuck. She wasn't sure how to address the issue of his possible cheating with Kasen. After having kept it a secret for so long, she didn't feel like she could just blurt out in that moment that Omar was stirring up so much trouble behind the scenes. She needed some time to clear her head and process the whole thing, so that she could decide how she wanted to break the news to Kasen. When she got home, she poured herself a glass of wine and looked through old pictures of her and Kasen together. Each picture reminded her of a beautiful and loving time they'd had together, and the more she saw, the more she realized that this man truly loved her. She finally realized that Omar had been lying, and when Kasen came home, she was going to tell him everything. Then they could go forward with their wedding plans, and she could become Mrs. Kasen Phillips. Instead, she had ended up in this house, on the brink of losing her mind. She hadn't seen Omar yet, but she was sure that he was someway or somehow involved in this too.

Voncile came back into the room, wearing a comfortable housecoat and smelling like fresh peaches from taking a shower. She pinched her nose as she entered the room then looked at Raine, who was still in the corner, trying to free her hands from the tight rope.

"Girl, forget it," Voncile said. "You're wasting your time. Those ropes aren't going anywhere, and even if you do manage to get them off, there is no way in hell that I'm gonna allow you to leave here."

In an attempt to intimidate Raine, Voncile sat directly in front of her with her legs crossed yoga-style. She untied the cloth from around Raine's mouth, watching Raine as she moved her stiff mouth in circles.

"What do you want from me?" Raine asked tearfully. "How long are you planning on keeping me here like this?"

Voncile shrugged. "Hopefully not too much longer, but we'll see. Are you hungry?"

Raine didn't answer as she narrowed her eyes and silently cursed Voncile in her head. That look cost Raine a hard slap across the face. Her head jerked to the side, and her hair shifted into another style from the force of the blow. Voncile pointed her finger at the tip of Raine's nose, speaking through clenched teeth.

"Don't you dare look at me like that. And when I ask you a question, you need to answer. So, let me try this again. Are you hungry?"

Raine's head remained lowered. She had no idea that Voncile was capable of doing something like this. She wondered how far Voncile was willing to go.

"Yes," Raine said in a soft tone. "Yes, I am hungry."

"It's late, but I'm thinking about cooking me some good ol' buttermilk pancakes, cheese eggs, and sausage. I don't have time to make anything like that for you, but I'll think of something. Meanwhile, what about going to the bathroom? You really need to clean yourself up. The last thing I want is you walking around my house smelling like a garbage truck. Do you smell this way around Kasen?"

The one thing Raine could attest to today was that this bitch was crazy. She didn't want to say or do anything else to set Voncile off. Raine knew that she had to be careful with her words.

"I don't smell like this around Kasen. And as for using the bathroom and getting something to eat, I would love to."

Voncile got up and left the room without another word, locking the door behind her. Feeling good about the way her plan was progressing, she danced her way to the kitchen to make breakfast. While flipping pancakes and scrambling eggs, she listened to jazz music, the same kind that Kasen sometimes listened to in his office. It made her think of him and their amazing dinner that night. Those lips were on her mind. She wondered if he was thinking about her as well, or if he was at home trying to cope with losing Raine. She considered calling to check on him, but she didn't want to be too obvious. They weren't really friends outside of the office like that. If she called out of the blue, asking a bunch of questions, he might suspect something. Instead, she planned to act as clueless as she could about the situation, in hopes that Kasen would eventually tell her about his tragic loss. Whenever he decided to spill the beans, she would offer her support to him. She would make herself available, and let him know that if he needed a strong shoulder to cry on, and a place to lay his burdens, she was there for him.

Voncile stacked three pancakes on a plate, along with minimal scrambled eggs and two sausages. She grabbed a little something from the pantry for Raine, and also reached for a big aluminum pot. She could barely climb the stairs with so much stuff in her arms, and when she unlocked the door and stepped into the guest room, she was out of breath. She put the plate on the floor, then the pot.

"You should try carrying all of this upstairs like I did," she said to Raine. "That stuff was heavy, especially that pot. Feel free to use it as a toilet. I'll get you some toilet paper before I go to sleep. And as for something to eat, you're going to love this. I used to have a cat named Daisy. This was her favorite dish. She couldn't get enough of it."

Voncile removed a can of gourmet cat food from her pocket, cracking it open. She put in on the floor in front of Raine, ordering her to dive in. Raine stared at the food in awe. She was too afraid to comment, but the one thing that she was sure of was that she wasn't going to eat a pinch of the cat food. She would starve to death before diving in, as Voncile had suggested.

Voncile got on the floor, sitting in front of Raine again. The maple syrup aroma from her plate roamed underneath Raine's nostrils. Raine's stomach grumbled. She hadn't eaten since the day before, but she would never be hungry enough to eat cat food.

"This is really good," Voncile said with a forkful of eggs in her mouth. "I wish there was enough for you, but unfortunately not. I'm hungry because your ex ate up my steak tonight. We had

fun during dinner, celebrating his breakup with
you. He seems so happy that you left him, and
the names he called you—girl! I didn't know he
could talk like that. Did you know his mouth was
that foul?"

"No," Raine said softly, feeling tears welling
up in her eyes again. "And I don't believe he's
celebrating."

"Then you're a fool, because he is." She pointed
to the cat food with her fork. "Eat up. There's
no telling when you'll get something else to eat
again, so you'd better start chowing down."

This time, Raine couldn't hold back. This was
ridiculous. "I've never had cat food before, and
I'm not going to start eating it today. I do thank
you for bringing me something, but no thanks
to that."

Voncile shot her an evil gaze. After she swallowed the mouthful of eggs, she let Raine have it.
"Just as I thought, you're a little ungrateful bitch.
You don't appreciate anyone doing something
nice for you, and I went out of my way to carry
all of this shit up here for you. But you know
what?" Voncile stood, raking the rest of her food
on the floor. "I will not bring you anything else.
If you get real hungry, eat that. I'm also taking
my stink pot back downstairs. You won't get it
back until you've earned it." Voncile stormed

toward the door. She slapped her hand against the light switch, turning the room pitch black.

Raine heard the click as Voncile locked the door again. She was sick to her stomach and she felt like crying, but she knew she had to hold it together. She had to think of some way to get Voncile to release her, because after another day of this, she wouldn't be able to bite her tongue, and she just might lose her mind.

The next morning, Raine was slumped over on the floor with her arms still tied behind her back. She had been trying to free herself for most of the night, but to no avail. Her whole body felt weak, and her arms were severely sore.

Voncile was determined not to let her get any rest. She unlocked the door then strutted into the room. "Rise and shine," she said loudly. "It's time to wake up. You can forget about getting any more beauty sleep, because the Wicked Witch of the West is here."

Raine's eyes fluttered. Her vision was blurred, and she strained to look at Voncile. As her eyes began to focus, she noticed Voncile was wearing one of her fitted dresses and a pair of peep-toe heels that Kasen had given her for her last birthday. Then she noticed that Voncile was carrying a large pot with her. At first she thought it might be the same pot she had brought in last night for Raine to use as a toilet. But then Voncile stepped closer and dumped the pot full of ice cold water over her head.

"At the car wash," Voncile sang out and danced around Raine. "Whoa, whoa, whoa, whoa, workin' at the car wash, girl."

"Pleeeease," Raine cried out. "Stop doing this! What did I . . . do to you, to make you do this to me?"

Voncile didn't respond. A crooked smile washed across her face, as she looked down at the puddle of water surrounding Raine.

"Can I please have a towel?" Raine barked with anger in her voice. She couldn't help it. There was no way for her to tolerate this. "Something . . . anything to wipe myself off." Raine's pajama top was clinging to her, and she was dying to remove her panties, which had a horrible stench coming from them at this point.

Voncile stepped up to Raine, laughing. Her heels sank in the soggy carpet as she squatted to Raine's level.

"Girl, you look a mess. If Kasen could see you like this, he would be disgusted, wouldn't he? I'll go get you a towel, but let me warn you again. Watch your tone with me. If not, your days here are going to get a whole lot worse. Trust me on that."

Voncile pivoted, quickly leaving the room. She returned in a minute, throwing the towel at Raine's face.

"I'm going to work. I have a little surprise for you later, too, so sit tight and please don't go anywhere," she said with a maniacal laugh. She left the room with the pot in her hand, locking the door behind her and beaming about what she envisioned the evening would bring.

Chapter 6

Kasen was glad it was Friday because he'd had a sleepless night, and he definitely needed some rest. Raine's departure was starting to take a heavy toll on him. Fortunately he only had two appointments in the morning. His intention was to leave around noon, go back home, and go to bed. One whole day was all he needed. Then he could chill for the rest of the weekend and try to figure out the best way forward without Raine.

Regardless of what she had said in her letter, part of him hoped Raine would change her mind and come back to him. He kept waking up in the middle of the night, thinking that he'd heard her come through the door. He swore her scent was somewhere in the house again, but when he looked around, there was no sign of her. She was gone.

Ready to get the day over with, Kasen dragged himself into the office in slow motion. Voncile was already there. Her bright smile always made him feel a little better. To know that he could count on her to keep his office running smoothly during this difficult time was a blessing. He considered her a gem. She never complained about much. In fact, the most she ever did was tease him when he forgot to do something, like when he'd forgotten her shake the other day. Voncile was a pretty easygoing person, and he appreciated that.

Kasen stopped at Voncile's desk. "I wanted to tell you what a nice time I had at dinner," he said. "You have no idea how badly I needed that. Thank you for just being there."

Voncile waved her hand at him as if to shoo away the compliment. "No need to thank me. I'm there for you any time you need it. Any time you want to talk, or just go out and have some fun, let me know."

"I will. And if we do go out, can I bring Omar along? I know what you said about him, but I really think you should get to know him better. Word on the street is he's not a two-stroke man either," he added mischievously.

Kasen laughed, so Voncile forced herself to laugh as well. Her insides were boiling, though. She just didn't understand why Kasen kept trying to force her to be with his friend.

"Even if he was a hundred-stroke man, I still wouldn't want to go on a date with him. You can leave him right at home. I'm only interested in entertaining you."

Yet again, Voncile waited for Kasen to bite, but he didn't. He viewed most of her little comments as jokes, especially since he flirted and joked around from time to time too.

"Okay, I'll back away from the thing with Omar," he said. "The last thing I want to do is offend you, and I definitely don't want to scare you away. I really need you here. You're doing an awesome job. So many of my patients speak highly of you."

Voncile gazed at Kasen as if she had just fallen in love for the first time. She only caught herself and straightened up when he gave her a strange look. Trying to gather her thoughts, she said, "You could never scare me away, so no worries. Besides, I love my job. It's truly the best working for you, and the majority of your patients are so cool."

Voncile's response made Kasen feel good. She always knew the right things to say. He felt so lucky to have her around.

"Back to this thing with Omar," she said, preparing to lay the next step in her trap. "Please tell him not to come in here anymore being so pushy.

You can also tell him that I'm not interested. I met someone after you left last night, and we're supposed to go on a date this weekend."

Kasen wasn't exactly jealous, but he was surprised that she was putting so much emphasis on a date with someone she had only met the night before.

"Omar and I will talk about his pushy behavior, and he's going to be disappointed that he blew it. As for you, young lady, be careful out there. Don't be moving too fast, and always carry mace."

Voncile chuckled as if he was being silly, but inside, she was thrilled that he was showing how much he cared. It made her feel bold enough to extend an invitation. "Hey, a few of my girlfriends are joining me this evening for a card game. We're going to whip up some of our favorite dishes, and some of those girls can really cook. If you're not doing anything, why don't you join us?"

"You know, I am pretty tired, and I was planning to have a quiet weekend. Can I think about it and get back to you later?" Kasen asked. He knew he needed to rest, but part of him was also afraid of being alone, because he knew it would be hard not to be thinking about Raine the whole time. Being with Voncile and her friends might be good for him.

"Okay, but I do hope you decide to come," she said as she bent over to reach for a file she had purposely dropped on the floor. The fitted dress she wore gripped her ass even tighter.

Kasen couldn't help but to zone in on her goods. His eyes scanned all the way down to her pretty feet in a pair of sexy, peep-toe shoes. In an instant, Kasen's face twisted, and any sexual feelings he'd been having were suppressed by his heartache. Voncile's shoes looked exactly like a pair that Raine had. They used to sit in a box at the top of her closet in the bedroom, the closet that was now completely empty. The memory of Raine left him feeling deflated all over again.

"I'll talk to you later, Voncile," he said as he picked up his briefcase and headed to his office with his shoulders slumped.

Kasen sat back in his chair in his office, wishing he could erase all thoughts from his head. He felt a headache coming on, so he opened his desk drawer, pulled out a bottle of aspirin, and tossed back two pills.

"So, you got a problem with calling people back now?"

Kasen looked up to see Omar standing in his doorway. "Come on in, man," he said.

Omar walked in and took a seat across the desk from Kasen. "I thought you were supposed to call me back and finish telling me what happened between you and Raine," he said.

"I was, but things got a little hectic around here. I crashed as soon as I got home," Kasen said, not wanting to admit that he just hadn't been ready to address the truth with his friend. He hadn't wanted to hear Omar say "I told you so."

Omar shrugged like it really wasn't that important to him anyway. "I understand. I've been feeling a little under the weather myself," he said. "But yo, so give me the scoop on Raine, man. What's going on with you two?"

Kasen was hoping the aspirin would start working soon, but he knew that if he started talking about how Raine had left him, then he would never get rid of his headache. "Actually, man, I have a patient coming in soon, so why don't we talk about this later?"

"I hear you," Omar said, standing up to leave. "Let me get out of your way then." He walked toward the door, then stopped before leaving the office.

"Oh, before I go," he said. "Do you think I could borrow a little money? My car is trippin' again. Cost me over a thousand to fix it, and it still ain't really running right."

Kasen shook his head. "I told you a long time ago to get rid of that hooptie. I don't understand why you just won't buy something you can depend on."

"Because money is tight and everybody can't go buy a new car every time something goes wrong with it like you do, Doc," Omar answered with a little hostility in his tone.

Kasen frowned at his friend, wondering where this funky attitude was coming from. Omar picked up on it and dialed back his sarcasm a little.

"Hey, sorry about that. I didn't mean to insult you. I'm just frustrated with my own situation, you know?" he apologized.

"I get it," Kasen said. "How much do you need?"

"You know what? Why don't we talk about it this weekend? We can get together and play a little golf. Maybe before then I can come up with another way to get the money, and then you won't need to loan me nothing."

Kasen wasn't sure he was going to have the energy to play golf with Omar, but he didn't want to disappoint his friend, so he just said, "Yeah, man, I'll call you tomorrow morning."

"Sounds good. Talk to you then. And tell the beautiful one out there I said hello. She wasn't at her desk when I came in."

Kasen nodded, realizing that he would have to tell Omar to lay off of Voncile, sooner rather than later. He'd add that to the list of conversations they needed to have, because he damn sure didn't have the energy to do it now.

Ten minutes after Omar left, when Kasen's headache was just starting to feel better, Voncile was at his door.

"May I come in?"

"Please do."

The second she entered, Kasen's eyes shifted to her shoes. He couldn't figure out why he was so damn consumed by her shoes today; if anything, he wished he had never noticed them.

"Is something wrong?" Voncile questioned when she noticed him staring at her feet.

Kasen's eyes shifted to hers. "No . . . nothing is wrong. What did you need?"

"Well, I have good news for you."

He leaned back in his chair, placing his hands behind his head. "I need some good news. Hit me with it."

Voncile laughed. "Both of your appointments cancelled for today."

"So that means I can get out of here, go home, and get some rest. That definitely is good news."

"Yes, yay for you. You definitely look like you could use some rest. I don't think I've ever seen you looking this worn out."

"Wow. Now there's some brutal honesty for you," Kasen replied, hoping his humor would stop her from prying any further about why he looked so bad.

"Oh, I'm sorry," she said. "I didn't mean to offend you. I'm just a little worried about you, that's all."

"I get it, and I appreciate your concern. I'll be fine," he said. "I just need some rest." *And some answers about why my relationship fell apart,* he thought.

"Well, if you feel like it, you know you're still welcome to come to the get-together at my house tonight," Voncile offered.

"I'll try," Kasen said, not wanting to make any promises.

"Great. We're supposed to meet up around seven o'clock. Hope you can make it. Who knows? It might do you some good. No offense, but I'll be so glad when the old Kasen returns," she said, sashaying out of his office.

Nearly an hour later, Kasen found himself parked outside of the elementary school where Raine worked. He had to see her, even though she had told him not to come after her. After several sleepless nights, he felt he deserved some answers. She had to look him in the eyes and tell him what was up. A stupid letter just wouldn't do. He didn't even care if she broke him down again. He just wanted it done in person.

Kasen sat in his car for a while, his eyes scanning the parking lot for Raine's car. He didn't see it, but sometimes she carpooled with another teacher, so she was probably still in the building.

Kasen turned off his car, but just as he put his hand on the door handle to step out, his cell phone rang. The name on the screen said MR. JONES. Kasen answered it without hesitation.

"Hello, Dr. Phillips." It was Mr. Jones's wife on the line.

"Hi, Mrs. Jones. How are you?" Kasen felt his stomach twist as he asked the question. It couldn't be good that it was his wife on the line and not Mr. Jones himself.

"Oh, I've had much better days, trust me. I just called to tell you that my husband has made his transition to go be with the Lord. Right before he passed away, he reminded me to call you. I wanted to thank you, again, for all of your help." Mrs. Jones paused for a moment to gather herself, and Kasen heard her sniffling away her tears. "I . . . I won't be having a funeral or anything like that for him, per his request."

Kasen took a hard swallow. This, along with the situation with Raine, was too much. "Thank you so much for calling me. Your husband was a very good man. He always told me I was a blessing to him, but the truth is, he was a blessing to me."

"To many of us," his wife added. "And I'm going to miss him dearly."

Kasen passed on a few more encouraging words to Mrs. Jones before ending the call. He hated to get bad news about his patients, especially Mr. Jones, who had just made some courageous changes to improve his life. Kasen said a quick prayer for him, and then exited the car sadly. *Could this day get any worse?*

He entered the elementary school, only to be stopped by a security guard who Kasen had seen several times before.

"What's up, Doc?" the security guard said, shaking Kasen's hand. "What brings you by today? Are you here to see Miss Raine?"

"Yes. Is she in her office?"

"I'm not sure. I haven't seen her in a few days, but you can go upstairs and see if she's in there."

Kasen thanked the security guard then headed up the steps to Raine's office. He didn't know what to expect. As angry as he was with her, he could only hope that he wouldn't have to raise his voice and go off on her. He kept telling himself to stay cool, doubting that he would be able to.

Kasen reached Raine's door and knocked. He waited a minute before knocking again, and still he got no answer.

"Oh, hello, Dr. Phillips."

Kasen turned around to see Mrs. Culbreath, the principal, standing behind him. "Hello," he said, greeting her.

"I was just coming to put these files on Raine's desk for when she returns from vaca—" She stopped abruptly. "Wait. I thought the two of you were on vacation together."

"She may be on vacation, and I would love to be, but I'm not," Kasen said, feeling his anger rising. She must have gone on vacation with the other man.

Mrs. Culbreath looked perplexed. "Oh, I see. I could've sworn that the message she left said she was with you. Maybe I should double check."

"When did she leave a message, if you don't mind me asking? I'm asking because I haven't seen her."

Mrs. Culbreath touched her chest. "Haven't seen her? Is she missing or something?"

He didn't want to alarm her. There was no need for the elementary school to be in an uproar over Raine's nonsense, so he quickly cleared thing up. "No, I don't think she's missing. According to a letter she left me, she kind of broke things off. I thought she might be here so we could talk."

The principal looked pretty uncomfortable now. Maybe she expected him to start going off. "Well, I'm sorry to hear about the breakup. I'm surprised, especially since all Raine talks about is you. But please understand, Dr. Phillips, that I can't allow you to stay in here. You're going to have to leave. If Raine wants to speak to you, I'm sure she will call you."

Kasen took that as the best advice he had received all day. He felt foolish now for chasing after Raine. She'd made it pretty clear in the letter that she didn't want anything else to do with him, not to mention the fact that she had laughed at his proposal. He had always told his patients that if a person didn't want to be with them, there was nothing they could do, and now it was time for him to take his own advice.

"Thank you, Mrs. Culbreath," he said as he turned to leave. "When you see Raine, please do me a favor. Don't tell her I stopped by."

She nodded, looking relieved that he was going. "You have a good day, Dr. Phillips."

Kasen made his way back to the car with his head hanging low. He wasn't an overly emotional man, but this thing with Raine was a hard pill to swallow. With his head now resting on the steering wheel, he thought about Raine, and he thought about Mr. Jones too. Tears welled in his eyes, and after one tear fell, so did another.

Why did she do this to me? he thought as his tears flowed freely. Kasen began to sob. He couldn't remember the last time he had allowed himself to get this emotional. No matter how much he told his patients to open up and bare their souls, he hated to do it himself. Reacting this way made him feel like less than a man. Crying was for punks, his father had always told him, and crying over a woman was a no-no. Kasen couldn't help it, though. His baby was gone. She had moved on with another man, and he was left to pick up the pieces alone.

"I can't believe you did this," he mumbled then sat up straight, trying to pull himself together.

A loud knock on his window startled him. He sucked in a deep breath and snapped his head to the side. A skinny bum with a scraggly beard was peering into the car. Kasen rolled down his window, thinking that he could reach under his seat for his gun if things got dicey.

"Can I help you?"

"Say, man, you . . . you got a quarter? All I need is a quarter or fifty cents to go do my laundry."

Kasen looked at the man's filthy clothes. He needed more than fifty cents if he was going to do laundry.

"A quarter?" Kasen questioned. "What can you do with a quarter?"

"I told you already. My laundry."

"Man, you can't do laundry with a quarter or with fifty cents. I'm going to give you five dollars, and whatever you decide to do with it is up to you. I really don't care, but I do want you to go get some help and get off the streets. You can get hurt out here, and everybody won't be as nice to you as I am right now."

The man licked his lips as he watched Kasen open the glove compartment and then hand him a five-dollar bill. The bum kissed the bill then lifted it up to the sky.

"Thank you, Jesus!" he shouted. "You're a miracle worker. Ask and I shall receive." He looked at Kasen with tears in his eyes. "Bless you, my brotha. You're so kind. If you want, I can sing a little something for you too. Would you like that?"

Kasen couldn't believe the man's excitement over five dollars. He was also aware that the man was trying to coax him into giving him more.

"Jesus is on the mainline," the man sang while clapping his hands and stomping his foot on the ground. "Tell him whuuut you want. Tell him what you—"

Kasen had heard enough. He put his hand up to quiet the man from singing. "I'm good, bro. Nice voice, and all the best to you."

Kasen put his car in drive, but the man kept at it.

"Wait! All right, I can sing another song. Listen to this right here." The man cleared his throat then swallowed. "God is the joy and the strength of my life. He moves all pain misery and strife. He—"

"Yes, He does, sir. Have a good day." Kasen had to laugh at the guy's persistence. Looking in the rearview mirror as he drove away, he saw that the guy was still singing and dancing holding the five dollars high up in the air.

Kasen was actually glad to have run into the guy. It made him think that his situation wasn't the worst thing that life could throw at someone. Women problems could be fixed.

Chapter 7

After Kasen left the office, Voncile sat at her desk for a while, fantasizing about what would happen if he did show up at her house later. She was determined to get a piece of Kasen, and she was willing to put any amount of money on it that his dick was finger-licking good. His stance and the way he strutted said so. The way he danced gave her a hint, too, and the way his package bulged in his slacks confirmed it. Voncile could almost feel it, like she could feel everything falling into place. If Kasen came over that night, he definitely wouldn't be there to play cards. It would just be the two of them alone— with the exception of Raine being tied up in the other room.

After a while, she got up from her desk and went to the restroom. She stared in the mirror at her beautiful face, which resembled her mother's. She missed her mother so much, and just the thought of her brought a tear to Voncile's eye. Then her mind drifted to those horrible years after her mother died, years during which she suffered terribly in foster care. She was a young, motherless girl with no one to protect her.

She thought of Mr. Jeffries, one of the counselors in the foster home. At first he had seemed like a knight in shining armor, rescuing her from the sadness and loneliness that was her life. He told her, "I'll be your daddy. All little girls need a man to protect them," and she fell right into his trap.

Voncile didn't know better. She was happy to go see him. He always had treats for her, and they watched cartoons together. After a while, though, the cartoons turned to porn. He would make Voncile watch videos with him in his office behind closed doors. Then he forced her to do things that the women in the videos did. She knew it was wrong, but she felt trapped and betrayed. This man who had promised to protect her was abusing her and making her feel like trash, yet she believed she had no way out.

Finally, she gathered the nerve to tell a female counselor about it, but instead of making things better, it completely shattered her trust in people. When she finished telling the woman what Mr. Jeffries made her do, the woman jumped up from her chair, but not to rush over and comfort Voncile. She snatched her by the arm and started yelling in her face.

"You listen to me, you little snot-nose bitch. How dare you go spreading stories like that. Don't you dare breathe another word of this to anyone, or next thing you know, you'll have the damn feds busting down the door, closing this place down."

Voncile wiped away her tears and tried to free her arm from the woman's grip.

The counselor continued ranting. "Where do you think you're going if they close this place down? They'll just send you somewhere that's ten times worse." She finally let go of Voncile's arm and sat back in her chair, panting hard from all her yelling and fussing. "Now get the hell out of this office, and don't let me ever hear you say anything like that again."

Voncile bolted from the room and did as she was told. She never spoke another word about the abuse that continued until she finally ran away from the foster home at the age of fifteen.

Still staring at herself in the mirror, Voncile wiped a tear that was sliding down her cheek. She was so glad that time in her life was over. Because of Kasen, she had good things to look forward to. Now she was thrilled, and no one, not one single person, would stand in the way of her happiness.

Voncile returned to her desk prepared to shut down her computer and go home, until she noticed that the door to Kasen's office was open. She stepped into his office, where she saw a man sitting in Kasen's chair with his back turned to her.

"Excuse me," she said.

The man lifted a brown paper bag to his lips, swallowed the last of the liquor, then turned around and tossed the empty bottle into a nearby trash can.

"Omar, what are you doing here?" she asked.

"I take it that Kasen has left the building," he answered.

"He just left."

"Good. I thought you might have left too, but then I saw your purse behind your desk."

"I'll be leaving in a few minutes. As you already know, I have a situation to take care of at home."

"How's that bitch doing?" he asked. "Is she giving you any trouble?"

"She has my whole damn room stinking, but other than that, she's doing better than I thought she would. She won't eat, though. I guess not everyone likes cat food."

Omar chuckled, shaking his head. "Are you kidding me? Did you really offer her some cat food?"

"Yes. I was only being thoughtful," Voncile said wickedly. "I may stop to get her something to eat on my way home, especially since I'm feeling real good today."

"Why's that?"

She shrugged, not wanting Omar to know she had invited Kasen over to her place. "No reason. I just am, and I'll be feeling even better if you show me how much you appreciate all of my efforts. I've done a lot for you, you know. It's just a matter of time before you have all of Kasen's money and assets in the palm of your hands."

For years, Omar had been very envious of Kasen. He had it all: the women, the house, good looks, a rewarding career . . . everything. All Omar wanted was a piece of it, at least in the beginning. He would borrow five or ten thousand dollars at a time, until he felt Kasen developing a little bit of an attitude about sharing the wealth. That was when he decided to devise a plan that would bring Kasen down.

He had always gotten a certain vibe from Voncile. Kasen thought she was so great, but Omar knew there was something devious behind that cheerful exterior. He knew she would be the perfect person to assist him with his plan. When he approached her with his idea, he soon learned that he had been right about her character. Without a second thought, she agreed to hook up with him and take Kasen for as much as they could get. They both agreed that removing Raine from his life would be the first step, because they had to make Kasen vulnerable.

Omar had no clue about Voncile's ulterior motive. Kasen's money meant nothing to her. She wanted him, and she saw Omar's plan as the perfect way to reach that goal.

In the meantime, she tolerated Omar and even let him get a piece of her sweet goodies once in a while because—well, a sister had needs, and until Kasen was in her bed, she would use Omar to satisfy those needs.

"Yes," Omar said. "I certainly do appreciate your efforts. Why don't you lock the door and I'll show you just how much."

Omar's lust-filled eyes examined Voncile as she went to the door and locked it. His dick shot up like a rocket, and he approached her from behind, pressing her up against the door. His hands roamed her backside.

Voncile shut her eyes, just for a few seconds. The sensation of him caressing her hips and thighs made her pussy leak. She was ready for

Omar to get down to business, but she wasn't going to serve him the full-course meal today.

Save some for Kasen, she thought as Omar massaged her breasts. *Don't give all of the goodies away*.

Omar lowered his hand to Voncile's waist, removing her belt. It dropped to the floor, and the rest of her clothes followed seconds later. Voncile turned around and stood proudly in her green silk bra and panties.

Omar's dick grew to new heights. He leaned in close to her ear, licking it and teasing her as he whispered in her ear, "You are so fucking sexy. That pussy of yours better be hot, slippery, and ready."

Voncile laughed at what she considered Omar's bullshit talk. It was up to him to make her pussy hot, slippery, and ready. "For starters, you can shut the hell up and remove your clothes. After you do that, I'm sure we can figure out how to prepare me for your grand entrance."

"Grand it will be. You can count on it."

He started grinding his goods against her, and she could feel the hardness of his muscle, which caused her juices to flow freely. He dipped his hand into her panties, slipping a few fingers into her dark cave.

"Mm-hmm. Hot and slippery," hc said. "Just like I wanted."

Voncile sucked in a deep breath. She grabbed the back of Omar's head, as he slid his wet fingers out and brushed against her clitoris with great speed. He gave her a sloppy, wet kiss as he continued to draw circles around her hard button.

"Turn around," he said suddenly, pulling his hand away and dropping his pants in one quick motion.

Before she knew it, he was plunging into her wetness, delivering long strokes that caused her pussy to pop loudly with each thrust.

"That's right," he said. "Talk to me, baby. I hear you. Hear you loud and clear." He grunted loudly as she tightened her walls and worked her magic on him.

She could feel every inch of his heavy meat serving her well. Her mouth was wide open. Each stroke took her to a new level. She couldn't help but to cry out and tell Omar how grateful she was for his satisfying dick.

"You are the truth," she shouted with tightened fists. "I love how you feel inside of me, but go harder, baby. I want you to go hard and beat this pussy up!"

Omar knew exactly how Voncile liked it: so hard that her legs weakened, almost buckling underneath her. He could tell that she needed a moment to gather herself, so he quickly pulled out of her, bringing an overflow of her hot lava with him. Needing a moment of rest as well, he backed up to a chair.

It wasn't long before Voncile went over to the chair, backing up to him and sitting down on his steel rod. Inch by inch, Voncile's tight pussy lips sucked him all in. No woman had ever satisfied Omar like Voncile; he was obsessed with her.

She gave him the slipperiest ride of his life, causing his whole body to weaken and slump in the chair. He was defeated by her, drained in a sense, because Voncile had mad skills.

Omar loved a woman who could handle him. He appreciated how aggressive Voncile was, and he definitely wanted to keep her all to himself. Sharing with Kasen was a no-no. He'd already made that perfectly clear to Voncile. She felt like she needed Omar's help to reach her ultimate goal, so she pretended that she was fine with his demands. She told him she had no interest in Kasen anyway, so he had nothing to worry about. When the time was right, though, he wouldn't stand a chance. If Voncile ever had to choose, hands down she would choose Kasen.

"We are so perfect for each other," she said, still sitting in the wetness of Omar's lap. "And I'm going to be so happy when all of this is ours."

"That has a ring to it, doesn't it? One day it will be ours, whether it's in the form of his life insurance policy, or with me draining his accounts as his guardian while he's in a mental ward. Do what it do, baby, and make that nigga go crazy."

After she and Omar cleaned up and left the office, Voncile was headed to her place to check on her favorite new roommate. The orgasm Omar had given her left her in a very good mood, so she decided to be generous and pick up some real food for Raine. She stopped at a fast food restaurant and then drove to her house, looking forward to a great night.

She just knew Raine would appreciate the burger and fries she was carrying into the house, but when she stepped inside and heard Raine yelling at the top of her lungs, she dropped the bag and raced up the stairs. She unlocked the bedroom door and stormed inside.

"What the hell is going on here?" she screamed.

Raine was on the floor, squirming around and stomping her feet as she continued to yell for help. Her eyes were swollen from all the crying she'd been doing.

Voncile stormed over to Raine, yanking her matted hair so hard that Raine ceased yelling. "Shut the hell up!" Voncile slapped her face. "How dare you ruin my day, bitch? How dare you!"

When Voncile finally let go of her hair, Raine dropped her head to the floor and whimpered quietly. She turned to look at Voncile and glared at her with pure hate.

"Why are you doing this?" Raine asked. "I don't get why you're doing this. What in the hell is wrong with you, Voncile?"

"There's nothing wrong with me!" Voncile screeched. "I call myself being nice to you. Stopped to get you a burger and fries, gave you a shower this morning, and even offered you a pot to piss in. The problem is, you don't know how to be nice to people. You've always had a problem being nice to me, and until you change your damn attitude, your ass will stay right here. You can holler all you want to. No one will hear you. You can kick the walls, pound your head against the floor, whatever. No one is coming for you."

She stared at Raine for a few seconds to let those words sink in. Then, just to dig the knife a little deeper, she added, "And just so you know, Kasen has already moved on. Shame on you for breaking his heart like you did. I don't blame him one bit for getting involved with someone else. Keeping a whore like you around did him no good, and he finally realized that. Now that he has moved on, you need to do the same—if I ever let you out of here."

Leaving Raine alone in the room, Voncile locked the door again and went to the kitchen. She was so upset that she paced the room with a cigarette burning in her shaking hand. Her breathing was heavy as she pondered what she was going to do about Raine. When she and Omar had devised their plan, they had agreed that Raine would be kept alive as a sort of Plan B. If they somehow failed to get Kasen to give up on Raine, then they could at least use her to get some ransom money so he could have her back. Of course, Voncile was not down with that plan, especially now. First, she obviously wanted Kasen all to herself, and second, Raine was getting on her fucking nerves. With Raine being in her house, she couldn't get much sleep. She feared Raine getting loose and, possibly, coming into her bedroom to cause her harm. Also, Voncile's house was isolated, but she still feared that Raine could escape and run to one of the neighbors' houses. Then Voncile would be in jail, and Omar might choose to let her rot there while he pretended not to know anything.

Voncile made a decision: She would go with the flow for only a few more days. After that, Raine would have to be moved to a more secure and secluded location.

The cigarette hadn't calmed Voncile's nerves like she wanted it to, so she opted for a shot of vodka. She downed the fiery liquid that caused her chest to burn, then took a deep breath and listened for signs of movement from Raine. Things had become awfully quiet up there, so she tackled the stairs again to check on Raine.

Raine was lying sideways, in a daze. Her eyes were wide open as she stared at the wall in front of her. She hadn't moved an inch; it didn't look like she had even blinked. Voncile thought she was dead, until she walked up to her and slapped her face. Instantly, Raine snapped out of it, but she was still as docile as she could be.

"Please," Raine begged, "just let me have a pillow for my head. I'm so sorry for all that screaming. I shouldn't have made you mad. I hope you can forgive me. All I want is for the two of us to get along while I'm here. Don't you want that too?"

Voncile pursed her lips then folded her arms. She patted her foot on the floor, responding to Raine in a sharp tone. "Don't you dare feed me a bunch of bullshit. We are not friends, and we never will be. As for the pillow, I'll think about it. Depends on how you behave. See, I am in control. Don't you understand that?"

To Voncile's surprise, Raine didn't respond aggressively. She actually gave her a smile, even if it did look a little forced. "Okay, I understand. But may I please use the bathroom to go clean up myself? As you can see, I'm a mess. I don't want to ruin your floors like this, and I know the smell on me is irritating you."

Voncile sniffed the air. "I don't smell anything, especially since I gave you a shower earlier. Now please don't get ahead of yourself and keep asking me for favors. I said I'll think about the pillow. That's all I will do."

"I won't push," Raine said politely. "And thank you. Thank you, again, for at least considering it."

Voncile pivoted then walked away, not noticing the evil glare that Raine shot at her behind her back.

Nearly an hour later, Voncile returned to give Raine a fluffy pillow. She also had another clean pajama top for her, along with a soft white towel. The pot was back in her hand, and inside of it was the burger and fries she had purchased for Raine earlier.

"See," Voncile said, setting everything neatly in front of her. "When you're nice to me, I'm nice to you."

Raine flashed another fake smile. "Thank you. But I need my hands untied so I can wipe myself down and change clothes. Do you mind freeing my hands?"

"Of course I don't mind." With a grin on her face, Voncile removed a 9 mm from her pocket and showed it to Raine. "I got this bad boy a few weeks ago. It's nice, isn't it? I paid a pretty penny for it, too. I hope like hell that I don't ever have to use it. After I untie your hands, I want you to be real careful, because if you do anything stupid, one little thing, I will be forced to splatter your damn brains."

Raine assured Voncile that she wouldn't do anything to upset her, but the second Voncile freed her hands, her eyes shifted to the door that Voncile hadn't shut all the way.

Voncile waved her gun in front of Raine's face. "I wouldn't think about it if I was you," she said as she slowly stepped backward and kicked the door shut. "I don't care if you were a damn track star in high school or something. You can never sprint fast enough to outrun a bullet, so you might as well forget about even trying."

Voncile leaned against the wall, carefully watching as Raine wiped her body with the towel. Raine pulled the pajama top over her head, wiggling it past her curvy hips. She tried to rake her matted hair back with her fingers, but it didn't do much good. She glanced at the door again, but when Voncile cleared her throat, Raine's eyes shifted to her.

"You really do have some nice clothes," Voncile said to Raine. "I went through some of your things yesterday. Saw sooo many things that I would love to have, and I couldn't help but to rock your dress and shoes earlier. Kasen paid me a nice compliment, and I noticed him checking me out all day. That man of *ours* is something else. He's a romantic little devil, too, isn't he?"

Raine cringed. "I like to buy nice things. And you can wear whatever you want to. I don't mind. I also don't mind that Kasen paid you a compliment. He's a nice man and very romantic."

"Yes, too nice," Voncile added, then began rambling on about Kasen. She got so wrapped up in the things she was saying that she momentarily forgot about Raine. Practically in a trance, she wandered over to the other side of the room, still gushing about how she knew Kasen was secretly in love with her.

Raine realized this was her moment, and she darted across the room so fast that she was out the door before Voncile snapped out of her daydream. Running as if her life depended on it, Raine had already made it midway down the stairs before she heard shots being fired. She saw a bullet blast into the wall next to her, and another hit the wooden rail, breaking it.

"Come back here, bitch!" Voncile yelled from close behind. She fired one more bullet at Raine, and when that bullet hit the same step Raine had landed on, she collapsed and went tumbling down the stairs. Raine landed face first on the floor, her body weak from her days in captivity.

Voncile stood over her, lifting her head and placing the gun against her temple. She pulled the trigger, but the gun made a clicking sound. She was out of bullets. Voncile laughed, pushing Raine's head forward.

"Girl, yo' ass is lucky. Real lucky. But if you want to know anything about being brave, let me show you how to do it." Voncile raised the gun, slamming it hard across Raine's face. Raine was knocked out cold.

Voncile quickly got to work. She had to clean up the mess before Kasen arrived.

Chapter 8

Kasen tried to rest for a while, but even though his eyes were closed, he hadn't really gotten any good quality sleep. He couldn't stop his mind from going over and over his relationship with Raine. He desperately wanted to figure out where he had gone wrong. Knowing the truth, that she had been seeing someone else, he reflected on some of the signs he had missed or ignored. There were times when Raine had not answered his late-night phone calls, claiming she'd been so sound asleep she never heard the phone ring. Now he wondered if there had been another man in Raine's bed all those times. Also, she had never wanted to take long vacations. She said it was because of work, but now he realized she was never completely relaxed on vacation, even if it was during a break when the schools were closed. Maybe it was because she was anxious to get home to someone else. Viewing her past actions through this new lens, he saw plenty of reasons to believe that she had been cheating. He felt like a fool. How had he ever let this woman trick him into proposing?

Kasen finally gave up trying to rest. He got up out of the bed and called Omar, thinking they could go play pool or something, but he got no answer.

Kasen desperately needed something to entertain him, to take his thoughts off of Raine. Voncile's offer from earlier came to mind. He wasn't necessarily in the mood to be around a bunch of women who would probably seek his advice about relationships, but even that would be better than sitting there beating himself up over the mistakes he had made in trusting a cheating liar.

He got dressed in casual attire: a pair of jeans, a black button-down shirt that hugged his muscles, and Ferragamo loafers. He covered his eyes with dark shades then hopped in his car, making a stop at the store to pick up two bottles of wine.

Voncile's place was almost an hour away from where he was, but he didn't mind the drive. It would give him time to clear his head so he didn't show up at the party in a terrible mood. He turned up the volume on the radio, crooning along with Tyrese Gibson's latest CD. Before he knew it, he was parked in front of Voncile's house.

From what he could see, it didn't appear that any action was going on. The only car parked in the driveway was hers. He could see a sliver of light coming from one of the rooms in the house, but otherwise it was dark. For a moment he considered putting the car in reverse to leave. Maybe she'd canceled the party or something.

"Oh, hell," he said out loud to himself. "I didn't drive all the way out here for nothing. Let me at least go give this lady the wine I bought."

He got out of the car and went to the door to ring the bell.

Voncile opened the door, wearing a short silk robe that revealed her thick thighs. The only makeup she wore was a sheer gloss that emphasized her pouty lips. She looked good, but she definitely wasn't dressed as if she had been expecting guests.

"Hey, Voncile. I'm sorry. Did I get the date wrong or something? I thought you were having a get-together tonight," Kasen said.

"Oh, shoot. Kasen, I am so sorry," she said. "I forgot to call and let you know that my plans changed. Two of my friends said they couldn't make it. The other one, her mother had to go to the hospital. I cancelled until next weekend."

He shrugged. "No need to apologize. I should have called before I drove all the way over here."

"No, this is on me. Please come in," she told him, stepping aside so he could enter the darkened living room. "If you're hungry, I did cook a little something for dinner."

"Are you sure? I mean, it looks as if you were on your way to sleep."

"Nope. I was just watching TV."

Kasen looked around the living room, which was spotless. It was rather cozy, too, with the lights dimmed and the fireplace lit.

"So what's that you're holding?" she asked flirtatiously as she sat down on the couch.

Kasen smiled and put the bottles of wine on the coffee table in front of her. "Well, I brought some wine for you and your guests," he said with an embarrassed laugh.

She patted the seat next to her. "That's sweet. Why don't you sit down here and I'll go get you a plate of food?"

Kasen took a seat. "Thanks, but I'm not that hungry. I haven't been eating much lately. Too much on my mind."

"Well, I'll tell you what." Voncile stood and reached for the wine bottles. "I'll go pour both of us some wine, and I'll also pull out a deck of cards. As we play a few games of spades, you can tell me why you haven't been eating much and what, exactly, is on your mind."

Kasen watched Voncile walk away, thinking about how sweet she was. Maybe he would actually feel better if he opened up about his troubles instead of always trying to hide behind some perfect image. After working with her for so long, he trusted Voncile to be a good listener and to have his best interests at heart. And hell, if their talk led to something more, then so be it. Getting with another woman might be the best way to get over Raine once and for all.

As soon as that thought entered his head, Kasen pushed it out. Voncile was an employee and a friend, and it was inappropriate to be thinking about her in a sexual way, he told himself. He was only thinking that way because Raine had injured his ego. Besides, Omar was into Raine, and Kasen was not one to push up on his friend's love interests.

Kasen stood up to distract himself from the thoughts he shouldn't be having, strolling around the living room to look at some of the pictures on Voncile's walls. Many of the pictures were of her. Some were of a lady who looked just like her; he assumed the pictures were of her mother. There was an older man who could've easily been her grandfather, and pictures of twin girls who looked to be about two or three.

Kasen stepped into the kitchen and caught a glimpse of Voncile's shapely ass through the clingy fabric of her robe. Just like that, his head was filled with lustful thoughts again.

"Hey, Von—"

Startled by the sound of his voice, she dropped the wine glass she'd been holding. It crashed to the floor and shattered.

Kasen rushed up to her. "I didn't mean to startle you."

"Oh, it's no problem," she said. "I don't know why I'm so jumpy."

She looked over his shoulder nervously, almost like someone else was there. Kasen turned around to see what she was looking at, but there was nothing.

"You sure you're okay?" he asked.

"Of course, silly," she said as she grabbed the broom to sweep up the shards of glass. "Let me just clean this up and I'll be right in."

"Let me get that," Kasen said, reaching for the broom, but she swatted his hand away.

"I said I'm fine, Kasen." Her tone was a little aggressive, which took him by surprise. He held his hands up as if surrendering to her authority.

"No problem. I'll just go sit in there and wait for you," he said and turned to leave the kitchen. "Actually, where's your bathroom?"

"It's down the hall over there, to your right." This time her tone was softer.

She sure is unpredictable, he thought. *Maybe that's why she never seems to have a man.* Then he caught himself and realized he was being unfair. After all, he had shown up at her house when she was dressed in her robe, obviously getting ready for bed. Maybe she was just being polite by letting him in. Maybe she didn't really want him there at all. He decided he would have one glass of wine to be polite and then he'd leave.

Kasen made his way down the hallway to the bathroom. As he stood in front of the sink drying his hands, he heard what sounded like faint moaning. Confused, he looked around as if he might find the source of the sound in that small room. Of course, there was no one in there with him. Still, he was sure he'd heard it, so he placed his ear against the walls to see if it was coming from an adjacent room. There was silence. When the moaning started again, his eyes zoomed in on a vent on the floor. Just as he bent down to check it out, there was a knock on the door.

"Are you okay in there?" Voncile said. "I'm ready to spank your tail at spades."

Kasen loved a challenge. He took a look down at the vent but heard nothing. With his attention now focused on beating Voncile at a card game, he left the bathroom. His face still wore a puzzled expression, though, and Voncile noticed it as soon as he walked out.

"Everything okay in there?" she asked.

"I think so, but I could have sworn I heard someone moaning. Are you sure this house isn't haunted?" he joked.

Voncile frowned, looking kind of angry.

"What, you don't like jokes about ghosts?" he teased, and luckily, it seemed to calm her down. Then her facial expression changed to one of shame.

"I am too embarrassed to tell you what that was," she said, walking back toward the living room.

Kasen followed behind her. "Too embarrassed about what?"

Voncile had placed two big pillows on the floor in front of the fireplace with a stack of cards between them. The wine glasses were nearby on a table. She sat on a pillow, inviting Kasen to do the same.

"You're not getting off the hook that easy," he said. "What are you so embarrassed by?"

Voncile reached for her glass of wine and took a sip. "You ready to play?" she asked.

He raised his eyebrows, still waiting for an answer to his question.

Finally, she relented. "Fine. If you must know, those moans are coming from downstairs. Sometimes I like to watch a little porn, but I keep it all in the basement in case . . . you know, I don't just go advertising to my guests that I watch porn. I must have forgotten to turn off the TV."

Now Kasen understood. He hadn't interrupted her on her way to bed. He'd interrupted her getting her freak on by herself. He had to suppress a little smile as he imagined her down there with her robe open and her legs spread wide, playing with herself as she watched porn. The image excited him.

"There's nothing wrong with that," he said, and then, throwing all caution to the wind, he added, "Maybe next time we'll check out a movie together." His lust had gotten the best of him.

For a split second he was worried that she would be offended. After all, she had told him how much she didn't like Omar's aggressiveness. She totally surprised him, though, when she handed him a glass of wine with a smile and said, "Sounds like a plan to me." They clinked their glasses in a toast.

"But before we get busy on this card game, let me run downstairs to turn off the TV. No need to run up my electric bill, you know?"

"I feel you on that. And when you come back, I'll be right here, ready to spank that ass."

She winked. "I'm looking forward to it."

Voncile walked away, giddy about how flirtatious Kasen was being, but also fuming about how close Raine had come to ruining everything. She went through the kitchen and unlocked the deadbolt that secured the basement door. Pulling the string on the single lightbulb at the top of the steps, she peered down into the musty room. Raine was in the far corner, her quivering body dripping with sweat. A sizeable knot had appeared on her forehead where Voncile had bashed her with the gun. The cloth that Voncile had wrapped around her mouth was still in place, but she could tell that Raine had been trying to remove it.

"You must really want me to knock your teeth out." Voncile's hand was attached to her hip as she went down the stairs. She tightened the gag around Raine's mouth so she wouldn't be able to budge if she tried again. "I have been nothing but nice to you, and what do you do? Try to run. Try to trick me and run, even when I told you that there was no way out of here. You need to listen to me, and when you start playing by my rules, your stay here will be much easier. Take two more days down here to think about what I said. Until then, I don't want to hear a peep from you. Not one word. No moaning and groaning, nothing. Do you understand?"

Raine slowly nodded. That was all she could do, considering the vulnerable position she was in. Besides that, she was obviously in so much pain, which made Voncile very happy. It served her right for messing up the flow between Kasen and Voncile.

Voncile locked the door to the cellar and put the key back underneath the small rug in front of the door; then she quickly returned to Kasen. Her whole demeanor changed when she saw him chilling sideways on the pillow, waiting for her to return.

"Sorry to keep you waiting," Voncile said cheerfully. "That chick in the porn movie was doing a lot of moaning. I had to stand there for a second to see what she was getting into."

"You mean what was getting into her."

They laughed as Voncile took a seat, purposely crossing her legs yoga-style so that Kasen could have a clear view of her goodies. She wasn't wearing panties or a bra, and the top part of her robe exposed just enough to keep him interested on both ends.

Kasen could barely concentrate on the card game. His narrowed eyes thoroughly examined

Voncile, and with her neatly shaved slit in his view, he had to keep shifting to try to hide the growing tent in his pants.

Trying to focus on the game and not embarrass himself, he fixed his eyes on the cards in his hands. He didn't have enough spades to beat Voncile, but beating her wasn't exactly on his mind. Laying her back on the floor and throwing her legs over his shoulders was.

It wasn't long before Voncile tossed a king of spades on the floor. Not one card in Kasen's hand could beat the king, so he laid all of his cards on the floor.

"You win; I lose," he said.

Voncile laid all of her cards down too. "No, actually, we both win. And I'm about to show you why."

Voncile leaned back on her elbows and untied her robe, causing it to fall open and expose her flawless body. Her firm breasts sat high. Her pussy looked good enough for Kasen to eat, and from the way he eyed it hungrily, she could tell he was ready. She spread her legs wide and touched her pearl, turning it in circles and inviting Kasen to enter the gates of her moist haven.

Locked in a trance, all he did was stare. He couldn't even move.

Voncile slipped a finger inside of herself. "Are you going to help me with this or not?" she asked softly. "I don't mind you watching, but I would prefer it if you made a move."

Kasen stood to remove his clothes, and Voncile had to bite her tongue to keep from crying out in pleasure. This was the view she had been waiting so long for. His body was carved to near perfection, just as she had envisioned. His abs were stacked with muscles, his broad shoulders resembled a linebacker's, and his dick was aimed in her direction, ready to fire.

Her coochie lips puckered at him, and he took the initiative to stroke his meat and step forward. Neither one spoke a word as he kneeled between her legs then moved her busy hands out of the way. He took over by slipping his fingers inside of her, toying with her clit. Her breasts rose, a perfect arch forming in her back. The smell of her sweetened juices filled the air. The temperature in the room increased, as did the size of Kasen's dick, which was now harder than a black diamond. Right before her eyes, Voncile witnessed it swell to a size that excited her beyond her wildest dreams.

"I need to feel it, Kasen," she moaned. "Nowww."

He sensed that his finger-fucking festivities weren't enough to please her, but without a doubt, he knew something that would. He leaned in closer and planted light kisses on her shapely thighs. She trembled from the feel of his tongue. He slid it over her clit, and then plunged it deep into her tunnel.

Voncile's fists tightened, and so did her stomach. She reached out to grab and gripped the pillow to keep herself from scratching his back in a fit of passion. Kasen knew exactly how to get her liquids flowing, and within a matter of minutes, she felt heat rising from the very tips of her toes to her vagina. It started to boil over, quickly erupting like a volcano. She sprayed Kasen's lips with her cream, and he loved every bit of it.

"I knew you had it in you," he said, showing a Crest smile. "I just didn't know you had all of *that* in you."

"Trust me, baby, when I say there's more. All you have to do is dig deeper. I assure you that's where you will find more."

Kasen placed Voncile's long legs over his broad shoulders, journeying to a place that caused her to lose her mind. Now she understood why he was known as a healing doctor. She wanted to pull her hair out, especially when his strokes became longer, more rhythmic, more satisfying. She was ready to give him another buildup of her excitement, but she did her best not to let him milk her dry. Her intentions were for Kasen to get his too, and thus far, he didn't seem ready.

Kasen wanted to take his time with Voncile. He was enjoying every minute of their encounter, especially since it was such a welcome relief from all he stress he'd been feeling lately. In fact, he couldn't help but wonder why they hadn't done this sooner. It didn't matter, though, because he couldn't think of a time in his life when he needed a good fuck more than now.

He was caught up in the moment now, and when Voncile positioned herself on all fours, Kasen prepared to shut her down for the night. He rubbed the soft mountains on her ass and carefully parted her cheeks so he could enter her haven once again. Her pussy was instantly stuffed to capacity, and with each thrust, her folds sunk in. She could feel every inch of Kasen's meat. There was no holding back on another orgasm, especially when he smoothly stroked her clitoris like a violin.

"I'm done!" she shouted. "I am sooooo done with you!"

Kasen was just about done too. He rocked his body with Voncile's, and as they crossed the finish line together, they fell forward on the floor.

When they finally caught their breath, Kasen sneaked a peek at Voncile. She grinned at him with a totally satisfied expression, and they both burst out into laughter.

"So that just happened, huh?" Kasen said in a teasing manner. "And you tried to wear me out, didn't you?"

"No, I didn't, but you sure did wear me out. And I enjoyed every minute of it. Wish we had done this sooner."

Kasen agreed. He didn't say it to Voncile, but she had given him the perfect way to forget how Raine had hurt him. He hadn't thought about her all night, and he was glad about it. To him, this was the first step to putting the whole situation behind him.

He cuddled Voncile in his strong arms, and as they both lay naked, gazing at the fireplace, he wondered where the two of them would go from there.

Chapter 9

Omar and Kasen sat at the busy Chinese restaurant chowing down on some of their favorite dishes as the waiters scurried around the packed room. This was their favorite place to go after a round of golf, and they would enjoy the food while they caught up on each other's lives. Omar wasn't a counselor, but he was a good listener. He usually gave good advice, too. That was why Kasen wanted to talk to him about Raine's sudden departure, to see if he had a different perspective that might help Kasen understand it all.

"Are you fucking kidding me?" Omar cocked his head back in shock when Kasen told him the details of Raine's good-bye letter. "Is this why you've been walking around all week with your head hanging low, not returning phone calls and shit?"

Kasen shrugged, pretending as if the letter didn't sting as much as it did. "I've been a little different, I guess, but do you blame me? I just proposed to her, man. Talk about getting my face cracked! You know I hate to admit this, but that shit hurt. It still hurts, and I'm trying to come to grips with her not being around anymore."

"So, are you telling me that you didn't know she was cheating? Come on, Kasen. I said it before: You know how to read people like a book. Why couldn't you sense that something was going on with her? And, I mean, come on. She laughed at your proposal, for God's sake! That didn't set off any alarm bells?"

Kasen shook his head, disappointed in himself for all the signs he had missed. "I don't know what was wrong with me, man. I let that shit go right over my head. I didn't sense a thing. Never suspected that she was with someone else. That letter was a total shock to me, and for her to bring up what I'd done in the past . . . I just can't believe she was holding a grudge all that time."

"Women do shit like that. They hold grudges for a long time. Then, bam. You get hit with shit like this. Happens all the time," Omar said.

"I guess so. It took a lot out of me, though. It'll be a long time before I ever trust another woman. This shit left a real bad taste in my mouth."

"Don't let this incident fuck you up, K. Every woman isn't like Raine. There are still some good women out there, like the two chicks over there who keep looking at us," Omar pointed out, trying to lighten the mood.

Omar waved at the two women who were sitting in a booth with wide smiles on their faces. Kasen barely looked their way. He tossed back a shot of Henny, his fourth of the night.

"Speaking of good women," Kasen said, "I want you to do me a favor and back off Voncile. She told me that you try to push up too hard when you come into the office."

Omar laughed at the idea that he could have offended Voncile. "Man, that chick will say anything to get your attention. You know me. Would I ever bother a bitch that wasn't interested in me?"

Kasen frowned at his friend's use of the B word, but he didn't call him on it. "Yeah, man, I do know you. That's the problem. You're not exactly Mr. Manners when it comes to trying to get some ass."

Omar shrugged like a little kid trying to get out of a punishment. "Okay, maybe you're right," he said. "But can you blame a brother? I mean, your secretary is hot as hell, K."

Kasen couldn't help but chuckle as an image of Voncile's beautiful naked body flashed in his mind. "Yeah, I won't deny that. But even so, how about you back off so I don't have to worry about her taking out a restraining order against you?" he said, only half joking.

Omar raised his eyebrows, looking a little pissed. "What's with the tone, man? If you want me to back off, then I will, but you don't need to lecture me like you my daddy or something. Just because you make more money than me doesn't make you better, you know."

Kasen was surprised by Omar's anger. He watched his friend down the rest of his Hennessy and decided maybe they'd both just had a little too much to drink. Omar always got a little testy when he was drunk.

"No problem, man. I didn't mean to offend you. She just asked me to talk to you about it, so that's what I'm doing. We're still cool, right?" Kasen asked.

Omar hesitated before answering, but as his facial muscles started to relax, Kasen knew they would be fine.

"Yeah, we're cool," Omar finally said. "Ain't no big thing. Voncile's not my type anyway. I like wild women, not timid and boring like she seems to be."

"I don't think she's timid at all, nor is she boring," Kasen said, remembering the way she came all over his face the night before, screaming and moaning at the top of her lungs. She had put on quite a show, and he had loved every minute of it. "And believe me when I say there is a very wild and sexy side to her," he added with a smirk.

"I guess our definitions of wild differ," Omar said. "I'm talking about a woman who doesn't mind getting buck wild in the bedroom; who knows how to work that pussy and put her creative mind to good use. Not someone who gets wild in the office by managing things. That's the Voncile you know."

Kasen laughed. He didn't want to put his business out there, but this was Omar he was talking to. Telling him what had happened between him and Voncile last night wouldn't hurt. At least, that was what Kasen thought.

"I do believe that we have the exact same definition. I know more about Voncile than you would think," he said. "I'll just say that it's been a long time since I met someone as creative as she is. You have my word that she is, indeed, a wild one."

Omar's face fell. It took Kasen by surprise, because usually Omar was the first one to ask for every detail of Kasen's sexual conquests. Now, he almost looked disgusted.

"Are you telling me you fucked her?"

Kasen was straightforward. "To be blunt, she fucked the hell out of me. We got into a little something last night."

Omar picked up his glass, which was now full of melting ice. He swallowed some of the cold water and cleared his throat. "Dude, you're over here telling me to back off so she doesn't file a report, and then you go and fuck her yourself? How about you take some of your own advice on this one?"

Kasen shook his head. "Yeah, I hear you, man, but given the week I've been having, it felt pretty damn good to end it that way."

Omar kept pushing his point of view. "K, that chick is not someone to mess with. Sometimes the way she looks at you makes me a little nervous. I mean, you missed all those signs with Raine. Are you sure you're not missing something with Voncile too? Something about her makes me think she could go a little *Fatal Attraction* on you."

Now Kasen was totally confused. A minute ago Omar was talking about how he wanted to get with Voncile, and now he was calling her crazy. He decided that Omar must be talking out of jealousy. He understood, because he had broken the code by sleeping with someone his friend was interested in. Usually he was more loyal, but Raine's betrayal really had his head messed up.

"Don't worry about it, O. I was just having some fun, blowing off some steam, and I think Voncile understands that."

"What if she doesn't?" Omar asked. "What if she wants more?"

"Right now, she can have more. More sex, for sure." Kasen laughed at his own joke, but Omar didn't find it funny at all.

He stood up from the table and put on his jacket. "Just don't say I didn't warn you," he said, although something in his tone told Kasen he wasn't speaking out of concern. It was almost like he hoped something bad did happen.

Before Kasen could ask him why he was so pissed off, Omar turned around and left the restaurant without another word. As usual, he stuck Kasen with the check.

Outside the restaurant, Omar sat in his car and called Voncile. She answered in a very tired and sluggish voice.

"Unlock the door for me," he said, sucking on a toothpick that dangled between his teeth. "I'm on my way there."

"Do you know what time it is?"

"Yes, but we need to talk. It can't wait until later."

Voncile hung up on Omar. That made him livid. Between her and Kasen, somebody was about to get hurt. They had both been working Omar's nerves, and for Kasen to sit there and talk about having sex with Voncile—how disrespectful was that? He knew damn well that Omar wanted Voncile, but being the golden boy, Kasen was used to having everything he wanted, all the time. He had the professional career, the money, and now Omar's woman. Kasen didn't give a damn about anyone but himself, and Omar was sick of it. He had been plotting to bring Kasen down because of his arrogance, and this just made him all the more certain that he was doing the right thing. Before, he had just been after Kasen's money, but now he wanted Kasen to lose everything—his money, his girlfriend, his career, and maybe even his life.

Omar sat in the car for a few more minutes, processing and reevaluating his so-called friendship with Kasen. He went way back to when they were in college and Omar needed Kasen's help in a major way, or else he was going to have to drop out. He asked Kasen for money—not even that much, just enough to help pay for his books.

Kasen said he didn't have it, but the next thing Omar knew, Kasen purchased a new car and was catering to as many chicks as he could on campus. Without money to pay for his books, Omar failed his classes. He was forced to drop out, and he never forgave Kasen for being so stingy.

Kasen had no idea that his friend harbored so much resentment, because Omar never said a word to him about it. Once Omar dropped out, however, Kasen felt guilty and started helping him out. He gave him money whenever he asked, even if it was money to gamble. He cosigned on a loan for a car, as well as a house, even though that eventually went into foreclosure.

Omar had considered cutting off the friendship when he dropped out of school, but once he realized that Kasen was now willing to give up the cash, he figured it was better to stick around and take advantage of it. That didn't mean he cared about Kasen, though. He still believed that Kasen was an arrogant son of a bitch who only gave him the money so he could feel superior to him. He always wanted to get a pat on the back for doing a good deed, and from time to time, Omar was willing to play along and stroke his ego, just so the cash would keep on flowing.

Things started to unravel when Omar needed an extra fifteen hundred dollars to pay his rent and a thousand for his light bill. Maybe it was Kasen's new degree in psychology that caused it, but all of a sudden he started acting like he was Omar's therapist, lecturing him about how he had to start taking responsibility for his actions, and how he should start searching for a career where he could support himself. All Omar heard was one grown man telling another grown-ass man what to do, and that pissed him off even more. As far as he was concerned, he wouldn't have gotten so off track if Kasen had given him the money to buy books in the first place. Kasen owed him, because he was the reason Omar dropped out of school.

Omar opened the glove compartment and pulled out a brown paper bag with a bottle inside. He twisted off the cap and turned the bottle up to his mouth, shaking it to make sure he got every drop of the little bit of liquor that was left in there. It felt good going down his throat, but it wasn't nearly enough to get him drunk, so he put the car in drive and sped to the nearest liquor store.

On the way, his mind wandered to thoughts of Voncile. When he first met her in Kasen's office, she had brought a brightness to his life that he hadn't felt in years. First it was just a physical attraction, but he sensed pretty quickly that she was just as lonely as he was, and he started coming to the office during hours he knew Kasen wouldn't be there, just so he could spend time talking to her. Before Omar knew it, they started to connect. She understood him. She listened to him, and she began to fill the void in his life. The fact that she had agreed to participate in his plot against Kasen was just icing on the cake.

Now, though, he felt betrayed by her. He had been sensing lately that, although she tried to hide it from him, she was becoming caught up in feelings for Kasen. Now that he knew they'd had sex, Omar felt it would be very difficult to get Voncile away from him. He might still eventually forgive her for giving up the goodies to Kasen, but in the meantime, he surely wanted some kind of revenge.

He wondered how she would feel if the tables were turned and he started having sex with one of her friends. The only friend he'd ever heard her talk about, and the only one he'd ever met, was a woman named Patrice. He had met her a while back, and Patrice was down with the whole plot against Kasen. She let it be known that she would be willing to participate in any way—for a price, of course. But Omar also knew that she would be willing to drop her panties if he asked her to. She had that look in her eyes whenever he saw her. It was something to keep in the back of his mind, in case he decided to put Voncile in her place for disrespecting him with Kasen. Patrice was just a phone call away, and he knew it would piss off Voncile.

Omar parked his car, hurrying into the liquor store to get a bottle of gin. When he got to the counter and pulled the cash out of his pocket, he realized he was a dollar and fifteen cents short. He had left his wallet at home that morning, so he couldn't pay with a credit card.

"Come on, man," Omar said. "It's just a dollar. I'll bring it back to you later, all right?"

"No, it's not okay. You can come back when you have all of the money. And not just a dollar, but a dollar and fifteen cents. When you get it, you can have it."

The man snatched the bottle from Omar's hand, but Omar snatched it right back, holding it close to his chest. "Snatch it away from me again and I will jump over this counter and beat yo' ass! I said I'll be back. As much money as I spend in here, you need to be giving me something free." Omar walked to the door, not even caring that he was on camera. He ignored the man yelling at him. As Omar headed to his car, the man rushed after him.

"You not pay for that!" he said, trying to take the bottle from Omar's hand again. "Give it back. Now!"

Somebody had to pay for what Kasen and Voncile had done, and unfortunately for him, the man had tripped at the wrong place, wrong time. Omar lifted his fist, slamming it directly into the man's face. He fell on the ground, holding his face, yet still fussing about Omar not paying. He shook his finger at Omar, who hopped in the car, ignoring him.

"You not pay, but you will. I promise you, you will pay for this!"

"And I promise you that I will run your dumb ass over if you don't move out of my way."

Omar sped off, swerving his car so he wouldn't run the man over, in spite of his threat. He twisted the cap off the bottle of gin and started guzzling it down. Minutes later, he found himself swerving in and out of traffic lanes. He figured he'd better find a place to chill, and his thoughts took him straight to Patrice's house. He rang the doorbell then leaned against the doorway, waiting or her to answer.

When she opened the door, he could tell that he had woken her up. She didn't seem to mind, though. She looked him up and down and smiled, obviously glad to see him.

"Whoa," she said, as he came in and stumbled his way over to her couch. "I know you weren't just out there driving like this."

"I was, but I wanted to find someplace where I could lay my head." He reached out for her hand and pulled her down on the couch next to him. She didn't resist at all when he rested his hand on her upper thigh, rubbing the silky fabric of her pajamas. "You look sexy tonight, Patrice."

"Thank you," she said, arching her back a little like she was posing for him.

His hand moved from her thigh to the warm space between her legs, and Patrice still didn't make a move to stop him.

"You know I see the way you watch me sometimes when you're over at Voncile's place, right? So why don't we stop pretending you don't want me, and you can give me some of that pussy."

To his surprise, that was all he had to do to get her. Patrice wasted no time straddling his lap, looking ready for whatever he wanted to give her.

Voncile's friend is about as loyal as Kasen, he thought with disgust. Still, she was eager to give up the pussy, and he was not the kind of man who would ever turn that down.

"That's a good girl," he said. "Hurry up and take those panties off and sit on my face."

Patrice stood up and removed her pajamas, standing totally naked in front of Omar. She nudged his shoulder and said, "Lie down."

He did as he was told, and then she climbed on top, placing her moist coochie directly over his mouth. Omar got to work, sucking and licking her, but he was so drunk from all the gin he'd had on the way over, he wasn't hitting the spots Patrice needed him to. She started gyrating her hips to try to help things along, but all of a sudden, Omar's mouth stopped moving.

"What the hell—?" she said out loud as she got off of him. "I know this motherfucker ain't—"

She looked down at Omar, and sure enough, he was sound asleep, snoring lightly.

"Damn it. Omar, get up!" she said, nudging his shoulder roughly.

His eyelids fluttered open. "Wha . . . what did you say?"

"Stop playing. Are we gonna do this or not?"

Omar struggled to lift himself from the couch. He reached for his jeans, removing a condom from his pocket. He gave it to Patrice.

"Hell yeah, we're doing this. Put that on me and let's rock and roll." He lay back on the couch, crossing his arm over his forehead.

Patrice unwrapped the condom and used her mouth to put the condom on him. That made him wake up—a little.

"Yeah, baby, I likes that," Omar said. "You are on the right track, 'cause I am almost there."

Minutes later, he seemed ready to aim and shoot, so she straddled his lap again. This time, she latched her coochie in the right place, and as Omar fully opened his eyes, Patrice started to ride him. She was doing most of the work, while he looked at her with a glassy film covering his eyes.

"How did you get up there?" he slurred.

"I put myself up here," she said, breathing heavy. "Now, are you down with this or not, Omar?"

"Yeah, sure, baby. I'm down," he said, but within a few seconds, his eyes were closed and he was snoring again.

Patrice climbed off of him and slapped his leg to wake him up. "You need to get your drunk ass out of here. I was getting some good sleep before you came over here with this bullshit. Talk about a waste of time."

Omar sat up, scratching his bald head. "What'd I do?" he said with a yawn.

"Not a damn thing," she said, sucking her teeth. "That's the problem. You brought your drunk ass over here and woke me up, but you can't even keep your eyes open or your dick hard. So now you got to leave."

"Look, bitch," Omar said, standing up and towering over her, "after the day I've had, I don't need no attitude from you."

She took a step back, clearly intimidated by him now.

"So just go get me some orange juice and an aspirin and I'll carry my ass out of here."

She sucked her teeth again in defiance, but she still turned around to go get him the things he'd asked for. On her way into the bedroom, she threw one last insult over her shoulder. "Voncile was right. Your dick ain't all that anyway."

That was the final straw for Omar. He had taken all the disrespect he could handle for one day, and now Patrice was going to have to pay the price. He rushed up behind her, grabbing her arms and pinning them against her back.

"Ow, you psycho! Take your fuckin' hands off me!" she yelled as he shoved her toward the bed.

Still half out of his mind from the alcohol and seething with anger, he bent Patrice over the bed and forced her legs open. Before he even had time to rethink what he was about to do, he had plunged himself deep inside of her.

"Still want to talk shit, Patrice? Still want to say my dick isn't good enough for you?"

Patrice cried out in pain. "Omar, stop! I never should have said that. I'm sorry! Just please, stop!"

He started to pump her with full force. "I may not be Kasen, but I still know how to fuck a woman real good. Admit it, Patrice."

"What are you talking about? What does Kasen have to do with anything?" she cried out.

Suddenly, he stopped moving. *What the fuck am I doing?* he asked himself. Finding out about Voncile and Kasen having sex had really messed with his mind even more than he had realized. He pulled himself out of Patrice and let go of her arms.

"I'm sorry," he said as he helped her get up. "I don't know what came over me." He hoped like hell that she would accept his apology, because the last thing he needed was for her to be calling the cops and having him arrested for rape.

Before he knew what was happening, Patrice had run to her nightstand and pulled a handgun out of the top drawer. She whipped around and waved the gun at him.

"You need to get the fuck out of here, Omar. Right now."

Omar nodded and raised his hands, slowly walking backward out of the room. Patrice followed him, still aiming the gun in his direction. She stood nearby as he got dressed, and then she escorted him to the door, slamming it behind him.

Omar was glad to be out of there with all of his body parts intact and no bullet holes. *I never should have come over here,* he thought as he got in his car and headed to Voncile's house. After all, it was her, not Patrice, who deserved all of his anger.

Chapter 10

"What do you want? Why do you people keep waking me up?" Voncile said when she answered her phone.

"I don't know what you mean by you people," Patrice said, "but I wanted to call and let you know that Omar almost left out of here in a body bag. He came here tripping, drunk as hell. I was lucky I had my gun close by. I didn't know he was like that. Did you?"

Voncile gasped. "I'm well aware of what kind of man Omar is, but damn, I didn't know he was capable of rape. What was he doing at your place anyway? He said he was coming over here."

"Girl, I'll be damned if I know what the fuck he was doing here. Like I said, that fool was drunk."

"Well, don't you worry. I will deal with him when I see him," Voncile promised. "In the meantime, this heifer over here is getting on my nerves."

"I'm not surprised," Patrice responded. "Let me know what I can do. And have your guard up tonight. Omar is on a rampage."

"Please. I ain't worried about Omar," Voncile said boldly. "I'll talk to you later, girl." She ended the call.

Voncile sat in her living room thinking about what Patrice had told her. She wanted to know why Omar had gone to see Patrice in the first place considering she was Voncile's friend, not his. And what the hell would have caused him to go crazy like she said he did? It wasn't long before Omar showed up and she got her answer.

He was pounding on her door loudly, and as soon as she unlocked it, he barged in, yelling in her face. "Why in the fuck did you have sex with him?" Omar barked. "That wasn't the plan, Voncile, and you know it!"

Voncile backed up quickly. "Whoa, wait a minute and calm down. You don't have to come in here yelling and screaming at me. And before you start yelling at me about Kasen, what's up with you going to Patrice's house? I didn't know the two of you were close like that." She tried to flip the script on him.

Omar shook his head. "I can't believe that bitch called you already, but since she did, let me just say to you that she is no friend of yours.

That ho tried to rape me. I went there to sleep off my headache from drinking, but I couldn't rest because she kept trying to get a piece of this."

Voncile cut her eyes at Omar. "I really don't care about all of that. She said you attacked her, and now you're saying she tried to rape you. Whatever, Omar. Just tone it down and tell me what's on your mind."

His voice was full of sarcasm. "Thanks for letting me get back to the subject I came here to discuss with you. We were talking about you and Kasen, remember?"

"Yes, you were, but allow me to clear the air. I didn't intend to have sex with him. He came over last night, told me that he had been going through some things, and then one thing led to another. I don't know why you're so upset. It's really not a big deal," she said flippantly. She knew he was pissed off, and she kind of enjoyed it.

Omar wasn't trying to hear that. His face twisted, and his voice went up several notches. "Bitch, it's a big deal to me! How could you think it wouldn't be? You let him come in here, knowing that Raine is here too? Why would you do something like that? For all I know, the two of you could be plotting against me. This is so messed up, Voncile. You fucked up!"

Voncile reached out to Omar, trying to calm him down. He caught her by surprise when he shoved her back, making her fall on the couch.

"Don't touch me, especially when I don't know where your hands have been," he shouted, spit flying from his mouth. "From what Kasen said, you did things to him that you have never done to me, you whore."

Voncile evil-eyed Omar. She wanted him to cut the crap, and she was livid that he had shoved her. She could barely think straight, but she knew she had to say something to get him to calm down before one of them got hurt.

"It's obvious that you're upset, but you're not going to get anything accomplished by putting your hands on me. I think it would be best for you to leave," she told him. "I'm not going to let you stand there and bully me, Omar. You should know me better than that."

"I thought I did know you. But then you went and fucked my friend—or should I say my enemy? I can't just sweep this underneath the rug even though you want me to. I don't operate like that, and *you* should know *me* better than that."

Voncile was pissed off now. If he thought she was going to let Kasen go now when things were just starting to heat up, then he was sorely mistaken.

"The bottom line is, in order for us to finish what we started, you will have to control your feelings and get over what happened between Kasen and me. Besides, the last time I checked, you and I weren't even in a relationship. Please tell me why we're arguing about who I have sex with."

Omar moved forward, gritting his teeth. "You really want me to tell you why? Is that what you want to know?"

Voncile didn't back down. She stood to confront Omar, crossing her arms in front of her. "Yes. I do want to know why."

His fists tightened. "I can show you better than I can tell you." Catching Voncile off guard, Omar raised his fist and punched her in the stomach.

She grabbed her stomach, doubling over in severe pain. She couldn't believe Omar had done that to her. The hard punch had knocked the breath out of her, but Omar didn't stop there. He pushed her back on the couch then he laid his body over her. His knee was pressed into her chest so she couldn't move. His evil eyes stared into her tearful ones.

"You gave him everything he wanted," Omar hissed. "I thought we were supposed to be in this shit together! How the fuck are we supposed to bring him down when you're over here doing shit that lifts him up? And then you have the audacity to snap your voice at me and catch an attitude like I'm the one who's wrong? Fuck that! Who's wrong, Voncile? 'Cause it damn sure ain't me."

Voncile couldn't say much with all of Omar's weight on top of her. Slow tears ran from the corner of her eyes; she couldn't believe this was happening. Her body weakened, and when Omar shook her around, demanding that she answer him, she quickly spoke up.

"I wa . . . was wrong," she strained to say. "Pleeease get off. I ca . . . can't breathe."

Omar pointed his finger between her eyes. "It's going to hurt more if you fuck him again. I'm warning you, Voncile. Keep your eyes on the prize, until we get this over with. Don't fuck up! Do you hear me?"

She nodded, but rage was in her eyes. How dare he treat her that way? How dare he put his hands on her and demand anything from her? His actions triggered something in her that she couldn't let slide. When Omar got up to walk away, he never could have imagined that Voncile, sweet little Voncile, was on the verge of causing his demise.

She picked up a heavy wooden bat that was in the corner. Omar was on his way out the door when she lifted the bat over her head and came crashing down with it. It landed on the back of his head.

"What the fuck!" he yelled as he stumbled from the blow.

Voncile didn't let another second pass her by. She struck him again and again and again. His blood splattered on the walls, and an eyeball broke from his socket. When his body hit the floor, Voncile stood over him, glaring at him with hate in her eyes. The bloody bat was still in her hand. Making sure that she hit a home run, she struck Omar in the face one last time.

"What do you have to say about that?" She swiped her hands together then spit on him. "You stupid fool. Didn't you know better than to come over here and put your fucking hands on me? Don't you know what kind of woman I am? I bet you won't put your hands on another motherfucking woman again! Will you, Omar? Speak up, my dear. I can't hear you! Were you wrong or right for doing this shit? Better yet, let me answer that for you. You were wrong, wrong, wrong!"

She tossed the bat on top of him then stormed down the hallway. Her breathing was heavy, chest heaved in and out. She was disgusted by how Omar had treated her. She had told him about her past; therefore, he should have known better. He was the only person who had known, aside from the counselor, that damn Mr. Jeffries, whom she had trusted.

Everything that had just happened with Omar sent Voncile's mind spiraling back to the traumatic events of her childhood. First Mr. Jeffries entered her thoughts, and then her mind traveled back further, to the reason she ended up in foster care in the first place. With Omar's blood on her face and hands, she stared at herself in the mirror as her mind went all the way back to the terrible day she witnessed her father murder her mother—the day that changed her life and affected her sanity forever.

Seven-year-old Voncile was standing in the hallway, listening to her parents fight for what seemed like the millionth time. Their voices were raised, and the tension was getting thicker as they spewed insults at each other in the kitchen. Voncile figured things were about to turn ugly. She wanted this to stop. With tears cascading down her face, she ran into the kitchen, still carrying her backpack from school. She stood right in front of her mother, trying to protect her.

"Stop it, Daddy! Stop being so mean to Mommy!"

Everything happened so quickly. Before she knew what was happening, her father had shoved her out of the way, snatched up her mother, and pressed a giant knife against her neck.

"This is for betraying me, bitch. I win, you lose," he said to Voncile's mother before slicing her throat open.

Her mother's body crushed to the floor, and Voncile ran to her, almost slipping in the blood that was collecting beneath her. Using skills she had learned from a first aid lesson at school, Voncile pressed her hands against the gaping wound. In her innocent mind, she thought she could stop the bleeding, but it was too late. Her mother had already stopped breathing.

"Mommy, noooo," she cried when she finally realized her mother was dead. "No, Mommy, come back."

Voncile looked at her father with an evil glare. He stood still, as if cement had been poured over him.

He started to speak. "I . . . I'm sorry, baby girl. I didn't mean to do—"

Joshua paused, dropped the bloody knife, and then he ran off. Seconds later, Voncile *heard the front door shut. She crawled on her hands and knees, through the pool of blood, over to the phone. She dialed 911 and begged for someone to come save her mother. She was still young enough to believe in magic, and was wishing with all her heart that they would bring her back to life. When the paramedics arrived, she learned the truth: she would never see her mother again. That was the day her life became a living hell. It was also the day a rage was planted deep in her soul that would never leave her.*

Years later, Voncile got a small bit of satisfaction when she found out her father was alive. Voncile had just turned eighteen, but she was far from an innocent teen. She was a real force to be reckoned with. People on the streets, where she spent the majority of her time, referred to her as Killa Girl.

After the murder, Joshua had managed to flee the area, and he went into hiding for a long time. Truth was, a black woman murdered in that part of town wasn't given much attention by the police. Voncile doubted they ever seriously looked for her mother's murderer, even though she had witnessed it and told them it was her father. When she was sitting in the station waiting for a social worker to bring her to the foster home, she overheard one of the cops saying, "That punk is probably already in the wind." Another one replied, "Yeah, some other thug will kill him sooner or later. No need for us to look too hard for him." Those words stayed with her forever, and Voncile vowed that she would personally never stop looking for her mother's killer.

When he thought enough years had passed, Joshua got bold and made his way back to the old neighborhood, getting a part time job at a local hardware store. Word got back to Voncile pretty quickly that he was around, and she wasted no time going over there to see for herself. She watched him from a distance for a few days, learning his patterns. He parked in the same spot every day, and always showed up five minutes before his shift was supposed to start. When she felt ready, Voncile made a trip into the store while he was working.

She walked up and down the aisles, pretending to be looking for something. Joshua saw her, and thinking she was just another customer, he approached her from behind. He admired her shapely backside, her long hair, and her high heels that made her look like a hooker.

"Say, baby, can I help you with something?" he asked.

Voncile swung around. Joshua's face fell flat and he stumbled backward a few inches. "Baby girl, is that you? Please tell me that ain't you in them hooker shoes."

Voncile smacked on gum and cocked her head back with a frown. "Old man, you need to back the hell away from me, because I do not know you."

Joshua started having flashbacks of the last time he'd seen his daughter. It was a day that had stayed with him for years. Ever since that day, his life had been speeding downhill. He could never quite get on his feet, and trouble seemed to follow him everywhere. He had been shot, robbed, and beat down by three niggas he owed some money to. He had turned to drugs after killing his wife, and his habit almost cost him his life when he was shot in the leg. Needless to say, it had been rough for Joshua, but he was happy about working again. What was missing was a good woman. He'd had many years to think about his fuckups with Sabrina, and thus far, he hadn't found anyone to replace her. All he found were crackheads like he was, and prostitutes who were willing to give him the goodies for a little bit of change.

"I . . . I apologize for bothering you," Joshua said to his daughter. He knew it was her, but

maybe she didn't recognize him. "I thought you were someone else." More than anything, he was ashamed of himself. As he watched Voncile walk out the door, he told his boss that he wasn't feeling well and needed to go home.

"No problem, man. Just be sure to clock out," his boss said.

"I will, and I promise to be back tomorrow. Just need to go lay my head down for a while and get some rest."

Joshua clocked out and left the hardware store, limping to his car in the midday heat brought about by a blazing sun. He couldn't wait to get into his car to turn on the air conditioner. But when he got inside, there was no relief.

Voncile was in the backseat with a sharp blade in her hand. He didn't have a chance to utter one word before she sliced his throat, just as he had done to her mother. Then she pushed him forward and stabbed him several times in the back.

"Guess what, Dad?" she said. "You lose; I win."

Voncile jumped out of the car and bolted from the scene. Unfortunately for Joshua, there were no witnesses to the crime, which was over in less than a minute. Just like they hadn't bothered to search for Sabrina's killer, the police didn't care enough about this drug addict's death to search for his murderer either. Voncile got away with murder that day, and it made her feel invincible.

Pulling her thoughts back to the present, Voncile splashed water on her face and washed her hands to get rid of some of the blood. She was still on edge as she realized the mess that she now had to clean up in the living room.

She returned to the scene of her horrific crime. Omar's body was lying in a pool of crimson blood. Getting right to work, she lifted his arm and started tugging. It was quite a struggle, but she managed to drag him all the way to the basement door. Knowing that she couldn't lift him, she used all of her strength to shove him down the stairs. His body bumped into the walls, broke several pieces of the railing, and then landed on the cold concrete floor.

Voncile rushed downstairs to move the body further into the basement. *Maybe Raine would like some company,* she thought with an evil laugh.

Raine was lying in the middle of the floor, flat on her back. Voncile turned on the bare light-bulb hanging from the ceiling, causing Raine to lift her head to see what had come crashing down the steps. Her eyes grew wide as she saw Voncile dragging Omar into the small space with her.

Raine started screaming, but it was muffled by the gag that Voncile kept tight around her mouth. Now, however, Voncile was getting a perverse pleasure from the whole situation. She felt powerful and in control. She was enjoying Raine's terror, and she loosened the gag around her mouth so she could taunt her.

"Go ahead and scream. Ain't no one gonna hear you down here." She glanced at Omar's bashed-in head. "And he sure isn't coming to your rescue anytime soon."

"Is that Omar? What did you do to him?" Raine asked in a small, terrified voice.

"This is what happens to people who try to screw me over."

Raine started crying. "Voncile, please. I don't want to be in here with him. I will do whatever you want me to do, but please don't leave me in here like this. I'm so sorry for upsetting you. I promise you that I'll never do it again."

Voncile waved her hand dismissively. "Oh, don't fret. Omar won't be in here for long, and trust me when I say he will not bother you. I have plans for him, but first I need to make sure my jigsaw is still working."

Raine made a gagging sound, like she was about to throw up.

Voncile laughed. "Oh, calm down. How else do you think I'm going to get his body out of here? You saw how hard it was to move his big ass. Of course, I could always just set him on fire. . . ."

Raine's eyes were wide with fear. To Voncile, witnessing her victim's fear felt almost as good as an orgasm.

"Oh, calm down," she said, still teasing her like a cat would tease a trapped mouse.

"I won't make you watch. Put your big-girl panties on and stand up," she told Raine.

Raine stood up on shaky legs, waiting for Voncile to direct her next move.

As she had done at least four or five times a day, Voncile checked to make sure the rope on Raine's wrists was still tight. Then, just to inflict some more damage, she gagged Raine's mouth by stuffing it with one of Omar's bloody socks. She shoved Raine toward the steps, daring her to run off again.

"Let's try this again," Voncile said. "You're going back to your room and this time, you'd better act as if you appreciate luxury living."

Raine nodded, signaling that she did. While Voncile held a tight grip on Raine's arm, they climbed the stairs all the way to the second floor, where Voncile put Raine back in the guest room. No matter how small the windowless room was, it was much better than being in that damp and muggy cellar.

Voncile sat Raine in the corner then removed the sock from her mouth. "Aw, you look terrible," she said, looking at Raine's swollen eyes. "Get some sleep. I'll bring you something to eat for breakfast in the morning."

"Thank you," Raine said in a very weak voice.

Voncile left the room feeling energized, ready to tackle the rest of her cleanup.

Chapter 11

On Monday, Kasen strutted into the office feeling more upbeat than he had been the week before. Sex with Voncile had definitely relieved some of his tension, and even though Omar was pissed at him for sleeping with her, he knew his friend couldn't stay mad forever. He would call him later and apologize, and things would go back to normal. They had never let a chick come between them before. Unfortunately, as soon as he saw Voncile, his good mood was ruined.

"You know your boy is trippin' right now, right?" She started in on Kasen as soon as he walked in the door.

He stopped in front of her desk, taken aback by her aggressive tone. "Good morning to you, too, Voncile," he said, trying to lighten the mood.

"Uh-uh. You don't get to shut me down like that. Not after what Omar did to me."

Kasen put down his briefcase and leaned against her desk, prepared to listen. "What did he do?"

"I don't know how that so-called friend of yours got my number, but Omar called me early Sunday morning, talking about why wouldn't I go on a date with him. He called me every nasty name in the book. Bitch, whore . . . you name it, he called me one. Said I didn't have to worry about him coming around the office anymore because he didn't want to be around a ho who had sex with his friend."

Kasen didn't know what to say. He just stared at her with his eyes wide open, revealing his guilty conscience.

"My question to you, Kasen, is why did you tell him about us? It really makes me look bad."

Kasen felt horrible. What he thought was innocent shit-talking between two friends had turned into a giant mess. What the hell was wrong with Omar? Why would he call Voncile, and more so, why would he call her all those vile names? Something was up with his friend, and he would get to the bottom of it, but for the time being, he owed Voncile an apology.

Kasen looked at Voncile like a sad puppy, trying to defend his actions. "I'm sorry that he came to you with such nonsense, and it was wrong for me to discuss our intimate moments with him. I made a big mistake, and I don't blame you for being upset with me."

"Thank you for the apology," she said, and Kasen could have sworn she was fighting to suppress a smile.

"Would you like me to have him call you and apologize?" he asked.

She answered in a hurry. "Oh, no. As far as I'm concerned, I'll be happy if I never have to see him again."

"Done," he said. "I will make sure he never comes around here again while you're at work."

"Thank you," she said, letting her smile break through this time.

Since Voncile had forgiven Kasen, he felt one hundred again. He strolled into his office and settled in behind his desk to get ready for his day. Before his first patient arrived, he reached for his phone to call Omar, leaving a message when the voice mail picked up.

"Omar, man, I don't know what is up with you, but that shit you pulled with Voncile was uncalled for. I have never seen you go off on a chick like that before, so I'm gonna give you the benefit of the doubt and assume there's something else going on that has you messed up. Whatever it is, Omar, you need to get yourself together. In the meantime, don't bring yourself around here to my office. She don't want to see you, and I don't blame her. Matter of fact, I think I need a little time to cool off too. Until you're ready to talk to me man to man without flying off the handle, don't bother to call me back."

Kasen ended the call with no regrets for what he'd said. Omar was out of line. His friend had some serious growing up to do.

Things got better for Kasen later in the day, when one of his patients, Mr. Davidson, sat across the desk from Kasen with a wide smile on his face and declared that everything between him and his wife was great. Kasen's advice had changed his world around, and his wife was now giving him the special attention he needed.

"Thank you, thank you, thank you again," he said. "It's been on and poppin' in my house. My wife has truly stepped it up."

Kasen smiled. This was the reason he loved his job, being able to help people change their situations.

"I followed your advice to the letter, Doc, and that was all it took. You are my new hero," Mr. Davidson said with a laugh.

"I'm here to help," Kasen said humbly.

"Well, I appreciate that, but I guess I won't be needing your services now that me and my wife worked things out," Mr. Davidson answered as he stood up and extended his hand to Kasen.

"I totally understand, and I wish you and your wife the best," Kasen said as he shook the man's hand.

Kasen watched Mr. Davidson exit his office with plenty of pep in his step. He wished all of his patients had the same results, and even though most of them did, there were some who took years to come to grips with their situations. His mind wandered to his newest patient, Patrice Davenport. He hadn't heard back from her yet, and he wondered how her situation was unfolding. He was tempted to call and check on her, but knew it was best to let a person make the decision themselves to ask for help. If they felt forced to come to therapy, they generally weren't very successful. He hoped she would call sometime soon.

Kasen stepped out of his office.

"Hey, Voncile. You want to go to lunch with me?" he asked.

She looked up from the papers on her desk and noticed his expression. "Well, don't you look happy," she said. "You must have had a good session."

"Sure did," he answered. "And now I'm ready to go out and celebrate for a few. Or at least go to lunch. You interested?"

"Oh, trust me, I'm always interested," she said flirtatiously. All traces of her earlier anger were gone, and Kasen was relieved about that.

Suddenly, his eyes traveled to her neckline, and a puzzled expression came across his face.

"Uh, that's a nice necklace," he said, his voice sounding tight.

Her hand went to her neck, clutching the pearl strand that hung there. "Oh, thanks. This old thing came from my grandmother. She loved pearl necklaces, and she gave it to me two weeks before she passed away. I can't remember the last time I wore it. For some reason, I was thinking about her this morning and decided to put it on."

"Well, it's a nice necklace. You should wear it more often." For some reason, he couldn't shake the feeling that something was not right. Then he realized what his problem was. The necklace reminded him of one that Raine used to wear all the time. He shook his head to clear his mind of Raine. Plenty of women wore pearl necklaces; he couldn't trip every time he saw someone wearing one. He just needed a little more time to get Raine out of his system, he thought.

"Thank you. Maybe I will wear it more often," Voncile said. She stood up from her desk. "Now what about that lunch?"

He held out his arm for her, and she placed her hand on it as he led her out of the office.

They went to a nearby pizza joint that had some of the best sausage and pepperoni pizza. Both of them were relaxed as they enjoyed their time together, getting to know each other as more than just work colleagues. Kasen entertained Voncile with stories about some of the things he had gotten in trouble for in high school. He didn't seem like the kind of guy who would do anything bad, but when Voncile learned that Kasen had put a rat in the principal's shoes, she was tickled pink.

"My parents were so pissed at me," Kasen said. "I got suspended in my senior year, and I almost wasn't able to graduate. Fortunately, after a little begging and pleading and a whole lot of community service work, I was in there."

Voncile laughed. "I think the worst thing I ever did in high school was bump somebody too hard in the hallway. I never got in trouble, because I hung with the quiet and nerdy girls that people didn't want to be around," she lied.

"Most nerds in high school are not the same people today," Kasen said.

"Who you tellin'?" she joked.

"I mean, look at you," Kasen continued. "You're beautiful, intelligent, funny, and sexy as hell. I know I haven't gone into great detail about some of the things that I've been going through lately, but I want to thank you for being so kind and understanding, especially about what I told Omar. I hope you can forgive me." Kasen actually surprised himself by heaping so many compliments on Voncile, but he had to admit it felt good to be flirting with another woman instead of indulging in a pity party about Raine.

Voncile blushed, looking deep into his eyes. "Of course I forgive you. I don't hold grudges, Kasen, and I'm sure you meant no harm. Omar is the one who got ugly when he didn't have to. Personally, I think he's very jealous of you. I never told you this, but when he stops by the office, he always speaks ill of you. He has said many negative things about you that made me wonder how you could ever consider him a friend."

Kasen leaned back and crossed his arms over his chest. He was surprised to hear Omar was not the person he thought he was, but he didn't want to dwell in the negative at the moment. He was enjoying his lunch with Voncile, who was becoming more beautiful by the minute in his eyes. "I'm sure he has said a lot about me, but I don't want to hear about it right now. Remember, I came out to celebrate Mr. Davidson's success today."

Voncile lifted her glass of water for a toast. "To Mr. Davidson, then."

Kasen clinked his glass against hers.

They returned to the office a little after two o'clock, and Kasen went right back to his desk.

A short while later, Voncile stuck her head in and said, "I hate to have to tell you this, but Omar called and left a message."

"He did? What did he say?" Kasen asked, hoping his friend was ready to apologize for his bad behavior.

"It wasn't good," Voncile answered.

"Well, what did he say?"

She sighed. "If you really must know, he called me another whore and called you a sucker. Told you to kiss his ass."

"What!" Kasen jumped up from his desk as if he wanted to go hear the message for himself.

"I deleted the message. Figured that you wouldn't want to hear it," Voncile said quickly, stopping him in his tracks.

Kasen shook his head with disgust. He couldn't believe that their friendship had gone down the drain so quickly, although a part of him knew his friend was a mess and always suspected that things could turn ugly before Omar got his shit together.

"Maybe that's a good thing," Kasen said, shaking his head. "If he happens to come here, be sure to come and get me. I don't want to call the police on him, but I will if things get out of hand."

"I will," Voncile said.

Acting on an impulse, Kasen walked quickly over to her and put his hand under her chin. "Meanwhile," he said, "I've been dying to do this all day."

Kasen placed his finger on Voncile's chin, turning her head to face him as he leaned in to kiss her. They savored the moment as the heat rose between them.

Obviously Voncile was on the same page as him, because suddenly she became the aggressive one. She unzipped Kasen's slacks, lowering them to his ankles. Her pussy was ready to receive him, but she needed something tasty in her mouth. She dropped to her knees, making his dick disappear. The feel of his mushroom head massaging her throat made her high. Her eyes were closed;

jaws were sucked in real tight. Kasen could barely contain himself. He was in a daze, thinking about how Voncile had quickly stepped up to the mic and delivered a masterful performance. With his back against the wall, his eyes were shut too. He raked his fingers through her hair, grabbing it tight when she sped up the pace.

"I swear," he moaned, losing all control in the sexy moment. "I could do this with you every day for the rest of my life."

Voncile backed away from his steel and stood with her back facing him; then she bent over far enough to touch her toes. With her legs open wide, Kasen plunged into her wetness, causing her pussy to lock on him like it was specifically created for him. The smell of sex in the air excited them both, and as their bodies rocked perfectly together, neither could ignore their instant connection.

"Are you ready?" Kasen said as his thighs slapped hard against Voncile's ass. "I want you to come with me. It feels so good when you do, and I. Am. Ready," he said, matching his words with the rhythm of his thrusts.

She pushed back, and he pushed forward. Her toes curled, his fanned out. Their breathing increased, and as they did a quick exchange of juices, their legs almost gave out on them. Kasen wrapped his arm around Voncile's waist just to make sure she didn't fall.

"Fuuuuuck," she cried out. "Mmmmm, Kasen, you are doing it, baaaaby! You are doing it!"

No question he did it well—so well that when Kasen eased out of Voncile, a flood of her excitement rained down her legs. His entire shaft was polished with a mixture of their cream, and it was, indeed, a beautiful sight for both of them.

They sealed it with a quick kiss. Voncile had a glow in her eyes that made her look like a new woman, and she looked beautiful to Kasen. It was almost enough for him to totally forget about Raine.

Chapter 12

Raine was completely out of it. She had no clue what day it was, what time it was, nor could she guess how long she had been in that room. Day in and out, she stared at the white walls, only daring to move when she knew Voncile wasn't in the house. She had gotten all the way to ten thousand when it came to counting sheep. Her thoughts of Kasen had stopped. There was no reason to think about the love of her life, especially since she didn't think she would ever see him again.

After what Voncile had shown her the other day, Raine knew that she was in the hands of one sick bitch. Voncile had come into the room with one of Omar's fingers. She laughed about cutting it off and said that it looked like a barbecued hot dog when she put it over a fire. Raine didn't see a damn thing funny, but at that moment, she laughed right along with Voncile. In fact, she started to talk to Voncile as if they were really friends, hoping that her new attitude toward Voncile would somehow get her to come to her senses.

With her hands still tied behind her back, Raine stood up and paced the floor. The other day, she had rammed herself into the door and wound up hurting her shoulder. It was bruised, but she didn't think it was broken. Voncile was not there during the day, so Raine used that time to try anything to get out of there. She kicked the door and slammed her body against it, but nothing worked. Raine felt like giving up.

Raine leaned over and vomited in the pot Voncile had left for her. She had been feeling so queasy lately, probably from the nasty food Voncile brought in when she bothered to feed her at all. She had also been feeling dizzy, probably because she was starving.

When she heard movement downstairs, she knew that Voncile was home, and she raced back to her spot and sat down. Shortly after, Voncile unlocked the door and came into the room, rolling a TV on a cart. She appeared excited about something.

"You look awfully happy, Voncile," Raine said, trying to keep up the friendly attitude she had been displaying lately.

"Girl, all I can say is things have been going very well for me. Eventually you'll see why, but for now, I brought this TV in here so you can watch it. I know you get bored sometimes, and there really isn't much in here for you to do."

"No, there's not," Raine said. "And thank you again. You've been too kind to me. I do appreciate your kindness."

When Voncile turned her back to plug in the TV, Raine rolled her eyes.

Voncile looked at the clear picture on the TV then turned to Raine. "Looks like you're in business. What channel would you like me to put on?"

"It doesn't matter. I'll watch *Sesame Street* if I have to."

Voncile laughed. She put the TV on BET and then headed to the door without another word.

"I don't mean to bother you," Raine called after her, "but is there any chance that you can untie my hands? I have come to the realization that I'm not going anywhere until you say so. I'm good with that, but my wrists are real sore and they sting."

Voncile hesitated, but then she walked over to Raine, examining her wrists. They were in bad shape. Raine's flesh was skinned and bleeding.

"I thought that bringing you a TV would be enough," Voncile said. "This is the last thing I'm going to do for you, so don't ask me to do shit else."

"I won't. I promise you this will be it."

Voncile tried to remove the rope, but it was so tight that she had to leave the room and go get a knife to cut it. She wasn't careful when she cut it either; she wound up taking a chunk out of Raine's wrist. It started to bleed, and feeling relief and pain at the same time, Raine used her pajama shirt, along with her other hand, to cease the bleeding.

"Is that better?" Voncile said when the bleeding had slowed down. "I hope so, because I need to hurry and get ready for my date this evening. He's coming over, and you'd better be on your best behavior. If not, your life ends tonight."

Raine tried to ignore the evil expression on Voncile's face. She was just happy to have her hands free. She wiggled her arms around, trying to eliminate some of the stiffness. Even if she wanted to take a swing at Voncile, she couldn't. She was too weak. A punch from her would do no good. Voncile wouldn't think twice about tying her up again, so for now, Raine left things as is.

She watched as Voncile walked over to the aluminum pot that Raine used as a toilet. Voncile turned her head to look at Raine.

"Are you sick or something?" Voncile asked.

"I . . . my system has to get used to the food you keep giving me. I'm not used to eating moldy bread and a bunch of leftovers. That's what's making me sick." She didn't dare admit to Voncile that she also had missed her period, and a part of her wondered if she might be pregnant.

Voncile rolled her eyes. "Well, I'm not gonna spend a bunch of my money trying to feed you. You do understand that, don't you?"

Raine nodded, even though she didn't understand. She didn't understand any of this. Voncile had yet to give her any real reason for any of this.

Voncile turned to leave again but then stopped dead in her tracks. She swung around, looking at Raine with a raised brow.

"Do you think you're pregnant?" Voncile asked.

Raine was absolutely shocked by the question. How could Voncile know this? "No," Raine rushed to say, knowing that she was lying, but also instinctively knowing that Voncile would not be happy if she was in fact pregnant. "I take my birth control pills faithfully."

"When is the last time you had your period?" Voncile questioned.

"I just came off, so I don't expect it soon," Raine said then quickly changed the subject, knowing that it was her best chance to avoid setting Voncile off. "Enjoy your evening. Whoever you have plans with, he sure is a lucky guy."

Her words put a slight smile on Voncile's face.

"Yes, he is lucky," she mumbled as she left the room.

After Voncile closed the door and locked it, Raine sighed with relief. She massaged her wrists, able to stop the deep cut from bleeding by continuously pressing on it. Feeling as free as she could possibly feel under the circumstances, she moved around the room, swinging her arms and lifting them over her head. Her bones creaked, and she cracked her knuckles and raked her fingers through her hair, trying to knock out some of the kinks.

Suddenly, she felt the urge to vomit again, so she rushed over to the pot. Her eyes watered, and then tears started to drip from her eyes. As much as she didn't want to admit it to herself, a small part of her knew that she was carrying Kasen's baby. That made her even more upset. She knew Kasen would be happy about this if he knew. She could almost see the smile on his face and the joy in his eyes. If her assumption was indeed true, not only would Raine have to fight to save her own life, but she had to save her child's life too.

***

About an hour later, Raine was lying on the floor with her head resting on a pillow. She stared at the TV, but she was so focused on the idea that she might be pregnant that it was more like the TV was watching her.

She lifted her head when she heard the door unlock. In walked Voncile, prancing around in one of Raine's scanty negligées.

"The only reason I'm wearing this one is because it still had tags on it. I can't stress enough how many nice pieces of clothing you have. I haven't had a chance to go through everything, but this here I couldn't resist," Voncile told her.

Raine sat up and forced herself to smile. "It looks nice on you," she said softly. "And red is definitely your color."

"I agree. Blue is too, but this red got me looking smoking hot."

Raine couldn't deny that the negligée looked good on Voncile, who had a flawless body with curves in all the right places. What man wouldn't appreciate the way she looked? But no matter how good she looked, Raine couldn't help but wonder what man was crazy enough to deal with her.

Voncile walked over to the TV. "Have you been watching this thing? The remote is in the same place I left it."

"I just left it on the same channel you put it on."

Voncile changed the channel, and then said, "Well, there's a good romance movie coming on around eight. Keep it there and check it out."

Raine didn't think much of it, until Voncile stepped away from the TV and left. Looking at the TV, Raine saw what looked to be the inside of a bedroom. It was clearly set for a romantic scene, with candles flickering, soft music playing, and a bottle of champagne chilling in an ice bucket. Raine felt disgusted as she realized that this was not a TV channel, but rather a video feed from another room in the house. This sick bitch wanted her to watch as she got it on with her date. That idea was sickening enough, but a while later, when she looked at the TV and saw Kasen enter the room with Voncile, Raine wanted to die.

Chapter 13

Kasen was looking forward to having sex with Voncile again. Even if it wasn't a love connection, at least it was something to help fill the void he felt ever since Raine left. Voncile was becoming everything Kasen needed her to be and then some during this difficult time. As each day passed by, his thoughts of Raine faded. Voncile had him underneath her spell.

As soon as he exited his car, there she was, sitting on the porch in a red negligee. Her legs were crossed, and the look in her eyes told him that she was ready for a repeat of what had happened in the office earlier.

Kasen walked up to her with his hands in his pockets. He flashed a grin then complimented Voncile on making his muscle rise and ready to turn tricks for her.

"How do you do it?" he asked. "All you do is sit there looking pretty and you got me standing at attention."

Voncile stood and walked up to him. Her hand landed on the heat he was packing. It was hard as ever. "Mmmm, isn't that interesting. I'm going to enjoy showing you something so new, so exciting, and very different tonight. Follow me."

As Voncile sashayed away, Kasen fell in line and followed. His eyes were fixed on her healthy, dimple-free ass cheeks. All he could think about was separating her cheeks and diving right in.

When Voncile opened the doors to what looked to be a barn converted into a bedroom, he was stunned. The setup was real nice and cozy. It kind of had a bed-and-breakfast feel to it. The bed was covered in a thick, paisley-printed comforter with several plush pillows on top. Candles were lit everywhere, and soft jazz music was playing from a small speaker on the night stand. Kasen was so impressed by Voncile's efforts that he pulled her to him, planting a soft kiss on her forehead.

"You are truly amazing," he said. "And without even knowing it, you are so on time."

Voncile laid her head against his muscular chest and wrapped her arms around his perfect waist, inhaling his masculine scent. "I'm no more amazing than you are." She pulled back and looked up into his eyes. "I know that you're still seeing Raine, and I don't want to interfere with that. Unfortunately for me, I'm finding myself falling in love with you. I'm trying to control my feelings, but I can't ignore that I feel a serious connection with you."

Kasen placed two fingers over her lips. "Raine and I are over. Done. You don't have to worry about her. But I have to be honest and tell you that I'm not ready to commit myself to another relationship. Let's not rush this, okay? In the meantime, let's focus on having some fun."

"Oh, we're gonna have some fun, all right," Voncile said. "You're going to have so much fun that you won't even remember your former girlfriend's name after tonight."

She walked over and picked up the bottle of champagne that had been chilling in an ice bucket, then crawled on the bed, getting on her knees. Slowly untying the straps on her silk negligee, she lowered it underneath her breasts.

Kasen looked at the firm globes with anticipation in his eyes. He couldn't wait to suck them, and when Voncile tilted the bottle, pouring a little champagne between her cleavage, Kasen stepped forward eagerly.

Climbing on the bed with her, he removed the negligee so he could admire her naked body in all its beauty. He massaged her breasts, licking up the droplets of champagne that were left behind.

Voncile moaned as she leaned back on the bed, spreading her legs wide. Kasen took the champagne from her and poured it all over her stomach. As the sweet liquid spread down between her legs, Kasen dove in and lapped up every last drop.

Once he'd brought Voncile to orgasm twice, Kasen stood up and removed his clothes, revealing his huge hard-on. Voncile smiled wickedly.

"You're going to get tired of fucking me," Voncile said. "How much do you want to bet?"

"I will never get tired of fucking you, and I'm gonna put it on you so good you damn sure won't get tired of fucking me either," he replied as he climbed back on the bed and pressed his body up against hers.

Voncile threw her arms around Kasen's neck, and when he slid into her wetness, she gasped in pleasure. Kasen closed his eyes and got to work, so he didn't notice when Voncile turned her face toward the tiny camera she had concealed in the bedroom and winked at Raine, who she hoped was watching every stroke.

***

Raine was staring at the TV in shock, watching as Voncile lowered her negligee and started pouring champagne on her breasts. The look in Kasen's eyes told Raine everything she needed to know: he wanted to fuck Voncile.

"Nooooo," she cried out. "Noooo, Kasen! Please, nooooo!" Raine pounded her fists on the door, hoping that he was somewhere in the house where he could hear her. She stomped her feet and yelled at the top of her lungs. "Come get meeee! Can you hear me? Please come get meeee!"

She went back to the TV, watching in agony as the sex between Voncile and Kasen intensified. Kasen's face was now buried between Voncile's legs. He was giving her the royal treatment—a treatment that Raine had gotten quite often. Now that Voncile was on the receiving end, she was scratching his back and telling him how good his tongue felt inside of her. She was screaming and shouting out words that weren't part of the English language.

Raine was purely disgusted and also felt totally betrayed. Even if Kasen believed that she had left him, how the hell could he have just moved on so quickly? Then a sick feeling came over her as she realized that maybe the reason he was over her so fast was that he had wanted to be with Voncile all along.

It became too painful for Raine to watch. Looking into Voncile's fluttering eyes one last time, Raine shut that shit down and kicked the TV, knocking it to the floor. Thinking fast, she grabbed a sharp piece of plastic from among the shards of the broken TV. She used the plastic to slice a small whole in the carpet, and then she slid her new weapon into the hole she'd made to hide it. She then returned to her lonely corner, crying her heart out about what her eyes had witnessed. If she ever got out of there, she would make Kasen regret ever being with Voncile.

Early the next morning, Voncile came into the room, dressed for work. She looked at Raine, who sat silently, with her back against the wall. She had not slept at all, because the images of Kasen and Voncile had kept her awake all night. Voncile, however, appeared high as the sky. She was beaming.

"Girl, what is wrong with you?" Voncile said in a mocking tone. "I can't believe you were that upset. What is Kasen supposed to do while you're away playing house with another man? You didn't think he would wait on you to come back, did you?"

Raine remained quiet, fearful of saying the wrong thing to Voncile this morning and really setting her off.

Not getting the reaction she'd hoped for, Voncile continued to tease Raine. She walked to the other side of the room and looked down at the pieces of the broken TV. "Awww, your feelings must have really been hurt. I guess mine would have been too." She turned around and smirked at Raine. "You should have told me that Kasen could fuck like that. Did you see him last night? I loved every bit of it. No man has ever sucked on my pussy the way he did."

She sighed happily, and the dreamy look on her face told Raine that she was reliving the good sex she'd had last night. "You know, we just can't get enough of each other," Voncile said. "Ever since you've been away, we've been indulging ourselves almost every day. All I can say is, what a man."

Tears welled in Raine's eyes, but she remained silent. She watched as Voncile trotted over to the stink pot, looking inside.

"I can't believe you vomited again. You need to stop this shit and get yourself together. I'm going to fix you something different to eat to-day. If you throw that up, then I don't know what I'll do."

Voncile snatched up the pot, carrying it out of the room and to the bathroom. She had left the door unlocked, and for a moment Raine contemplated making her move to escape, but as if she had read Raine's mind, Voncile rushed back into the room and dropped the pot back in the corner.

"There," Voncile said. "All clean. I'll see you later."

Raine stared at her, wondering if this crazy woman expected her to say "Thank you." She was so frustrated she wanted to scream. Her body was exhausted from this whole ordeal, but she imagined herself having the energy to jump up and claw out Voncile's eyes.

Voncile was obviously enjoying every cruel thing she said to Raine, like she was trying to kill her by breaking her heart. "I asked Kasen to go on vacation with me," she said. "What do you think? Any suggestions of places you've been to with him before?"

A single tear escaped and ran down Raine's cheek. That made Voncile smile.

"If I do go, though, I'll have to decide what to do with you. I'm getting to the point where I don't need you anymore. So, sit tight and don't let the bed bugs bite." Voncile laughed as she left the room.

As she heard the lock turning on the door, Raine shouted out, "There is no bed in here, bitch! You and Kasen both can go to hell!"

Voncile stormed back into the room. She punched Raine in her face then grabbed the back of her head, damn near breaking her neck as she forced Raine to look up at her.

"Don't you dare speak to me that way in my house! Kasen and I are going to be together for a very long time, and there isn't a damn thing that you can do about it!" She banged Raine's head against the wall then let her hair go.

Raine kept her head lowered, so Voncile wouldn't see the pure hatred in her eyes.

"Good-bye, tramp. And get some sleep. You look terrible. It's no surprise why Kasen would leave your ass to be with me."

Chapter 14

Kasen went into work early, even though he and Voncile had had a very late night. He thoroughly enjoyed their time together, but then he had tossed and turned in his bed all night. He was worried that Voncile was getting too attached. To him, it was too early to be throwing around the word "love." It was too soon to start a real relationship, yet she not only wanted to spend the entire weekend with him, but she also suggested they should go on vacation together. To Kasen, spending that much time together would make them a couple—like he had been with Raine. He surely wasn't ready to take that risk again. He didn't know what else he needed to say to Voncile so she would ease up a little, but he meant what he'd said about taking things one day at a time. He was starting to think that getting sexually involved with his secretary was a risk he shouldn't have taken.

As he sat at his desk thinking about the situation, Voncile came strolling in. "Good morning," she said, greeting him with a huge grin on her face.

Yet again, the dress she wore looked so familiar to him. He started to think that he was going crazy, and he didn't dare ask Voncile where she'd gotten the dress from, especially since he had already inquired about the necklace and was wrong. He gazed at her with a very awkward feeling inside.

"Hello, Voncile," he said. "How are you today?"

"I'm feeling damn good this morning," she answered. "You worked out all my kinks last night, lover."

He tried to smile, but he still felt uncomfortable. "Voncile, please sit down for a minute. I'd like to talk to you."

The smile left her face, but she was still trying to keep the mood light as she said, "Yeah, you worked me out for sure. In fact, I need to go get my hair done because you had me sweating last night. Do you mind if I leave early today? The only time my beautician can see me is at two."

"No problem," he said, almost wishing she would leave earlier so he could get rid of the bad feelings he was experiencing.

Voncile sashayed over to the chair and sat down. He thought she was going a little overboard to impress him. Now that she was closer, he got a whiff of her perfume. He had held back from asking about the dress, but now he couldn't help it. He had to ask.

"What fragrance is that?" he asked with a peculiar look on his face. The scent was just like Raine's. It made him think of her.

She gave a weird little laugh and said, "Truthfully, I didn't even look at the bottle when I snatched it off my dresser this morning. Do you like it?"

"Yes, I do. I love it . . . and I'm very familiar with it."

Voncile adjusted herself in the seat. "Familiar with it how?" she asked, sounding a bit nervous.

Kasen instantly regretted bringing it up. After all, he had screwed this woman every which way last night, so it wouldn't be very respectful this morning to ask her to listen while he talked about his ex and how much he truly still missed her. He decided to change the subject.

"Oh, I don't know. Maybe I smelled it in a store or something. Anyway, have you heard from Omar again? I tried to reach him this morning, but I keep getting his voice mail," he said.

"No, I haven't heard from him, but I told you what his last message said. He wanted to be as far away from us as he could get. I guess we should believe him."

"He may have said that, but that's not like Omar. We've had our differences when he did some stupid shit in the past, but he always calls to apologize. It seems strange that he hasn't called, especially after the voice mail message I left him."

Voncile shrugged, looking around the room like the subject was boring her. "I guess you know him much better than I do. If he calls, I will definitely let you know."

"Great."

Voncile leaned in toward the desk and tried to look deeply into Kasen's eyes. She appeared to be getting ready for another round of office sex, but Kasen had other things on his mind. He definitely needed to address their situation before Voncile got even more attached and things got out of hand. He had a professional practice to run, and didn't want things to blow up in his face because his secretary couldn't stay focused on work.

He cleared his throat and leaned back a little bit to put some distance between them. "Listen, Voncile, I just want to be clear about us, okay?

Last night was spectacular, and you are breaking a brotha down, but I was serious when I said I want to take this one day at a time. That means we don't have to spend time with each other every day. And as far as when we're here in the office, let's try to keep things strictly business, okay?"

Voncile stared at him for a few seconds without saying a word, and Kasen was a little worried she was about to go off on him. He was relieved when she finally spoke up calmly.

"So does that mean we're not going away together this weekend?" she asked.

"I don't think so. I'm going to be busy this weekend. I have a friend who I haven't seen in years, so I invited him to come hang out." He had made the plans in a hurry that morning, mostly so he would have an excuse not to go away with Voncile.

"I understand, Kasen. And you're right; we don't have to see each other every day," she said. Kasen couldn't help but notice that her facial expression did not match her words. She was agreeing with him, but the way she narrowed her eyes, she looked like she was cursing him inside her head.

"Okay, good. I'm glad you understand my point of view," he said, still with that awkward feeling in the pit of his stomach. "Now if you don't mind, I need a little privacy to prepare for my first patient."

Voncile stood up and left the room without another word. Kasen shook his head. The sex between them sure was good, but he wondered if he should be listening to that little voice inside him that was telling him she might be the kind to become obsessive. Normally he would call Omar to get his opinion in this situation. He really wished his friend would call so they could clear the air. It was terrible how both his fiancée and his best friend had disappeared from his life at the same time, leaving him no one close to talk to.

Later that afternoon, Voncile knocked on the door to his office while he was in the middle of a session.

"I'm getting ready to leave. Is there anything else I can do for you before I go?"

"No, I'm fine. Have a good evening," he said, wondering why she had bothered to interrupt his session to tell him that. He would have to remind her about professionalism next time he saw her.

"You too. And good-bye, Miss Sanders. Good seeing you again. Kiss that beautiful grandbaby of yours for me, and tell your daughter I said hello."

"I surely will," Miss Sanders said with a smile.

As Voncile left and closed the door, Miss Sanders said, "That secretary of yours is so sweet, Dr. Phillips."

"Yes, she is," Kasen agreed, relieved that his patient wasn't bothered by the interruption.

A few minutes later, he finished up his session with Miss Sanders and walked her to the elevator. "Have a nice weekend," he told her as she stepped on and the doors closed.

He turned around to head back into his office when suddenly the door to the stairway burst open and Voncile came running out. Her hair was a mess, her mascara was smeared all over her face like a raccoon, and the top of her dress looked like it had been torn. She fell to her knees, panting and crying.

Kasen raced to her side. "What happened?" he said, pulling her up and wrapping his arms around her shaking body.

Voncile sobbed like a baby. "Omar was in the backseat of my car. He tried to hurt me, Kasen! He tried to rape me!"

Her words felt like a punch in the gut. Kasen had no idea Omar would do something like this. Friend or not, he wanted him arrested. "Don't worry. Omar will be arrested. I'm going to call the police, and I want you to tell them everything that happened."

He felt Voncile's body tighten up. She pulled away from him, her tears suddenly vanishing. "I don't want to get the police involved."

Kasen was confused. "Why not? He hurt you, Voncile. He needs to be locked up."

She hung her head like she was embarrassed and said, "I have unpaid parking tickets, and there's a warrant out for my arrest. If the police come here, I'll be arrested."

"I'll pay the tickets and make them release you. You have to let me call the police on Omar. If you don't, he's going to get away with this. You don't want that to happen, do you?"

Voncile started pacing nervously, and Kasen felt bad for pressuring her to do something she clearly didn't want to.

"Can't you just install some cameras around the parking lot? You can protect me, Kasen, can't you? We don't need to involve the police." She sounded like a scared child, and Kasen immediately felt an instinct to keep her safe.

"I will do whatever to make sure he doesn't hurt you again. I'll put some cameras around here, and some at your house, too. But please consider talking to the police."

"I will," she said. "Just not today. Let me cool out for a moment and get my thoughts together."

Kasen felt terrible for what had happened to her. He would honor her request and leave the police out of it for now. Since she didn't want law enforcement involved, he would have to handle it another way. He couldn't wait to get his hands on Omar—if only he knew where the hell his friend was hiding.

Chapter 15

Voncile left the office knowing that Kasen was in her corner. It had been a stroke of genius on her part to go into the stairwell, rip her dress, smear her makeup, and then run back in there crying rape. He had nearly broken her heart when he said he wanted to slow things down between them, but she was sure that after the damsel in distress act she had performed, he'd be on board with the relationship moving forward. He was a sucker for a woman in need. He was a therapist, after all.

She was pretty proud of herself for thinking on her feet like she did when Kasen wanted to call the cops. The truth was that she didn't have any unpaid parking tickets, but Kasen was such a sucker for a vulnerable woman that he believed her without question and promised not to call the police. Even if he decided to go look for Omar on his own, Voncile was not worried.

He definitely wouldn't find him, because Omar was gone, gone, gone. Voncile had made sure of that, and she was about to make sure Raine was gone too.

She had just about had it with Raine. Voncile could only be so nice. She wasn't going to tolerate Raine's smart mouth anymore. It was time to get her out of Voncile's house, especially since she predicted that Kasen would be spending more time there. After a while, it would look suspicious if she always took him to the barn to get their freak on. She didn't want him questioning why they couldn't go into her house, but she was afraid to take him in there in case Raine started that damn moaning and groaning again.

Raine was becoming too bold lately. Voncile could tell that she had been trying to get out of there. There were many small dents on the door, as well as on the walls, as if she had been kicking at them. The knob was loose, and Raine's body showed visible bruises that Voncile hadn't put there. Still, Voncile hadn't brought any of that to Raine's attention. There was no need to warn her. If Raine ever managed to make it on the other side of that door, Voncile would blow her fucking brains out.

Voncile entered her house with the mail in her hand, thinking about how anxious she was to finish off this ordeal with Raine being in her house so she could move on with Kasen. If only Omar hadn't talked her into keeping Raine at her place, she could have been done with her already.

She thumbed through the mail while standing in the foyer. A letter addressed to her from the IRS put her in a bad mood before she even opened the envelope. Coming from the government, it was never good news. As she started to read the letter, she heard a loud banging sound that shook the house, bringing her mood even lower. The pictures on her living room walls went from straight to crooked. The crystals on her chandelier wiggled around, and a book that was on one of her shelves hit the floor. She didn't know what the hell Raine was doing upstairs, but Voncile realized that it was a good thing she had come home early.

She rushed to her room, snatching the gun from underneath her mattress. Today was the day. The day Raine would die. This was it, and Voncile was about to let that bitch have it in a major way.

She quickly unlocked the door and went inside, but what she saw actually amused her. Raine stood there with a piece of sharp plastic in her shaking hand. Voncile laughed as she aimed the gun at Raine.

"Okay, bitch, try me. Go ahead and lunge out at me with that right now. See what will happen to your ass. If you want to live, you damn well better think twice."

Raine held a tight grip on the piece of plastic. She knew there was no way for her to defeat Voncile with a gun aimed at her. At that moment, Raine completely gave up. She dropped the plastic on the floor and fell to her knees.

"Kill me!" she screamed out. "Please kill me now!"

Voncile pursed her lips and rolled her eyes. "I hate weak bitches who don't know how to fight. You give up too easily. You don't deserve Kasen. He doesn't need a woman like you in his life, and I'm so glad that he now has me."

Raine clutched at her stomach, but instead of running over to the stink pot, she vomited right at Voncile's feet. Voncile was so ready to pull the trigger, but then an unwelcome thought entered her mind like a lightning bolt.

"You are pregnant, aren't you?" she said. "That's why you've been throwing up, and you know darn well that you're carrying Kasen's baby."

Raine spat on the floor to clear her mouth. "No. I swear I'm not. It's the food."

"Food my ass. Back up and go sit in your corner." She went and snatched up the piece of plastic in case Raine thought about trying to use it again. "I'm going to the store, and I'll be right back. Save me some pee. I'm finding out today if you're really pregnant."

Voncile left in a pretty decent mood considering the circumstances. She was already formulating a plan in her mind that would use Raine's pregnancy to her own benefit. She was willing to do whatever to keep Kasen on her team, and a positive pregnancy test was a good way to do it.

She purchased a pregnancy test at the drugstore then returned home with it. When she got back to the room, Raine was lying flat on her back, staring at the ceiling like a zombie.

"Here," Voncile said, handing her the pregnancy test. "Get your crazy ass up and go take a piss over there."

Raine was moving slowly, but she did finally get up and open the box. She lifted her top then straddled her legs over the stink pot, peeing on the stick. When she was done, Voncile rushed over, snatching it from her hand. They both waited nervously, even if it was for different reasons. Seconds later, the test was confirmed.

"Positive," Voncile said with a smile. She looked at Raine, whose facial expression was flat. "Aren't you happy about this? We are going to have a baby. I can't wait to tell Kasen!"

Raine collapsed onto the floor.

What seemed like hours, days, maybe even weeks later, Raine woke up not knowing where she was. Her vision was blurred as she looked around at the spacious bedroom that was decorated in bright pink, yellow, and green. Considering the fact that she had been sleeping on a floor up until now, the king size bed she was in felt like the most comfortable mattress she had even lain on. The soft comforter felt amazing against her skin, and the plush pillows made her think she had died and gone to heaven. There were two windows to her left, covered with white blinds. An old-fashioned white dresser was between the windows, and an oval-shaped mirror hung next to a closet. On the other side of the room was a sitting area with two chairs facing each other. A TV was mounted above a fireplace, and the room smelled like fresh strawberries.

Raine jumped up, thinking she had been rescued, but as she attempted to get out of the bed, she realized her hands and ankles were tied to it. Her head dropped back on the pillow. She looked up at the spinning ceiling fan, wondering where the hell she was.

Her answer came when Voncile came through the door with that same ol' dumb smile on her face. Raine surely wanted that bitch to disappear, but it didn't look as if that was going to happen anytime soon.

"How are you doing?" Voncile asked, sitting on the bed as if she were deeply concerned. "I hope you and the baby are okay."

Raine squeaked out a one-word answer: "Fine."

"I know you're hungry. My friend made you some chicken and dumplings, buttermilk biscuits, and she baked you a peach cobbler. I can't cook like she does, and I'm sure you'll enjoy her meal. Don't forget to thank her. She's a real nice person, and we both did all of this for you."

Voncile looked around the room proudly, waving her hand Vanna White style to call attention to the decor. Raine didn't say one word, not even when Voncile's friend entered the room, carrying a tray. The food smelled delicious, and when she laid the tray down, Raine had to admit that it looked good.

"Thank you," she finally said, looking from one woman to the next. "Thank you both, but how am I supposed to eat with my wrists tied to the bed?"

"See what I mean, Patrice?" Voncile said as she untied Raine's wrists. "She gets real snippy and demanding at times. You're going to have to watch her. If things get out of hand, you already know what to do."

Raine massaged her sore wrists for a minute before spooning up some of the food that smelled like heaven compared to what Voncile had been feeding her. She put the food in her mouth, closing her eyes as she savored the flavor.

"This is delicious. Is there a chance that I can have some more once I finish this?" she asked the woman that Voncile had called Patrice.

"Hell no," Voncile answered. "We don't want no fat kid. You need to eat healthy for that baby. You will be on a strict diet. You really shouldn't even be having that cobbler or that biscuit, but since you're looking as if you need to gain back some weight, I'll let you have it this time."

Raine didn't bother to reply. She just enjoyed her food, finishing it in less than five minutes. Voncile took her tray, and right after Patrice escorted Raine to the bathroom, she was then tied back to the bed and left in the room alone.

While the room was, without a doubt, better than the other room, Raine still wasn't okay about being there. She wanted to go home—home to a private island where she and her baby would never have to see Kasen or Voncile again.

Chapter 16

Kasen's friend Jansen was in town, and they had gone to play golf together. They hadn't seen each other in almost two years, but they talked from time to time over the phone. They had graduated from college together, but Jansen went a different route, becoming involved in real estate sales. He made a fortune and never looked back. He had tried to get Kasen and Omar involved in the business, but neither of them wanted to pursue another career. Jansen understood why Kasen wouldn't want to. After all, he was already making a lot of money as a therapist. But with Omar, he didn't get it. Omar needed all the money he could get, but when Jansen inquired about it many months ago and Omar declined, he didn't push. Omar always had been a little unpredictable that way, so when Kasen told him about Omar's recent actions, a part of him wasn't surprised.

"I hate to say I told you so, but Omar has always been troubled. You knew that," Jansen said.

"Yeah, but you know me. I try to give people the benefit of the doubt. Omar gets off track, but then he gets back on. This time, though, he completely lost it. To do Voncile like that was totally uncalled for. I don't have much else to say to him."

"To do any woman like that is uncalled for. He is a womanizer, and he's abusive. Always has been, always will be. Look at what he did to that chick when we were in college. We should have known then that his ass wasn't right."

"Yeah, he did beat her up pretty bad, didn't he?" Kasen said. "Then he tried to blame it on her. I just hope that I don't have to see him again, 'cause if I do, I don't know what will happen."

"I feel you, man. I was thinking about stopping by his place to holla at him again about investing in some property. I would like to help the brother out, but I can't do anything unless he's willing to offer some apologies and correct himself."

"Maybe going to his place is a good idea. I've been thinking about going there myself. Maybe he'll listen if we're both there delivering the message," Kasen said.

Kasen and Jansen finished up at the club-house. Jansen had rented a Mercedes truck, so they rode to Omar's place in style. They went to his door and rang the bell several times, but he didn't answer. Jansen pulled out his cell phone to call him, but the phone went immediately to voice mail.

"No answer," Jansen said. "I wonder why that fool won't answer his phone."

Kasen knew that Omar kept a spare key under the flower pot right outside his door, so he lifted the pot and took the key. He opened the door, and they went inside the beautifully decorated modern apartment that made Omar look as if he had some serious dollars. The black leather sectional in the center of the room was topped with red and black pillows. Fine art covered the walls, and the open kitchen had stainless steel appliances. Kasen noticed that Omar had remodeled the place, and he had seriously upgraded everything. None of this was cheap.

"Omar!" Jansen shouted as he moved toward another room. "Are you in here?"

Kasen searched around too. In the kitchen, he noticed a pot on the stove with dried corn in it that looked like it had been sitting for days. There was also a cereal bowl with curdled milk in it on the kitchen table. Dirty dishes were piled up, and the kitchen had a sour smell, as if it hadn't been cleaned in quite some time. Omar had never been the cleanest guy, but this was just ridiculous.

Kasen went to find Jansen in Omar's bedroom, sitting on his bed, looking at some pictures. They were well aware that Omar liked to take pictures of naked women, to keep score every time he slept with someone. He had been doing it ever since college, and he saved every photo, pulling them out often to look at his past conquests and show them off to anyone who was willing to look. The pictures had Jansen engrossed.

"If he hit that, he is one lucky man," Jansen said, holding up the picture of a beautiful Latina. He kept flipping through them, making comments that made Kasen want to see them too.

Jansen passed a few to Kasen, who flipped through them quickly. Sure, a few of those women were pretty damn hot, but something felt wrong about ogling the pictures that were taken for Omar's benefit. He was sure the women in the photos wouldn't be happy knowing that they were looking at them now.

Kasen tossed the pictures back to Jansen. One of them fell on the floor, sliding a few inches underneath Omar's bed. Kasen got on the floor to retrieve it. That was when he saw another stack of pictures with a rubber band around it. Normally, he wouldn't dare look through Omar's things, but the picture on top caught his eye. The woman was bent over, showing her slit to the camera, but Kasen knew that ass very well. Pulling the picture out to get a closer look, he saw the woman's face and realized it was Voncile.

His breathing halted for a few seconds, and his mind raced. He narrowed his eyes and looked at the picture again, just to be sure. The lump in his throat was stuck, and he zoned out, staring at the photo.

Jansen reached for the stack of pictures in his hand, but Kasen snatched them away.

"We did not come over here to look at his pictures," Kasen said abruptly. "Let's get out of here."

Jansen put the pictures back in Omar's drawer where he'd found them. Kasen, however, tucked the stack of photos into his pocket as soon as Jansen turned to walk away. They grabbed two beers from the fridge then left.

"So you don't have any idea where he is?" Jansen asked Kasen as he drove off.

Kasen was too distracted to answer. His mind was stuck on Voncile. How did Omar get those pictures of her? Were the two of them involved? Why would Voncile lie and pretend that she wasn't interested in him? Something wasn't adding up.

"I'm sorry, man. What did you say?" Kasen asked.

"I asked if you had any idea where Omar is."

"No, I don't. The last time I spoke to him, he got pretty pissed off at me. At the time, I didn't understand what he was mad about, but now I think I know why."

"Well, if you hear from him, let me know. I'm going back to the hotel to get some rest. Let me know what time you plan to pick me up."

"Probably around nine. Is that cool?"

"Sounds like a good time to me."

Kasen and Jansen had plans to go out that night, but Kasen couldn't wait to get back to his car and look at the rest of those pictures. When he was alone, he removed the rubber band from the pictures and found plenty more shots of Voncile. She had gone all out for the cameraman. Kasen didn't know she could open her legs that wide or that she was that flexible, and seeing her in so many positions made him think about the sweet, innocent woman who claimed she was so afraid of Omar. While some women turned up the heat in the bedroom, Kasen just couldn't believe that Voncile would take pictures like these and give them to Omar. He wanted to call her and inquire, but he wasn't even sure how he would approach the subject without embarrassing her. He was sure she never intended for anyone else to see those intimate pictures of her.

Later that night, Kasen and Jansen sat in a busy nightclub, dressed to impress in tailored suits that placed them in the VIP section. The club was thick with celebrities, as well as with everyday clubbers, who were there to celebrate birthdays or simply get their party on. Rap music thumped loudly, and the white-and-yellow lights, rotating from up above, lit up the entire dance floor. Kasen and Jansen sat at a circular booth with three women and a man Kasen knew from the clubhouse. There were champagne bottles on the table and several joints in an ashtray. Kasen didn't get down like that, but Jansen definitely did. He was a party animal, and had applied just the right pressure to convince Kasen to go out that night.

Since Kasen hadn't seen Jansen in quite some time, and he hadn't been to a nightclub lately, he didn't mind. It would be good, he decided, to take his mind off all the craziness happening in his life at the moment. He was having a good time, and when one of the young women at the booth asked if he wanted to dance, he accepted her offer.

"Sure. Why not?" he said. Kasen removed his jacket, tossing it on a chair. The silk button-down shirt he rocked tightened on his muscles and caused quite a stir. Women peeked over their shoulders just to get a glance at him. Kasen didn't mind the attention at all. It felt good, especially when he stepped on the dance floor and saw so many women watching attentively, as if they wanted to jump up there and eat him alive.

"You are definitely an attention grabber, aren't you?" the woman he danced with said. She had men checking her out too, especially when the short dress she wore crept up her thighs as she danced.

She and Kasen tore up the dance floor. They laughed when the song was over, and exited the dance floor with sweat on their bodies. Kasen's shirt was so wet that it stuck to his chest. He wanted to remove it. As hot as it was, he wouldn't mind rocking a wife-beater, like some of the other brothas did. Removing his shirt caused more attention to swing his way. His tats were on display, and his muscles were stacked for all to see. Women pulled on him from left to right. He was flattered, but all he wanted to do was go sit down and cool off.

He stepped into the VIP section, anxious to get back to his seat and down another drink, but he stopped in his tracks when he spotted Voncile sitting next to Jansen. Her layered hair was cut short and spiked in the front. The loud pink dress she wore stretched across her perfect breasts and heart-shaped ass. Her ribbon-tied heels were tied all the way up to her knees, and the smile on her face implied that she and Jansen were getting to know each other.

Kasen didn't know Voncile hung out in places like this. In fact, he was pretty sure she didn't, and the fact that she was there now didn't feel like a coincidence to Kasen. He was still upset about those pictures, and her strange appearance at the club didn't help matters.

He stepped up to the booth.

"Hi, Kasen," Voncile said with a smile. "I saw the two of you when you came in, and I wanted to introduce myself to your friend. Why didn't you tell me that he was so funny, and that he looked like Boris Kodjoe?"

Jansen blushed, looking like he loved every bit of this. Kasen knew exactly what was on his friend's mind. Voncile was sexy as hell, and Kasen was sure that Jansen couldn't wait to get her back to his hotel room and show her what her presence had done to him. Kasen, on the other hand, wasn't impressed. He thought that Voncile was sitting too close to his friend. He also didn't appreciate her hand on his leg.

"I didn't tell you because I didn't think it was important," Kasen snapped.

Everyone around the table looked at Kasen, even the chick he had danced with. They could sense that he was irritated by Voncile's presence.

Voncile didn't seem to care about his feelings. She shrugged, turning her attention back to Jansen. "Would you like to dance? They're playing my song, and it's been a long time since I've been turnt up."

Jansen didn't hesitate. He followed behind Voncile like a puppy dog, gazing at her ass and no doubt imagining how many positions he would put her in that night.

Something about this whole situation just didn't feel right. Sure, Kasen had told Voncile that they should take things slow, but that didn't mean he wanted her to flaunt it in his face when she flirted with someone else. Also, considering what had happened not too long ago with Omar attacking her, she didn't seem bothered in the least. As he watched Voncile and Jansen on the dance floor, he became more and more pissed off by her behavior.

"Hey, sexy. You wanna go over there and chill with me?" one chick asked Kasen.

"No." He didn't bother to look at her.

Another chick squeezed the muscles on his arm. "Umph. I would love to get into your head, if you know what I mean."

She was ignored too. Kasen kept his eyes zoned in on the dance floor, where Jansen was grinding against Voncile's backside. She grinded right along with him, snapping her fingers in the air. Jansen kept whispering in her ear, and each time, Voncile nodded her head and laughed.

Kasen had seen enough. He rushed down the long stairs, bumping plenty of shoulders as he made his way to the dance floor. He reached for Voncile's arm, snatching her in his direction.

"What?" she said, pulling away from him with an annoyed look on her face. "Why are you pulling on me?"

"I'm not pulling on you," Kasen said, dialing back his anger a little. "I just need to speak to you somewhere in private, if you don't mind."

Voncile rolled her eyes then looked at Jansen. "Excuse me," she said. "I need to go take care of something."

Jansen cocked his head back. His face was scrunched, like he didn't appreciate Kasen trying to interfere with him trying to get some ass.

"What's the problem?" he asked Kasen.

"There is no problem," Kasen answered. "I just need to get at her, like I said."

Jansen stood there looking frustrated as he watched the two of them exit the club together.

As soon as Kasen and Voncile got outside, stepping to the side of the building, Kasen let her have it. "What the hell are you doing in there?" he barked.

"What does it look like I'm doing? I was trying to have a good time. Is something wrong with that?"

She was tipsy and slurring her words a little, which irritated Kasen even more. "This is not like you, Voncile. Why are you acting this way?"

"Acting like what, Kasen? I'm just having fun dancing."

"Yeah, well, you're dancing with my friend. And your dress is too damn short and too damn tight."

Voncile smiled, looking like she'd won a victory. "If I didn't know any better, I'd say you're jealous right now."

Kasen shook his head. "No, I'm not jealous. I'm pissed." And then, he finally admitted what his real problem was. "I'm pissed off about the pictures I found at Omar's house today."

Voncile's eyes opened wide and she stumbled back a step. "You were at Omar's today?"

"Yeah. He wasn't there," Kasen answered, "but I found some pictures of you that tell a very different story than what you've been telling me."

"What are you talking about?" Voncile asked.

"Naked pictures at Omar's crib. You were telling me he was coming on too strong and you had no interest in him, and then I find the pictures. What the hell, Voncile? Were you fucking him?"

Voncile appeared to be nervous. She looked down at the ground for a minute then shifted her eyes back to Kasen. They were wet with tears.

"Tell me the truth," he said. "If you fucked him, you fucked him. I don't know why you lied to me about it from the start, but it does kind of explain his actions. What guy wouldn't be jealous when you're fucking him and then you turn around and fuck his friend?" He stopped short of blaming her for the breakup of his friendship with Omar, but now he understood that Omar must have been so hurt when he found out Kasen had sex with Voncile. Kasen never would have done it if he'd known about their relationship. Her deceitfulness had done a lot of damage, and now Kasen didn't know which way to turn. Could anything be fixed?

She sighed and launched into her explanation. "Yes, Omar and I used to be involved. I never wanted you to know because I was ashamed of being with a man like him. Your friend was abusive, and I tried my best to end it with him. It wasn't as if we were ever in a relationship. All he ever wanted from me was sex, and vice versa. We hooked up a few times right after I met him at your office. It was one big mistake, and I regret giving myself to him."

Kasen was still upset that she had lied, but her story about being abused by Omar could definitely be true. Jansen had just reminded him earlier about how Omar had hurt that girl back in college, plus Omar had attacked Voncile this past week. His friend definitely had that violent tendency in him. Kasen didn't really like the way Voncile had handled the situation, telling lies like she did, but part of him understood why she chose to do it.

Voncile stepped forward, pressing her body against Kasen's. She touched the side of his face as she looked into his eyes. "I'm so sorry for not telling you, but I didn't want you to think less of me for being involved with someone like him. I hope we can put this behind us. Please don't be upset with me, Kasen. I just made a bad choice, that's all."

Kasen pushed her back gently to put some distance between them. "Look, Voncile, I don't know what to think about any of this right now. My head is fucked up from everything that's been going on lately, and finding those pictures has me even more on edge. I don't know why any of this is happening to me, but I need to step back and figure it all out. Let me go get my friend and get out of here, because I just don't think I can deal with you right now."

He started to walk away from her, until she screamed out his name.

"Kasen, stop!"

He turned around, feeling agitated but somehow unable to remove himself from the situation. She was such a needy person, and the therapist in him could never resist a woman in need of help.

"What, Voncile?"

"I can't believe you're this upset with me," she said. "Please don't be mad. Can't you see how much I really love you and want to be with you?"

Once he heard the word "love," he knew it was time to put some distance between them. They clearly had different views on what this little sexual fling meant. For him, it wasn't love; that was for sure. "I'll see you at the office on Monday, Voncile," he told her then went to find Jansen.

Later that night, he lay in bed, replaying the night's events in his head. Voncile had gone from being the victim of an attempted rape to a vixen in the club all in the course of a few days. Which one was the real Voncile? And why had he been so easily pulled in by her deceptive tactics? He was a therapist, trained to read people's feelings, yet he'd been blinded to her games. Raine's abandonment must have had him more messed up than he had realized—messed up enough to fall for anything as long as he was getting some good pussy. He made up his mind to keep his eyes wide open when it came to Voncile from this point on.

Chapter 17

Monday in the office was extremely tense between Voncile and Kasen. They barely said two words to each other, and Kasen kept to himself, staying inside his office with the door shut even when there was no patient in there. The atmosphere was totally uncomfortable, and Kasen was beating himself up for being stupid enough to get involved with an employee in the first place. She was a great asset to his business, but now he didn't know if he'd be able to keep her. At the same time, he couldn't fire her, because then she might claim sexual harassment. He had put himself in a terribly awkward position, and he had no one but himself to blame for his weakness. If he could turn back time, he never would have had sex with her the first time. Instead, all he could do would be to end the affair as gently as possible to avoid any major conflicts that would disrupt his practice—or possibly even destroy it.

Kasen was grateful whenever a patient came to the office that day, because listening to their problems helped take his mind off his own for a while. It felt especially great when Myra Carter, his last patient of the day, let him know how helpful his advice was to her. It was the kind of validation he needed to hear after doubting his judgment all day.

"You are so on point, Doc," Myra said. Her gambling addiction had gotten out of control, and Kasen had given her a list of things to do to take her mind off money. "I will try your suggestions, and I finally feel hopeful that I can beat this addiction."

Kasen stood up to shake her hand. "That's what I like to hear. I look forward to hearing about your progress at our next appointment."

"Oh, me too. I can't wait to be free of this burden," she said, putting her purse on her shoulder and standing up to leave. "Thank you again, Doc. And before I go, do you mind if I ask you a personal question?"

"Well, I suppose," Kasen said. He usually didn't share personal information with patients, but he was feeling so good after her compliments that he decided to make an exception this time. "As long as I have the option to not answer," he joked.

She laughed. "No, it's nothing bad. It's just that I noticed you're not wearing a ring, and if you're not married, I thought maybe you'd like to meet my niece, Frances. She's intelligent, she's beautiful, and I think the two of you would make a fantastic couple. It's not easy to find a good man like you these days, you know."

Kasen gave her a charming smile. "Well, I am flattered, but I don't think that would be a good idea. I'm not married, but I am involved in something kind of complicated right now. I'm afraid I wouldn't be very good company, and I'm sure your niece deserves someone who can give her his undivided attention."

"Okay, but you're missing out. I may just send Frances up here to meet you anyway. If you see her, you might change your mind," she said with a mischievous wink.

Kasen shook his head. "You are persistent; I'll give you that," he joked as he walked Myra to the door.

As they stepped into the waiting room, he saw Voncile at her desk, slumped over, with her head on the desk as if she were sleeping.

Myra turned and gave Kasen a puzzled look. "Is she okay?"

"Oh, don't you worry about Voncile. She probably just had a late night," he answered, trying to sound nonchalant, as if it was totally normal for someone to be knocked out in the middle of the day at work.

He rushed Myra onto the elevator and said good-bye, then headed back to Voncile's desk, shaking her shoulder.

Voncile stirred, raising her head from the desk. Her eyes were red, and the papers she'd been resting on were wet. It became obvious that she hadn't been sleeping; she'd been crying.

Kasen pulled up a chair and sat across from her desk. "Voncile, we need to talk and clear the air. This can't be happening at the office."

She dabbed her eyes with a tissue then wiped her nose. "I know, but I just can't help it, Kasen. I can tell that you don't want me around anymore. You've barely said one word to me today."

Kasen reached out to touch her hand. He knew he needed to let her down gently, because he could tell this was going to be hard for Voncile.

"It's not that I don't want you around. I love having you around, and my patients love you too. It's just that . . . we made a mistake by becoming physical. I am not proud of the way I acted at the club, and I definitely don't like to see you crying. I never want to be the source of your pain, so I think it would be best if we end our involvement and try to go back to the way we were before—you know, doctor and secretary, strictly professional."

Voncile's expression hardened, and her tears dried up in an instant. "Well, it's too late for us to have regrets now. Definitely too late." She reached for her purse and pulled out the pregnancy test, holding it out to Kasen.

He looked down at it, refusing to take it from her. "Is that what I think it is?" he asked.

She placed the stick on the desk so the double plus signs were clearly visible to Kasen. "I'm pregnant," she said.

Kasen felt like he had been punched in the gut. This was the absolute worst news she could have given him when he was trying to backtrack and get out of this toxic relationship. How the hell had he been stupid enough to not use a condom? He had been so caught up in the moment with Voncile and so torn up by Raine leaving him that he hadn't been thinking straight. Now he might be stuck in a big way.

"Are you sure it's mine?" The words slipped off his tongue before he could stop himself. He knew they were offensive to Voncile, but just like their relationship, he couldn't take it back now.

Voncile narrowed her eyes and spoke in an angry hiss. "How dare you, Kasen. I am not a whore. You are the one and only man I am sleeping with."

"But the pictures—"

"Oh, shut up about those fucking pictures! They were taken a long time ago, and I already told you, I know that my involvement with Omar was a mistake," she said.

Just like my involvement with you was a mistake, Kasen thought.

"Look, Voncile," he said, "I'm not trying to run away from my responsibility. We can go to the bank right now and I'll give the cash to go get an abortion. I'll even make the appointment for you if you want."

Voncile's face twisted into an ugly, angry mask. She jumped up from the chair and snatched her purse from the back of her chair. "Abortion my ass!" she shouted. "I don't believe in killing babies. To hell with you, Kasen. We don't need you, and you can kiss my ass!"

Voncile stormed out of the office, leaving Kasen shaking his head, feeling as if he were standing in the wreckage of a tornado. How the hell had his life gotten to this point? More importantly, how was he going to get out of this mess? No matter what she had said, he still didn't completely believe the baby was his.

He would certainly want a paternity test, but Voncile was so volatile and unpredictable that he would have to be careful how he approached this situation going forward.

Chapter 18

That night, Voncile was out of control. She looked like a madwoman as she paced the kitchen floor with scissors in her hand. Pictures of Kasen were scattered on the counter, many cut into tiny pieces. After the way he reacted to the pregnancy test, she had totally lost it. That test was supposed to guarantee that they would be together, but he turned around and started talking about abortion.

"Fucking bastard!" she shouted, pounding the counter so hard the whole kitchen shook. "How"—*bam!*—"can"—*bam!*—"you not"—*bam!*—"want your own child?" *Bam, bam, bam!*

She sliced through the air with the scissors, screaming loudly to release some of her rage. She had been taking such good care of Raine, and by all means, she was going to have that baby. Kasen was going to take care of it too. No way in hell was he going to walk away from her. She had to think of a new plan fast.

The ringing of the doorbell stopped her ranting and raving for a minute. Picking up the trash can, she swiped all of the destroyed pictures into the trash, then hastily wiped the tears off her face. Taking a deep breath to compose herself, she made her way to the door.

"Who is it?" she asked softly.

"It's me, Voncile. Kasen."

She felt her heart rate racing. Taking a few more deep breaths to try to prevent herself from hyperventilating, she finally opened the door.

"You really shouldn't be here, especially if all you came here to do is give me money for an abortion," she said, proud of herself for not breaking down in tears at the sight of Kasen.

"I didn't come here to do that."

She stared at him, waiting for more of an explanation.

"Well, can I come in?" he asked.

"I'll come outside and talk to you." She hadn't been prepared for him to come by, and she hated for anyone to be in her house if it wasn't spotless.

She stepped outside and sat down on the steps with Kasen.

"I came to apologize for what I said," he started. "You caught me off guard, and I blurted out the first thing that came to mind, but I was speaking out of fear. I was not planning on becoming a father, so it scared me."

"Well, I wasn't planning on becoming a mother either," Voncile said.

"I know," Kasen replied, "and that's why I need to apologize. My reaction wasn't fair to you. If you don't want an abortion, then I won't force you to get one."

Voncile felt like singing. "So we're going to do this parenting thing, then? I knew you'd come to your senses. We are supposed to be together."

Kasen looked at her with discomfort written on his face. "Hold up, Voncile. I'm not saying we're going to be together. I'm saying that if you want to have this baby and it's mine, then I will take responsibility and help you raise the child."

Voncile wiped away the tears that started rolling down her cheeks. *Calm down, girl. Do not let him see you get emotional. Play it cool,* she told herself.

"I don't want to hurt you," Kasen continued, "but like I told you before, I just can't do this relationship stuff right now. I didn't tell you everything about what happened with Raine, but I'm still bitter about what she did to me, and I need some time to figure out what went wrong before I can enter another relationship. I will support you all the way with this baby, but I can't give you anything more."

"I understand," Voncile lied. Hell no, she didn't understand. How could he not want to be with her? They were perfect for each other.

"I'm glad you understand. And again, I'm really sorry for the way I acted earlier. Whatever you need just let me know. And if you want me to go to your appointments with you, I'll make arrangements to be there."

"Thanks," she said in a sarcastic tone, "but I don't want you by my side at the appointments if we're not even a couple."

Suddenly, Voncile couldn't help herself. She knew she was supposed to be playing the understanding, submissive woman, but she felt the need to speak her mind.

"As a matter of fact, I don't even know if I will be able to sit in that office every day knowing that I'm pregnant with your child yet you don't want to be with me. Maybe I should start looking for another job," she said. In truth, she didn't want to stop working with Kasen, but she realized that at some point when her stomach didn't start growing, her pregnancy story wouldn't hold up. It would be easier to hide that from him if she wasn't at the office every day.

As if on cue, her tears started again. She was hoping they would gain her some sympathy from Kasen, but instead, he looked even more uncomfortable as he stood up to leave.

He held out his arms as if he wanted to give her a hug. She hesitated for a minute, but then couldn't resist the desire to feel his arms wrapped around her. She stood up and leaned into his embrace.

"Listen, I know this is not the ideal situation for your first pregnancy, but let's focus on the good things. Number one, we're having a child, and that's a lot to be thankful for. Two, you still have a job if you want it. I'll leave that choice up to you, but please don't let this situation affect your career. And three, we're still good friends. We're going to be awesome parents, and us getting along is going to be crucial for our child. Let's kick this off on a good foot and do the right thing." He kissed the top of her head the way a big brother or a father would. It certainly wasn't the kind of kiss Voncile longed for.

She tilted her head up and stared into his eyes, hoping he'd get the hint and lean in for a passionate French kiss. He didn't. Instead, he stepped back out of their embrace.

"I'm taking a few days off of work to think about what I need to do to prepare for our child," she said. "If you need me for anything, you can call me." This was her last ditch effort to get him to change his mind. If she was gone for a few days, he would miss her so much that he'd be begging her to come back. Then she would have the leverage she needed to get their relationship back on track. And just in case that didn't work, she could always call on her friend Patrice for some help.

Kasen gave her a peck on the cheek. "Get some rest. We'll talk soon."

Oh, I'm going to make sure we're doing much more than just talking soon, Voncile thought as she watched him get in his car and drive off.

Chapter 19

Raine was starting to feel as if this was her new home. Reality had finally set in that Kasen wasn't coming to rescue her, especially since she'd been moved to a new location. Being with Patrice, though, was much better than being with Voncile. Patrice was difficult, but compared to Voncile, she was the perfect hostess. Even on her worst days, Patrice never seemed as angry or vicious as Voncile.

Every time Voncile stopped by, she had an attitude. Sometimes she'd be mumbling under her breath, and some of the things that Raine heard made her think that things weren't going well with Voncile and Kasen. She sure wasn't bragging about their relationship the way she had been not too long ago. A small part of Raine wanted to rub it in Voncile's face, but she was sure that any mention of Kasen would get her slapped across the mouth and eating rotten left-overs again. She didn't want that kind of trouble, especially since she seemed to be on Patrice's good side more than on her bad side.

Sometimes, Patrice would just come into the room to lay down her burdens or simply talk to Raine about what was on TV. Raine thought that Patrice seemed a little weird too, but she also seemed lonely, like she wanted a friend more than anything. Raine wondered if Patrice was only participating in this kidnapping because she thought she was helping a friend—although she couldn't imagine how anyone could consider Voncile a friend. That bitch was barely human, as far as Raine was concerned.

Raine sensed that there was a chance she could one day get through to Patrice and ask her to set her free. So, she kept on being kind and speaking to Patrice as if she had a new best friend.

As Raine was watching TV, Patrice came into the room with dinner on a tray. This time it was a delicious-looking Caesar salad with buttery croutons, a glass of iced tea, and a cup of Jell-O for dessert. She set down the tray and untied the restraints so Raine could eat.

"You keep spoiling me like this and I will stay here forever," Raine said, lying through her teeth.

Patrice laughed. "Girl, please. After you have that baby, you are out of here. You're only here because Voncile is paying me good money to keep you for a while."

Raine felt a chill pass over her. She didn't know what their plans were for her after the baby was born, but she knew it couldn't be anything good. That's what scared her more than anything. She couldn't imagine her baby being taken away from her, and as the days ticked away, she knew she had to do something to make Patrice understand how wrong this was.

"When you say after the baby is born I'm out of here, what do you mean?"

Patrice shot her a dirty look. "Stop asking me questions and eat your food."

Raine knew she had gone a little too far. Their bond wasn't strong enough yet for her to be trying to get information from Patrice. First she would have to break down Patrice's loyalty to Voncile, and it wasn't time for that yet.

Raine did as she was told and ate her food. She was almost done with her salad when Voncile came in, fussing and cussing about something.

"We need to talk," she said to Patrice. "I'm so done with this Negro, and I need your help."

They left the room, standing just outside the closed door. All Raine could hear was the high-pitched, agitated tone of Voncile's voice. Shortly thereafter, Patrice returned to the room, but Voncile didn't.

"What was that about?" Raine questioned boldly, feeling desperate for some kind of information. Voncile's bad mood could mean dire consequences for her, and she wanted to be forewarned if at all possible. "Is everything okay? Voncile sounded pretty angry."

Patrice threw her hand back and pursed her lips. "Everything is fine. Voncile just gets so worked up at times, especially when things don't go her way."

"Yes, I know. I think she's a good person, but she just needs to chill and let the chips fall where they may." Raine wanted to grab her own throat and choke herself for complimenting Voncile. It pained her to even lie about how she felt.

"Exactly," Patrice cosigned. "But I can't tell her nothing. She has this little idea in her head that things are going to work out how she envisions them, but life isn't as cut and dry as she wants. I think she's gotten her wakeup call from Kasen. It doesn't seem like he's her Prince Charming after all."

Raine was grateful for even this little but of news, and she felt a smug satisfaction knowing that Kasen might have kicked Voncile's ass to the curb. She wanted to know more, but she had to be careful. Turning Patrice against Voncile had to be handled carefully.

"What did she expect from him?" Raine asked, trying to sound merely curious and not critical of Voncile. "Did she think he was going to marry her? I mean, Kasen really isn't the marrying type. He's a liar and a cheater. I hope she knows that now."

"When I met him, he came across as a genuine, caring man," Patrice said.

Patrice didn't sound perturbed, so Raine figured she must be doing a good job of hiding her hatred for Voncile. She continued to ask questions.

"Oh. So, you met him before?"

"Yes, I met his fine self before. I made an appointment and pretended to be looking for help with a sex addiction. Voncile thought it would be a good idea if we distracted him a little."

"What do you mean?" Raine asked. "Were you supposed to distract him with sex? Did you think he was going to try to have sex with one of his patients?"

Patrice's eyes grew wide. "Hell no! Voncile damn sure wouldn't have gone for that. She just said he's a really good doctor and he cares about his patients. She thought if I made up a really crazy story, he'd be so interested in helping me that it would keep his mind off of you."

Raine wanted to cry, but she held herself together. "And did it work?" she asked.

Patrice shrugged. "I don't think so. In the beginning she said I should be making at least two appointments a week to keep him busy, but then after the first one, she kind of dropped the plan. I think he started showing interest in her faster than she expected, so she decided she didn't need my help for that part of the plan."

Raine felt vomit rising into her throat at the thought of Kasen falling for Voncile so easily and so stupidly. He damn sure wasn't the man of character that she had once thought he was.

"Well, I hope she's figured out that he's not so wonderful after all," Raine said, although she was thinking that Kasen and Voncile probably deserved each other.

"I don't know about that," Patrice said. "I mean, things aren't great with them right now, but Voncile said she's got another plan that she needs my help with so they can get back on track. She needs me to distract him again."

Raine made her first attempt at breaking down Patrice's loyalty. "I don't mean to start anything, but you're a nice lady, and I would hate to see you being used. Do you ever get a feeling that she's asking you to do all the dirty work? If either of you get caught, you'll be the one to go down. After all, I am in *your* house. That may not turn out to be a good thing if the police ever find me."

Patrice sat silent for a minute, maybe two, then stood up abruptly. "Are you done with your food?" she asked.

"Yes, I'm done. Thanks again for the blessing. You are a good person who deserves to be treated like one."

Yet again, Patrice didn't comment, but Raine could tell she was in deep thought. She hoped that they were thoughts about what a bitch Voncile was.

Patrice picked up the tray and headed toward the door. Just to show Patrice that she could trust her, Raine called out to her, "Um, I think you forgot something." She forced a smile and held up her hands, which Patrice had forgotten to tie to the bed again.

Patrice shrugged. "Don't worry about it. Move around and enjoy yourself for the night." She turned around and left, locking the door behind her.

Raine let out a huge sigh of relief when Patrice was gone. She reached down and untied her ankles, stepping down off the bed. It felt so good to be free to move around the room, and she also felt like she had made a little progress with Patrice. She was confident that if she kept at it, she would be able to flip Patrice's loyalty soon and get herself and her baby out of this hell.

She rushed over to the window and opened the blinds, but her only view was a piece of plywood that had been nailed over the window. The same was true for the other window, so even if she had wanted to risk jumping from the second floor bedroom, the blocked windows made that impossible.

Raine checked the door knob even though she'd heard Patrice locking it when she left. It was useless. The room was totally secured. Raine's excitement was deflated a bit, but she was still relieved to be untied. She made her way to the bathroom and turned on the shower, removed her gown, and stood underneath the warm spray. Raine felt as if she had just entered the gates of heaven. She had never been this excited about taking a shower, and she didn't come out until the water had turned cold.

After she dried herself with a fluffy towel, she searched the drawer for something clean to put on. Many of her own clothes, which Voncile had taken from Kasen's house, were in there. Patrice had even taken the time to fold them for her.

She reached for a sweater that Kasen had given her, holding it close to her chest. She had been trying her best not to think about him ever since she witnessed him having sex with Voncile on the live video feed. It broke her heart to know that he had moved on so soon. She wondered if he had made any effort at all to find her. Her feelings alternated between being furious at him for forgetting about her so quickly, to longing to feel his strong arms around her, rescuing her from this nightmare. At times like this, as she touched the soft sweater and remembered the day he'd given it to her, she missed Kasen. She also regretted the way she had reacted to his proposal. What if she hadn't laughed, and instead had said yes? Maybe they would have gone out to celebrate, instead of her going home alone the way she did, and then she would never have been kidnapped.

Raine put down the sweater and found a comfy yellow nightgown to put on. As she removed it from the drawer, a diamond bracelet fell on the floor. She picked it up, holding it tightly in her hand. Tears welled in her eyes as she thought about how excited Kasen had been the day he gave it to her.

It was about a year into their relationship, and Raine had been in Kasen's kitchen, cooking dinner for two. He said he was going to be late but wound up coming home an hour early. Raine was not ready. Dinner wasn't ready, and she had just put the spaghetti in water. Her head was wrapped with a scarf, she wore no makeup, and the top she was wearing had two holes in it. She hated to look that way around Kasen. Not that she feared that he would like her any less, but she preferred to be at her best when her man was around.

He had crept up from behind, slipping his arms around her waist.

"Doggone it, Kasen. You're early. I haven't had time to do anything, and I look like a hot mess."

He planted a soft kiss against her neck. "Yes, look at you. You're beautiful, sexy, God-fearing, ambitious, inspiring. . . . Do I need to go on?"

Raine blushed. "No. No need to go on, but I wish I'd at least had time to shower before you got here."

He nudged his head toward the bathroom. "If it makes you feel better, then let's go shower together. I need to clean up too."

Kasen had removed his clothes then carried Raine to the bathroom, where he removed her clothes. The lovemaking session was so passionate that Raine found herself near tears. It was the first time she told him she loved him, and when he presented the diamond bracelet to her, it was the first time he said those words to her too.

"I have a good feeling about our relationship," he had said that day. "And one day, I could see you being Mrs. Kasen Phillips."

Now, standing in a yellow nightgown as a captive in Patrice's house, her romantic memories of that day were spoiled by the painful reality that he was having sex with Voncile. This thought caused her mind to travel to the time that Kasen had cheated on her during their relationship. For a while she thought she had moved past that pain, but now it came back full force, as if it had been waiting all along to overwhelm her again.

Maybe that was just the one I found out about, she thought. *There could have been dozens more, for all I know. Did I ever really know the real Kasen?*

As a fresh wave of tears came over her, Raine climbed back in the bed to cry herself to sleep.

The next morning, Patrice entered the room, dressed in a sleazy, low-cut top that had her breasts nearly popping out. The skirt she wore made it look as if it was difficult to breathe. Her hair was in a long, sleek ponytail that swung from side to side, and her makeup was caked on.

"I have an appointment-slash-date this morning," Patrice said. "I'll be back, and I want you to be good while I'm gone."

Raine sensed that this "appointment-slash-date" had something to do with Kasen, because Patrice had revealed last night that Voncile needed her to distract him again. There was no other explanation for Patrice to be dressed like a hooker-clown, since she was naturally beautiful and didn't usually wear things like this. She didn't know the details of the plan, but from the way Patrice was dressed, she was pretty sure that it included some type of seduction. The real question was would Kasen be stupid enough to fall for it? She hoped not, because even if she was mad about him sleeping with Voncile, she didn't want him to end up like Omar.

Suddenly Raine came up with an idea that she hoped might send some sort of message to Kasen.

"You look nice," she said as Patrice tied her up again. "But you need some flashy jewelry with that hot outfit. I hope you don't mind that I took a shower last night, but maybe it was a good thing, because when I was looking for something to sleep in, I found one of my pretty bracelets. It's in the top drawer over there. Go look at it. I think it would be perfect with what you have on."

Patrice went to the dresser and picked up the bracelet, admiring the glittering diamonds as she held it up in the light. "Ooooh, this is pretty. How much did this set you back?"

"It was under a grand. I wanted to treat myself to something nice. You have to do that once in a while, you know?"

Patrice nodded in agreement.

"I've only worn it one time," Raine said. "I don't mind if you wear it for your date today. As a matter of fact, I insist."

Patrice put on the bracelet, admiring it on her wrist. "Thanks, girl. It sets this outfit off just right. There ain't no way he won't notice me now," she said excitedly as she sashayed out of the room.

Raine lay back on the bed, hoping that Patrice was right—and that Kasen might put the pieces of the puzzle together and get her out of this hell.

Chapter 20

Like clockwork, Kasen was at work, preparing himself to do what he did best: make his patients feel good. Voncile wasn't there yet, and after their last conversation, he wasn't sure she was coming in at all. He had hoped she would call to let him know either way, but by ten o'clock after his first appointment was done, there was no sign of Voncile.

As he leaned back in his chair, Kasen thought about the fact that she was the third person to disappear from his life in a very short time. He didn't like losing people. Even when a patient improved and decided they no longer needed therapy, he would feel some regret about not seeing them again. Now that it was people he genuinely loved and cared about who were gone, he was feeling pretty damn terrible. He wished he could be one of those people who brushed it off and kept moving during hard times like these, but he couldn't stop thinking about his losses.

He had dreamed about Raine the night before. No matter how much he wanted to pretend he was over her, he knew he wasn't. He missed her terribly. In his dream, she wasn't happy either. She no longer wanted to be with the person she was with, and she came to Kasen, telling him she was pregnant by her lover. Kasen was disgusted, and as he started yelling at Raine, he woke up in a cold sweat. The dream had seemed so real that Kasen was still a little on edge this morning. He wondered what the dream meant. As a therapist, he knew it wasn't a coincidence that he was dreaming about Raine being pregnant by someone else when Voncile was pregnant—supposedly by him—in real life. What was his subconscious trying to tell him?

Without even thinking about it, he picked up the phone to call the one person he would normally talk to in a sticky relationship situation like the one he was in: Omar. He quickly came to his senses, though, and dropped the phone back on the receiver. Talk about messed up: not only was he mad at Omar for the way he had been behaving lately, but he also had to consider the fact that Omar could possibly be the father of Voncile's baby. This was one twisted web they were all caught up in, and he didn't want to confront Omar about it over the phone. He would go to his house again later.

Just as Kasen hung up the phone, Patrice Davenport appeared in the doorway. He recognized her right away, even though she looked quite different from her first visit. She was still an attractive woman, but the caked-on makeup made her look casket ready. The bright red lipstick and fake lashes were a bit much.

Kasen stood to greet her. He didn't want her to run away again, especially since he was there to help.

"I know I don't have an appointment," she said, "but when I tried calling, no one answered."

"My secretary is out for the day, but you came at a good time," he said. "My next appointment isn't until twelve thirty. Please, come in and have a seat."

"Thank you for seeing me. It's been rough since my last visit," she said as she took a seat in the chair in front of his desk.

"Why don't you tell me what's going on?" Kasen said, picking up a notebook and a pen as Patrice launched into a lengthy, explicit description of numerous sexual encounters she'd had recently. It sounded like the woman was having more sex than a porn star.

She concluded her story with, "I mean, why does sex have to feel so good to me?" She massaged her hands together as if she were nervous. "I keep running from one man to the next, and every time a good-looking man strolls by me, sex is all I think about. I can't control my thoughts, and I need to figure out a way to focus on something else for a change."

"First of all, it's okay that sex feels good. It's supposed to. What you need to be asking yourself is why do you run from one man to the next? Let's explore what is missing in your life and how you might fill that void with something other than sex. I want you to dig deep, Patrice. You have to go real deep in order to get to the root of your problem. Are you ready?"

She leaned back in her chair and crossed her legs so that her skirt hiked way up, revealing her lace panties. "Yes, I'm ready . . . but I want you to dig deep too. I can't even have a friendly discussion with you without thinking about you being inside of me. I want to fuck you so bad, Kasen, and I've been thinking about it every day since I left here. I think the way for me to overcome all of this is for you to let me play out some of the things in my head. I'll talk about how much I value myself and reveal what I think is bringing all of this about once your dick is deep inside of me. That's a sure way to get me to tell it all." She uncrossed her legs and spread them wide to put her goodies on full display.

Kasen responded with silence. He knew that some people had severe sexual problems, and this woman clearly needed some help. If he approached her the wrong way and she felt rejected, she might get up and bolt from his office like last time. He was mulling over the right way to respond.

"I've offended you, haven't I?" Patrice said. "I can tell by the look in your eyes. I wholeheartedly apologize for coming here and speaking my truth."

"I'm not offended," Kasen said. "Actually, I—"

"Oh, what a relief." Patrice closed her legs again and leaned far across the desk toward him, laying her hands on top of the pad where he'd been writing notes.

Kasen's eyes zoned in on the bracelet on her wrist. Suddenly, something in him just snapped. "Where in the hell did you get that from?"

Patrice followed the direction of his eyes, pulling her hands back casually as she said, "Oh, this? I bought it for myself. Sometimes you just have to do something nice for yourself, you know?"

Kasen wasn't satisfied with her answer. His subconscious mind was screaming at him to keep pushing. "What store did you buy it from?"

Patrice started wringing her hands and gave a nervous laugh. "I forgot. Why?"

Kasen moved quickly around the desk, and before she could react, he had grabbed Patrice's hands.

"Doctor Phillips, what are you doing?" she protested.

Kasen didn't answer. He flipped the bracelet over to reveal the engraving on the other side. It was a tiny heart, along with a date—the date he had given the bracelet to Raine. He had asked the jewelry designer to engrave it on the one-of-a-kind bracelet so that Raine would always have a reminder of the first time he said the words "I love you" to her.

He tightened his grip on Patrice's arms as she struggled to break free.

"Where in the hell did you get it from? Do you know Raine? Is she the one who gave it to you? Tell me now!" he said through gritted teeth.

"I don't know what you're talking about," Patrice shouted. "I told you I bought it for myself!"

"No you didn't. I had it special made, and now you're going to tell me how you got it before I—"

Patrice stopped struggling and slumped down into the chair. "Fine. I get it. You're a big, tough man and you're going to hurt me. Some healer you are," she said, insulting Kasen's professionalism in a way that caused him to snap out of his rage and let her arms go. He still hovered over her, though, not allowing her to stand up and leave.

With his chest heaving and his heart pounding, he begged Patrice for more information. "Look, I'm sorry about what just happened, but that bracelet belonged to someone very special to me. Someone who disappeared from my life without a trace. I shouldn't have put my hands on you, but I need to know where she is. Please tell me whatever it is you know." Kasen couldn't make sense of the whole situation, but he had no doubt that Patrice knew much more than she was letting on.

Patrice sat still, with her mouth clamped shut.

"Please," he asked again. "I loved her with all my heart."

This seemed to surprise her. She looked up into Kasen's eyes, and he could have sworn she was about to cry. "I've never had a man love me like that. I want that kind of love."

"I know you do," Kasen answered, speaking calmly because he felt like he was close to getting her to open up with the truth if he could just avoid scaring her away. "I'm sure you can find the right man, and I will help you do that. You can come for as many sessions as you want. Every day of the week, if need be. But first I need you to tell me what you know about Raine."

Patrice looked at him silently for so long that Kasen was scared she was not going to speak again. Finally, she started explaining.

"She was with a dark-skinned brotha at a gas station," Patrice said. "He smiled at me, so you know me with my sex addiction, I approached him. I didn't know he had a woman in the car until I gave him my phone number. That's when she jumped out."

Kasen frowned, wondering who was the man she was with. Was that who she had run away with?

"Raine tried to step to me, yelling about, 'stay away from my man!' She's a little crazy, you know. But I'm no wallflower myself, so when she reached out to slap me, I grabbed that bitch and started swinging."

As he listened to her story, he was having a hard time imagining Raine reacting with such violence. The Raine he knew was way too classy to get into it in a gas station parking lot like that.

"Anyway," Patrice continued, "her dude grabbed her up pretty quick, threw her back in the car, and they were out. When I looked down, I saw the bracelet on the ground. I took it and I kept it. That's it. End of story. You happy now?" she said, sounding sassy now.

Kasen may have been a fool at times, but he wasn't a damn fool. "Bullshit!" he yelled in her face. "Stop lying and tell me where you got the damn bracelet from! You came to my office for a reason. Tell me what the hell is going on!"

Patrice leaned back to put a few inches between them. "I just told you," she said nervously.

"Uh-uh." Kasen shook his head. "It's bullshit and you know it. At what point during that fight did she stop and tell you her name?"

"What? Now I think you might be crazy, Doc."

"You had a fight at a gas station with a random woman and somehow you know her name is Raine, and somehow you happen to show up in my office right around the time Raine disappears? Ain't that much coincidence in the world."

Suddenly, Patrice was out of her chair, taking a totally different approach to this situation. Now she wasn't cowering and afraid of Kasen. Before Kasen even knew what was happening, she had popped her breasts out of the top of her tight shirt and pressed herself up against his body. She hiked up her skirt and yanked her panties to the side. Her behavior was so sudden and so bizarre that it took Kasen a minute to respond.

"Patrice—" he started, reaching around her back to try to pull her skirt back down. She wiggled just the right way so that instead of grabbing the hem of her skirt, he grabbed her ass cheeks.

"Mmm, that's it," she moaned.

"Oh my God!" Voncile's voice suddenly came from the doorway.

Kasen froze when he heard her. His head was spinning. How could Voncile show up right now, of all times? Deep down he knew that all of these strange coincidences were somehow related, but he couldn't wrap his mind around what that connection was.

In spite of Voncile's presence, Patrice kept doing her thing, grinding on him and grabbing his hand to put it on her breasts. "Squeeze my titties," she commanded.

"What the hell is going on here?" Voncile shouted as she rushed into the room, shoving Patrice out of the way.

For someone who claimed she was no wall-flower, Patrice sure backed away from Voncile in a hurry. She looked scared as she put her clothes back in place to cover herself up. Without another word, she jetted out of the room.

"How could you do this to me, Kasen?" Voncile said, standing in front of him sobbing. "I'm pregnant with your child and this is how you treat me? Really?"

Kasen was so overwhelmed by all of this that he couldn't even speak. He felt like he was in some crazy alternate universe.

"So now you're fucking your patients, huh, Kasen?" Voncile said with a twitching eye. "I thought you said you needed to be alone for a while."

Kasen dropped down into the chair with so much on his mind: Raine, Omar, Voncile, the bracelet, and now this situation with Patrice and the bracelet. He didn't have enough energy to explain to Voncile about what she had just walked in on. There was no question that he had made some really bad mistakes lately, but he just didn't understand: Why was this happening to him? He felt cursed.

"I don't want to talk about this right now. Please leave, Voncile. I will contact you later."

"No! I want some answers now!" she screamed at full volume. "How long have you been fucking her? Don't sit there being a coward! Why don't you get it all out in the open? Is she the only patient you've been screwing around with, or are there more?"

Voncile's shrill voice gave Kasen a severe headache. There seemed to be no end to her madness, so he shot up from the chair and grabbed his jacket, brushing past Voncile as he exited the office. She followed behind him, ranting and raving.

"Where is the got-damn respect for the mother of your unborn child? I deserve to have some answers, Kasen!"

He headed to the stairs, and she stayed on his heels, refusing to give up. "Kasen, do you hear me talking to you? Why are you ignoring me? What in God's name did I do to you to deserve this?"

Kasen got in his car, slamming the door behind him. Through the windshield, he could see Voncile's tear-stained face. She looked like a madwoman with her hair all over the place, snot running from her nose, and mascara smudged under her eyes. Too caught up in his own pain, he didn't feel an ounce of sympathy for her. He revved the engine then sped off, swerving to avoid hitting her as she lunged toward the car. As he exited the parking lot, he let out a roar to release some of his pent-up rage.

Chapter 21

Patrice raced home in a rage. She had actually been enjoying the game she was playing, pretending to be a sex addict for Kasen, until he saw the bracelet on her wrist. Then he flipped so completely that for a minute she feared for her safety.

He had recognized the bracelet right away, and although Patrice was a good liar, there was no denying it once he flipped it over and saw the engraving. For a minute she thought that she'd be able to calm him down once she hiked up her skirt. No man had ever been able to resist her pussy before. She had actually been a little turned on herself, considering Kasen was so fucking hot. Patrice thought she was going to kill two birds with one stone—calm him down and also get some real good dick—until Voncile busted into the room.

That was another thing she had to worry about now. The look in Voncile's eyes told her there was going to be some major fallout. When it came to Kasen, Voncile was crazy jealous, and she had made it explicitly clear that Kasen was off limits. Patrice was supposed to distract Kasen with her little sex addict act, but when it came to actual physical contact, Patrice was to keep her hands to herself. Now she had crossed that boundary, and there would be hell to pay the next time she saw Voncile.

She pounded the steering wheel in frustration. This was all Raine's fault. She had probably known all along that Kasen would recognize the bracelet; that was why she insisted that Patrice should wear it. That bitch had set her up, and now Patrice was going to make sure she paid the price for it.

Raine was asleep in the bed, dreaming that she was safe in her own home, when Patrice rushed into the room and snatched the covers off of her.

"Get up!" Patrice yelled, shaking the bed violently. "Why did you do it, bitch?"

"What do you mean?" she asked. "What did I do?"

"That stupid bracelet. Kasen saw it and almost broke my arm trying to get it off. You knew he would do something like that."

Raine looked at her with wide, frightened eyes. She had just started to develop a bond with Patrice, and this could ruin everything. She shook her head vigorously. "No, I didn't. I wouldn't do that to you, Patrice."

"I should beat your ass for putting me in a predicament like that."

Raine's hands flew protectively to her belly. "Please don't. My baby—"

Patrice shoved Raine's shoulder hard, and Raine scooted back on the bed to try to put some distance between them.

"You should have thought of your baby before you started playing games!" Patrice yelled at her. "Now I'm gonna teach you a lesson. You had it so good over here with me, but now you ain't getting no food until I feel good and damn ready to feed you again. And who knows? It might be a week before I feel like it."

"Patrice, I swear I didn't set you up. Think about it. How could I have known that the bracelet would cause you any trouble? You never told me you were going to see Kasen. Remember? You just said you were going to an appointment-slash-date."

That caused Patrice to stop ranting for a minute. She had a puzzled look on her face, like she was thinking through what Raine had just said. Raine could tell she had struck a nerve, and there was still hope that she could talk her way out of this. That hope was smashed when Voncile came rushing into the house and ran up the stairs.

"Patrice!" she screamed, swooping into the room. "What the fuck did I tell you about Kasen? He is mine, mine, mine! And then I walk in and find you grinding your pussy all over him and his hands all over your ass? Bitch, you know that was against the rules."

Raine tried to wrap her head around what she was hearing. Not only had Kasen slept with Voncile, but now he was having sex with Patrice too. What had happened to the man she loved?

"No, it's not what you think," Patrice protested. "I was just trying to distract him, and words alone weren't doing it. I hate to break it to you, Voncile, but that guy is still hung up on Raine. You should have seen the way he flipped out over seeing her bracelet on my wrist."

Voncile narrowed her eyes as she looked down at Patrice's wrist. "You wore her bracelet to Kasen's office? What the fuck were you thinking?" she yelled. "I always knew you weren't too bright, but I had no idea you were straight up stupid."

"Don't call me stupid," Patrice hissed at her. "Last person who did that got her ass beat good."

Voncile rolled her eyes. "Oh, please. Your ass didn't even finish tenth grade and now you want me to tell you you're a fuckin' genius or something?" She laughed in Patrice's face. "You know what? You can forget about the rest of the money I owe you. You couldn't follow the rules of the job, so there's no reason for me to pay your stupid ass."

Patrice lunged at her. "I told you not to call me stupid!"

Raine watched as Patrice's body made impact against Voncile's and they crashed to the ground. They rolled around on the floor, pulling hair, scratching and clawing at each other's eyes, tearing clothes, and basically trying to cripple each other. Voncile finally got the upper hand, and she sat on top of Patrice's chest, panting and sweating as she looked down at her.

"Don't you ever try me like that again," she said through gritted teeth. "'Cause I swear the next time I won't let you live." She raised her fist high above her head, crashing it down on Patrice's face. Patrice was knocked out cold.

"That was for trying to fuck my man, you stupid ho." With that, Voncile pulled herself up from the floor and stumbled out of the room. Raine didn't dare move until she heard the front door open and then close.

"Patrice," she called out quietly, "are you okay?"

Patrice regained consciousness and groaned in pain as she rolled over and then stood up. She walked, hunched over, to the bed and plopped down on the edge.

Raine kept her distance, but she wasn't really scared. Patrice was much too weak to hurt her now. Even so, she still didn't want to be on her bad side.

"I'm really sorry that just happened to you," she said. "I don't know what happened in Kasen's office today, but Voncile had no right to go off on you like that. She is not your friend, and I hope you understand that by now."

Patrice turned her bruised and bloodied face to look at Raine. "Oh, you don't have to worry about her. I got something for her ass that'll turn her world upside down."

"What are you going to do?" Raine asked, hoping Patrice didn't think she was being too bold.

"I don't know, but that bitch is gonna be sorry she ever put her hands on me."

Chapter 22

Kasen put the key in the door, entering the house where he grew up.

"Ma!" he called out. "You in here? It's me, your handsome son!"

A moment later, his mother came down the stairs, her hair in pink rollers and a smile on her face. "Why are you down here yelling?" she said lightheartedly.

"Aw, Ma, you're not happy to see me?" he joked.

She laughed and opened her arms wide, giving him a tight squeeze. "You know I'm always happy to see you, baby."

He gave her a kiss on the top of her head, then turned to head into the kitchen. "I'm going to get a beer. You want one?" he asked.

"No, thanks," she said as she entered the kitchen behind him.

"Where's Pop?" Kasen asked.

She rolled her eyes. "Chile, who knows? Probably on vacation somewhere with one of his hoes. I haven't spoken to him in a few days. All I can do is pray for him and hope that he's okay."

Kasen's parents were still married, but their union was anything but healthy. Lately, they'd been talking about going their separate ways, mostly because his mother was finally tired of her husband's cheating, which had been going on for years. Kasen didn't agree with his father's behavior, but he loved both of them, so he tried to stay out of it as best he could. He had, however, requested that the two of them agree to go to counseling to see if their marriage was worth saving. His parents were stubborn, though, and neither one of them had made an appointment yet. They might have been proud that their son was a therapist, but that didn't mean they believed in therapy for themselves.

"I'm sorry to hear that, Ma," he said as he took a seat at the kitchen table and cracked open his beer.

She waved away his concern. "Don't you worry about us," she told him. "Now tell me what's going on with you. Something is wrong. I can see it all over your face."

Kasen had always had a tight bond with his mother, so he wasn't surprised that she sensed his mood right away. They might not talk every day like some mothers and sons, but sometimes she could read him so well it felt like she was inside his head.

"There's a lot going on, Ma."

"I know there is. You got lines in your forehead I ain't never seen before. Now why don't you tell me what's wrong?"

Kasen took a long swig of beer and then launched into his story, starting from the day he proposed to Raine and ending with the scene in his office yesterday with Patrice and Voncile.

"Son, you weren't kidding when you said there's a lot going on. Something definitely ain't right, starting with this Voncile woman. Whatever you do, you make sure you get a paternity test the second she pushes out that baby. I never did trust that heifer from the first time I met her in your office. She always gave me the heebie-jeebies."

Kasen was surprised. "You never told me that. Most of my patients really like her."

"Well, I ain't most of your patients," she replied. "I got a sixth sense around certain people, and she just always rubbed me the wrong way. Same way your friend Omar does."

"Him too? Ma, how come you never said anything about either of them?"

"You are a grown man—and a therapist to boot. I figured when it was the right time for you to know, you would notice it on your own."

Kasen shook his head. He sure as hell wished he'd noticed it before his whole world fell apart the way it had. "What about Raine? Don't tell me you had bad vibes about her too."

"No, not Raine. She's sweet, and you two are good together. Matter of fact, I wish that she was the one pregnant with your child right now. I'll tell you what, though. My sense is telling me that she's not the kind of person to just walk away from your relationship like that. Something's not right, Kasen."

He dropped his head into his hands. "I know, Ma, but I can't for the life of me figure out what is really going on here."

"Hmph. Maybe you should start with your shady friend Omar. You need to pin him down to get the truth about him and that slut Voncile. I'm gonna get down on my knees and pray that the baby she's carrying is his and not yours."

"Can't say I disagree with you on that one," Kasen said, downing the rest of his beer.

While it hadn't solved all of his problems, Kasen's talk with his mother had made him feel a little better. At least his head was a little clearer and he could think straight again. He had to come up with a plan to get to the bottom of this, and he would start by going to Omar's house again. It was time for the two of them to have a showdown. He was sure Omar had information—good or bad—that would help him start putting this puzzle together.

Just like last time, he got no answer when he knocked on the door, so he picked up the spare key and let himself in again. This time, the place was not such a wreck. The dishes had been cleaned and the place smelled a hell of a lot better. Omar's bed looked like it had been slept in, so at least Kasen knew he'd been there some time recently.

He wrote a note, short and simple: *Call me ASAP. We need to talk.*

After Kasen left Omar's place, he took the hour's drive to Voncile's house. Maybe by now she had calmed down enough that they could talk like rational adults. He needed her to understand that the scene she had witnessed in his office was not what she thought it was. Even if they weren't going to be a couple, he wanted to keep the line of communication open with Voncile in case the baby did turn out to be his. He didn't want her to think he was screwing his patients, because her jealousy was off the charts.

If she became a vengeful baby momma she might try to report his conduct to the medical board unless he set her straight real soon.

Kasen knocked on her door but got no answer. He rang the bell and still got no answer.

"If you're in there, Voncile, please open the door. We really need to talk."

Nothing. Instead of leaving, he walked around to the back of the house. With all the strange things that had been going on lately, he was feeling desperate for answers, whether or not Voncile was there to give them. He checked the back door, which was locked, and then started trying the windows. To his surprise, he found one that was unlocked, so he slid it up as high as it would go, and climbed inside.

Before he knew it, he was standing in her kitchen. To be honest, something about the whole damn house felt creepy to Kasen, and it only became more so when he spotted the scissors on the counter and shreds of paper on the floor, leading to the trash can. Peeking inside the can, he soon realized that Voncile had cut up many photos of him. He didn't even know why she had that many pictures, but there were enough to concern him. What the hell was going on? First he found her naked photos in Omar's house, and now his photos were showing up in Voncile's house.

Curious about what other unexpected things he might find, Kasen roamed around the house. Voncile was a very tidy woman, and unlike the shredded photos in the kitchen, everything else seemed to be organized and in the right place.

He climbed the stairs then entered the bedroom to his right. It was empty, but Voncile had started to paint the room a soft blue. Obviously that was going to be the baby's room, and Kasen figured that Voncile must have wanted a boy. For a few seconds, the thought of having a son crept into his mind. He actually relished the idea of having a boy to raise, and he wondered if he would ever be able to make peace with Voncile so that he could have a relationship with his son—if the child was his.

Shaking the thoughts from his head, he closed the door and went on to the next bedroom. That room was empty too, and it was also dark and stuffy. He realized that the reason for the stifling air was that there was no window in this room. An eerie feeling came over him as he entered this room. He was drawn to the corner, where he noticed lots of scratches in the paint and dents in the wall. Kasen squatted down to get a closer look and felt the hair on the back of his neck raise up when he saw what was scratched into the wall: *HELP*.

He backed out of that room in a hurry and closed the door. Heading back down the stairs, his mind raced with questions. Who had scratched that word into the wall? Why did someone need help? Desperate to find any kind of answer to this mystery that felt like it kept growing deeper, he went to the one place he hadn't yet checked in the house: the basement.

It looked pretty dark and uninviting down there, but Kasen moved forward anyway. He pulled the string to light the single bulb and walked slowly down the stairs. There was an old freezer and refrigerator in the corner, a wooden work bench in the center, and a few clothes hanging on a rack near a washer and dryer. It looked like a pretty typical basement to him. He walked over to the cedar closet and pulled open the door. Inside, he found only a pile of rope and a tray like the kind someone would use to serve breakfast in bed. That was an odd thing to keep in a basically empty basement, he thought.

Turning around to leave, Kasen looked down and saw something metallic sticking out from under the washing machine. *Is that what I think it is?* he wondered. Bending down to pick it up, he confirmed that it was in fact an iPhone. He pressed the button, but the screen stayed black.

Without hesitation, he slipped the phone into his pocket and ran back up the basement stairs. He'd been in this creepy-ass house long enough, and he wanted to get out before Voncile came home.

When he got into his car, he plugged the iPhone into his charger then drove away from the house with a cold sweat running down his back. He had a bad, bad feeling about all of this.

After a few miles, he looked down at the phone and pressed the button to see if it was charging. The screen came on, and he nearly drove off the road. It was Omar's phone. For a second he felt great relief because he thought the phone would help him put all the pieces together. He pulled over to the side of the road thinking he would check Omar's call history for some clues, but all he got was a screen telling him to enter the passcode. Without Omar's code, the phone was useless to him. Kasen was so upset that he threw the phone, cracking the screen and causing it to go black again. He took a deep breath to try to calm himself, because sadly, he could feel that he was losing it.

Chapter 23

A nightmare about Kasen being killed had made Raine wake with a start, and now she was lying on drenched sheets, feeling like she was drowning in her own sweat. Her heart was still racing, but she was relieved to know it was only a dream. In spite of everything, she knew that deep in her heart she still loved Kasen, and she longed to be with him again. A single tear rolled down her face, and like every single day that she had been there, she fantasized that she would find a way to escape.

Patrice hadn't been in to see her all afternoon. The last time Raine saw her was at breakfast, when she had listened to her rant for at least an hour about the brutal fight between her and Voncile.

"I agree. She was totally wrong for coming at you like that," Raine had told her more than once, understanding that it was in her best interests to stay on Patrice's good side. By the time Patrice left the room, she had calmed down a little, but she was still distracted enough that she forgot to tie Raine to the bed again.

Raine was relieved to be free to roam around the room, but, of course, she still wanted desperately to escape this house. As she got up off the damp sheets, she stared at the door, wondering what was on the other side and what it would take for her to get out of there.

Nearly thirty minutes later, Patrice opened the door, carrying a tray in her hand. The expression on her face let Raine know that Patrice was still agitated.

"I wish you would cheer up," she said, her voice full of fake concern, as Patrice moved closer to the bed. "And before you chew me out, my hands are untied because you forgot to tie them up earlier. I don't want you to think I somehow cut the ropes."

Patrice shrugged as she looked at Raine's free hands. "Whatever. Just eat your food and I'll deal with the ropes later."

She placed the tray on Raine's lap. Raine looked down at the juicy pork chops, covered with mashed potatoes and gravy.

"This looks delicious," she said, and she really meant it. She hadn't realized how hungry she was until the delicious food was in front of her.

"Thank you so much. I appreciate your kindness. One of these days, you should let me cook for you."

Raine was attempting to make small talk, just to keep Patrice in the room with her. So far, her plan was working. Patrice stood with her back against the dresser, her arms folded in front of her.

"I might just let you cook for me someday. Lord knows I'm getting tired of being ordered around by people—especially by someone who doesn't give two cents about me."

"I assume you're talking about Voncile," Raine said.

Patrice grunted in disgust like she couldn't even stand to hear the name.

"Have you heard from her?"

"No. I've called that bitch four times today, and she won't answer her phone. I'm not gonna kiss her ass much longer. If she doesn't respond today, things are gonna change around here. She can't disrespect me and then expect to use my place as a dumping ground for her little scheme."

Raine tried to swallow a mouthful of food past the lump that formed in her throat. Was Patrice saying that she would send her back to

Voncile's house? Raine didn't know if she could survive being locked up in that empty room again, always fearing when Voncile might come in to abuse her.

"You know, it's been a long time since I had a pork chop this good. Even my mother couldn't do it like this," Raine said, trying to change the subject to calm Patrice down.

It didn't work. Patrice was stuck on only one topic. "I don't know why I let her treat me like this. She's not really my friend. A friend wouldn't do half of the things she's done to me over the years."

Raine decided that since Patrice wasn't going to drop it, she'd better continue to support her. It was risky, because if Patrice got mad enough, she might send Raine back to Voncile's; but maybe there was another option. Maybe Raine could convince her that the best revenge would be to let her go.

"Well, you sure seem like a good friend and a good person," she told Patrice, heaping on the false flattery.

"Damn right I am. And I used to think Voncile was too, but ever since she got with Kasen, she acts like she's better than everyone," Patrice said.

"I thought you said they were having problems."

Patrice rolled her eyes. "Yeah, things aren't going the way she wants them to, but it just makes her even more jealous and possessive. I mean, shit—She was ready to beat my ass just for rubbing my titties on him."

Raine had no idea what had happened in Kasen's office, nor did she really want to know the details. What she wondered was, who were these sick women who seemed to use their bodies as weapons every chance they got? She tried to ignore her rising disgust for Patrice as she continued sweet-talking her.

"Yeah, it definitely isn't right that she put her hands on you," Raine said, even though she knew damn well that Patrice had lunged at Voncile first. "I can't believe she did that to you, especially since you seem like such a good friend."

"I will make her pay for putting her hands on me, that's for sure. No one makes me bleed and gets away with it."

Raine continued to take smalls bites of the food on her tray as her eyes traveled with Patrice, who had begun pacing the floor, biting her nails, and making weird faces every time she mentioned Voncile's name.

"I'm gonna call her one more time," Patrice announced, stopping her steps and pulling her phone out of her back pocket.

Patrice stood with her back to Raine as she made the call, but it was obvious she had gotten her voice mail again when she started yelling, "Listen, bitch. This is my last time calling you. You need to get over here ASAP and apologize for what you did to me. You also need to give me my money and come see about this heifer and her baby. Play mad all you want, but it will do you no good, because after tonight, the ball will be in my court, and you will not appreciate what I'm going to do."

Raine's heart began pounding as she listened to Patrice's threats. She was starting to feel like Patrice might actually harm her to get back at Voncile. While Patrice continued to scream obscenities into the phone, Raine slowly moved the plate of food off of her dinner tray. She stood up and moved quietly, closing the distance between her and Patrice, who still had her back turned.

Patrice ended her call, mumbling, "If that bitch don't call me back soon and bring me my money, I might just let your ass free. I bet she wouldn't like that."

"Just like you're not going to like this," Raine said, raising the heavy dinner tray over her head.

By the time Patrice turned around, it was too late for her to react. Raine smashed the tray down on her head, and Patrice crumpled to the floor.

"I'm out of here, bitch! Now!" She struck Patrice several more times until she was sure there was no more movement. Raine didn't care if she was dead or just knocked out cold.

She hurdled over Patrice's body and rushed to the door, poking her head out into the hallway. She'd never heard another person in Patrice's house, but she wanted to make sure the place was empty before she ran. With no one in sight, she bolted down the stairs in her bare feet, wearing only a thin T-shirt and a pair of sweat pants with holes in them. She burst through the front door, out into the darkness.

She hadn't felt the fresh air in so long that it caused her to gasp at first. Then she began sucking in deep breaths to enjoy the cool air flowing into her lungs. It tasted like freedom. Under a dark, moonless sky, she made her way quickly down the gravel driveway, which seemed to go on forever. She barely felt the sharp rocks under her feet, as her attention was focused solely on getting to the end of the property and onto the road.

At the end of the driveway, she found a deserted road. She had no idea where she was or which way she should go, so she crouched in the bushes to gather her thoughts. She wanted to cry tears of relief because she was out of that house, but also tears of frustration because now she didn't know where to go. Then she thought of her baby and pulled herself together. She had to keep her head on straight if she was going to figure out a way out of there, preferably before the sun came up. If Patrice was still alive inside, it was only a matter of time before she would wake up and come looking for Raine.

When Raine saw the headlights of a car approaching, she stood up, telling herself "It's now or never."

She stepped out of the bushes and jumped into the road, yelling, "Stop, please! I need help!"

The fearful woman slammed on her brakes to avoid hitting Raine, but then she quickly locked her doors. With wide eyes, she took a good look at Raine, with her messy hair and ripped sweat pants. After only a moment of hesitation, she pressed on the accelerator, swerving her vehicle away from Raine and speeding off.

"Noooo!" Raine shouted after her. "Please, stop! Pleeeeease!"

Another car was coming, so Raine did a repeat, running right in front of the car, waving her arms wildly. The driver hit the brakes, causing his car to skid within inches of her body. Raine pounded her fist on the hood of his car.

"Please, please, help me!" she cried. "I need your help! Don't go, please!"

The male driver sat nervously in his car while he tried to figure out what was going on. He felt horrible that he'd almost hit the poor woman in the street who was yelling for help. As he unbuckled his seat belt to get out and talk to her, another car whizzed by.

The woman in that car screamed at Raine, "Crazy bitch! What in the hell have yo' ass been smoking? You gon' get kilt out here if you don't move!"

Raine rushed up to the man who had gotten out of his car by now. "I'm sorry for jumping in front of your car," she said, pulling on his jacket. "But I really need your help. I . . . I was kidnapped. I need to get to my fiancé and tell him that I'm okay."

The man put his hands gently on her shoulders. "Ma'am, if you were kidnapped, you need to go to the police."

Raine shook her head adamantly. "Please, I'm begging you. I need to go to my fiancé first so he knows I'm okay. He can take me to the police." Raine didn't say it, but she was worried that Voncile might be trying to get to Kasen at that very moment. She wanted to get there to put a stop to Voncile's plot sooner rather than later.

"Okay, if you say so." The man removed his jacket and placed it around Raine's shoulders. He escorted her over to the passenger's side and helped her get in the car.

Raine's whole body quivered as the man drove her away from the place she'd been held captive for so long. She finally felt safe enough to release her pent-up tears. She covered her face with her hands, sobbing like a baby. She was so relieved to be out of that house, but more than anything, she was happy that she would finally see Kasen again.

Chapter 24

Voncile had listened to every single one of Patrice's messages. She was livid with Patrice, but after the last message, where Patrice had threatened to throw a monkey wrench in her program, Voncile started to worry. She wasn't prepared for an abrupt change of plans. If she had to apologize to Patrice for beating her ass, so be it. It was important for Voncile to stay on good terms with Patrice, at least until the baby was born.

At this point, she didn't trust Patrice anymore, especially not after she'd seen her throwing herself at Kasen in his office. Voncile hadn't been able to get that scene out of her mind. As far as she was concerned, Patrice was a traitorous bitch trying to steal her man. Once Voncile had gotten what she needed out of her, she would make her pay for her disloyalty.

Thinking angrily about the mess she was in, Voncile swerved in and out of traffic. She was on her way to Patrice's house, driving recklessly.

She hammered the horn when a female driver cut in front of her to get into the left turn lane. Voncile caught up with the woman at the red light and honked the horn to get the ghetto fabulous woman's attention.

She lowered the driver's side window. The woman lowered her window as well.

"You do know that you almost made me tear up my car back there, don't you?"

"Should've, would've, could've. I didn't, so what's the big damn deal?" the woman spat back.

"The big deal is, you weave-wearing bitch, you need to slow down and watch where the hell your ghetto ass going."

The woman laughed and shook her head. "Heifer, you don't know me. I will jump out of this car and beat yo' crazy-looking ass!"

Crazy, Voncile thought. *Did she just call me crazy?*

The light turned green and the woman sped away. Voncile decided that if someone wanted to call her crazy, then she would show her just how crazy she could be. She cut off another car and sped up until she was practically on the ghetto chick's bumper. After a short distance, the other driver looked in her mirror and saw that Voncile was tailing her. She stepped on her brakes, almost causing Voncile to hit her car.

"Shit!" Voncile yelled out. "This bitch ain't no joke!" She let her foot off the gas a little to fall back so she wasn't so close to the other car.

When she saw that they were approaching another red light, Voncile realized she had a decision to make. She could either jump out of her car and beat this woman's ass—and risk being arrested for it—or she could carry herself over to Patrice's and take care of the drama over there. Deciding that her relationship with Kasen was the most important thing, she knew she had to go check on Patrice and Raine.

At the traffic light, she pulled up next to the other car, held up her middle finger, and screamed, "It's your lucky day, bitch! But if I ever see you again, trust that I will whip your ass!" With that, she stepped on the gas and ran through the red light, continuing on her way to Patrice's house.

As she drove, Voncile snatched her cell phone from the seat, trying to keep her eyes on the road as she called Patrice. She was frustrated when her voice mail came on. Putting as much sugar in her voice as her foul mood would allow, Voncile left a message.

"Girl, where are you? I hope you're not still mad at me, are you? I'm on my way there to give you your money, okay? Don't be mad. Love ya."

Voncile was willing to say and do anything to keep Patrice on board with her plans. She'd thought about how much damage Patrice could do, and the truth was that Patrice could ruin everything. Voncile needed Raine and that baby to stay healthy, and she needed Patrice to help her with that. She didn't trust herself to keep Raine at her own house anymore. She hated that bitch so much that she knew she was capable of snapping and killing Raine before she even delivered the baby. Now that Kasen thought she was pregnant, Voncile needed that baby like she needed air to breathe.

Minutes later, Voncile drove though the wide gates at Patrice's house, drove down the long driveway, and parked her car. She had managed to calm her rattled nerves, a little, but when Patrice didn't open the door, Voncile caught an attitude. She pounded the door with her fist, rattling the glass panes.

"It's me, Patrice. Come open the godda—" She paused, remembering that she had to play nice so they could soon reconcile their differences. "Open the door, please. We need to talk."

Patrice didn't come to the door, but when Voncile reached for the knob, she discovered that it was unlocked. She would have to talk to Patrice later about being so damn careless.

She walked inside and called out to Patrice but got no answer.

"Yo, where are you? I got your message, and I'm sorry about what happened between us." Voncile stepped through the living room and then checked the kitchen, but Patrice wasn't in either place. The house was still quiet.

Voncile was starting to feel slightly uneasy as she headed up the stairs. "Look. I was just mad, okay? You know I'm gonna give you all of your money. I may even throw in an extra grand because you've done everything I asked of you."

It wasn't until Voncile reached the top stair, when she looked to her right and saw the door to Raine's room wide open, that she really began to panic. Her heart raced as she rushed toward the door. Inside the room, she saw Patrice holding her head, struggling to get off the floor. A stream of dried blood covered the side of her head where there was a nasty gash. She was down on one knee, squinting to look at Voncile through blurred vision.

Voncile let out a scream when she looked over and realized that Raine's bed was empty. "Where did she goooooo? Is she gone?"

Patrice could only moan in response.

Voncile felt the rage bubbling up within her like a volcano about to erupt. The baby Voncile had planned to pass off as hers was gone; that meant someone had to pay. She charged forward, gripping her hands around Patrice's throat.

"How the fuck did you let her get away?"

The gurgling sound Patrice made was an indication that she couldn't speak clearly. Voncile released her tight grip, shoving Patrice back on the floor.

"I can't believe this," Voncile shouted at the top of her lungs. "After all my time and effort, you let her get away!" She stood in the middle of the floor with her fists squeezed so tight that her nails pinched her skin. Her face was bright red, and her eyes flared with the fire that was consuming her soul. Her whole body vibrated as she hollered about the loss of her baby.

"Why did you let him get away from me? You let that bitch take him from me, and I will never get to see him again!"

Patrice was on her hands and knees as she witnessed Voncile become completely unhinged. "I'm sorry," she uttered weakly.

"Sorry?" Voncile said, jerking her head to the side. "A child should always be with his mother, no matter what! You let her get away with my child, so take that sorry and shove it up your ass!" Voncile reached to her left, picking up a heavy ceramic lamp. With gritted teeth, she raised it up high then smashed it in the center of Patrice's forehead.

Blood splattered in every direction as Patrice collapsed to the floor again. Patrice's body lay motionless, but that wasn't enough to satisfy Voncile.

"Take that and go straight to hell, you bitch!" she screamed as she raised the lamp again and bashed it into Patrice's skull repeatedly. Within a few minutes, Patrice's face wasn't even recognizable.

Voncile tossed the lamp aside then wiped her hands on her pants. "How about that?" she said, spitting on Patrice. "You're good now, aren't you?" She rolled her head around on her neck, feeling a little better now that she had released some of her frustration.

"Now let me go find my baby," she said as she darted out the door.

Chapter 25

Kasen was so uneasy about what he'd seen at Voncile's place that he decided to drive to the police station to talk to someone about his concerns. He had tried to tell himself that Voncile was the same person he'd always thought she was when he hired her—a good person—but he couldn't ignore the fact that his friend's phone was in her basement. How did it get there? Then there was the word *HELP* scrawled in that room, the cut-up photographs of him, the general sense of creepiness he got from being in her basement. . . . The list went on and on, until he knew he had no choice but to report it to the police.

Kasen walked into the police station with one hand in his pocket, the other swinging by his side. The hefty white officer behind the counter glanced at the well-dressed black man with jealousy in his eyes. When Kasen approached the counter, the officer held up one finger.

"I'll be with you in a sec." He pointed to several chairs against the wall, where three other people sat waiting. "Have a seat over there."

Kasen cleared his achy throat. "I don't want to be rude, but this is urgent. Is there someone else on duty I can speak to about a missing person?"

The officer stared at Kasen for a few seconds, irritated by the uppity man. "No one gets special treatment around here. Go sit, be a good boy, and I'll call you in a minute."

Kasen wanted to fire back, but he'd been taught for as long as he could remember not to say or do anything to provoke a police officer. Today was no exception, especially since he was in dire need of help, so he obeyed the officer and took a seat in one of the chairs. He watched as the officer did basically nothing, opening and closing drawers until he found a pack of gum, then fumbling around with a stack of papers in front of him that he was obviously pretending to read. Minutes later, he picked up a pen and started tapping it on the counter. Not once did he look Kasen's way.

Finally, Kasen had seen enough. He cleared his throat loudly to get the officer's attention. When the officer raised his head, Kasen pointed to his watch, implying that the clock was ticking. With a smirk on his face, the officer smacked his gum then hollered for another officer to come up front.

"Someone here needs to speak to you," he said. "He says it's important."

The officer who was called upon stepped forward, but when Kasen got up from his chair, he was quickly informed that it was not his turn.

"Not you," the unprofessional officer said. "The one next to you. He's been waiting longer than you."

The young black man next to Kasen stood and whispered, "It's about time." He walked by Kasen, leaving him stunned and aggravated.

"This is ridiculous. I have a real emergency, yet I'm being asked to sit my black ass over there and wait? Either you get somebody out here to talk to me right now, or else I'm going to contact my lawyer and start causing a bigger fucking scene!"

All eyes were on Kasen, who represented well for the out-of-control, angry black man. His loud voice garnered attention from the other officers who had been milling around, pretending as if they were preoccupied too.

"What's going on here?" another officer asked, tugging at his too tight pants. His big belly was on overload, and his hand was inches away from his holster.

Kasen's eyes shifted to the gun, and he knew it would be wise for him to change his tone. He went back to the counter, ignoring the first officer he'd approached, and spoke to fatso in a much more respectful way.

"I apologize for getting loud, but it's imperative that I speak to someone now. My girlfriend is missing. She's just disappeared. I have no idea where she's at."

Kasen's conciliatory tone hadn't moved the officer who had been giving him trouble, but fatso was willing to listen.

"Step around the counter and follow me back to my office. I can create a missing person's report for you."

"Thank you, sir," Kasen said, feeling relieved. He followed the officer into a messy office that smelled like onions and pickles.

"Sorry about the smell. Just had a double cheeseburger, loaded with the works."

"No problem. I'm just glad you're taking the time to do this."

Kasen took a seat in front of the officer's desk. The officer moved several papers and folders aside, then placed one piece of paper in front of him. Then he adjusted himself in the chair that was too small for him, reaching out to shake Kasen's hand.

"My name is Officer Stan Goodson. You are?"

"Dr. Kasen Phillips. Thanks for your time. I really appreciate it."

Officer Goodson nodded then picked up a pen. "So, tell me about this girlfriend. How long has she been missing?"

Kasen was almost embarrassed to say. He knew that the answer to that question was going to disturb the officer.

"She's been gone for several days," he lied.

"Several days? As in three days, a week, two weeks . . . what?"

"Well, see, she left about a month ago because we broke up. Well, technically she broke up with me. She wrote me a letter that said it was over. I haven't seen her since then, but I know something is wrong."

Officer Goodson frowned. "Sounds to me that she doesn't want to be found, especially if she left you a letter calling off the relationship."

"I know that's how it sounds, but she would never just up and disappear like that. She hasn't been answering her phone, and no one at her workplace has seen her."

Officer Goodson wrote something on the paper. "What's her name? And give me a description of her. Is she black, white . . . what? Also, about the letter. Did it imply that another man was involved?"

Strike two, Kasen thought. He really didn't want to mention Raine's race, nor did he want to reveal what was actually in the note. He did, however, know that it was important for him to be truthful.

"Another man was mentioned, but even though the letter said she was leaving me for him, I'm starting to think that wasn't possible. We—"

Officer Goodson put up his hand to interrupt Kasen. He had other things to do; this was a waste of his time. "I know it's hard to let go sometimes, but if a woman doesn't want to be with you, she doesn't want to be with you. Move on, and don't do anything stupid that will put you behind bars for good."

This was not going well at all. Kasen wiped a hand across his sweaty forehead then cleared his throat. "I assure you that that will never happen. I would never do anything to hurt Raine, and I'm only here because I believe she's in danger."

"Do you have proof of that?"

"No, but I have a patient who came in wearing Raine's bracelet. I gave Raine the bracelet as a special gift. I know for a fact that she wouldn't give it to anyone."

"So, your patient had the bracelet? Do you know where she could have gotten it from? Maybe your girlfriend sold it. If she ran away, she could have pawned it."

Kasen took his own advice that he'd often given to his patients: *Count to ten, think of something positive, and calm down.*

"Sir, I'm telling you that she didn't run away. My best friend is also missing, and I found his cell phone in the basement of my secretary's house. I think there's some kind of connection."

Officer Goodson chuckled. "Hell yeah, there is. Your girlfriend took off with your best friend. I can't say how your secretary fits into all of this, but did she say why she may have had his phone?"

"I haven't told her yet that I have it. We're not exactly on the best terms right now," Kasen answered.

Goodson put down the pen and looked directly into Kasen's eyes. "You're not on good terms with her, yet you were in her basement where you found your friend's phone?" He leaned across the desk toward Kasen and eyed him suspiciously. "Would you mind telling me why you were in her house? I don't think you're telling me the whole story here, Dr. Phillips."

Kasen wouldn't be able to maintain his composure much longer. The pitch of his voice went up a notch as he tried to defend himself from the officer's accusation. "Sir, you just don't understand, or maybe you're trying not to comprehend what I'm saying to you. I don't have all of the missing pieces to the puzzle, but I'm sure of one thing: Raine is somewhere in trouble. I need help finding her. Now. Before it's too late."

Officer Goodson stood then tugged on his pants again. "Look, people come in here all the time claiming that their loved ones are missing. Nine times out of ten, that is not the case. Now, your girlfriend may be gone, but from the way it sounds, I think you're getting all worked up for nothing. Nonetheless, I'll pass this information on to one of our detectives. I'll ask him to look into it, and then we can go from there.

He slid a slip of paper across the desk and held a pen out to Kasen. "Write your name, address, and phone number down, and a detective will be in touch with you soon, Dr. Phoenix."

Kasen stood up, refusing to take the pen. "I don't know who the hell Dr. Phoenix is, but maybe you should go see him so he can help you control your cholesterol intake. As for the detective, forget it. You motherfuckers around here aren't interested in helping me, and if something tragic happens to Raine, I'm going to come back in here and drill my foot in all of y'all asses."

Officer Goodson's bushy brows moved inward. "Was that a threat? If so, we don't take those lightly around here. Refrain from using such language or you, sir, will be arrested."

"Good. Maybe my arrest will cause you assholes to utilize those papers y'all been shuffling around. Have a nice day, sir. It is my hope that I won't have to see you again."

Kasen shoved the chair away from him and stormed out the door. The gum-smacking officer was still behind the counter, and now there were more individuals sitting impatiently in the chairs.

"What a damn shame," Kasen said as he walked by the officer on his way out the door.

"What you say, boy? Speak louder. I can't hear you."

It took an enormous amount of Kasen's strength—and good sense—for him to keep it moving. He didn't reply, nor did he bother to turn around. Being in jail would prevent him from continuing to search for Raine. That was his only mission, and there was no way in hell he was going to give up.

Chapter 26

Kasen returned home, still fuming over his visit to the police station. He couldn't believe those assholes. Not only was he pissed that they hadn't taken his report seriously, but they had also treated him with such disrespect that they caused him to step outside his usual calm demeanor. The worst part of it all was that he still needed to speak to a detective somehow, and he had doubts that those cops would even pass the information on. Not sure how to proceed, he put in a call to his attorney.

"I don't care how late it is, just call me back. There's so much that I need to tell you, and I really need your help," was the message he left when he got the attorney's voice mail.

Kasen ended the call, wondering who else he could reach out to. Patrice definitely knew more than she had been willing to admit. Her behavior in his office had been crazy, but she was his only hope at this point, so he decided to call her to see if she would tell him anything else. He went to his home office and checked his online patient files to get her phone number. There were two numbers listed, but after trying to call each one, he discovered that they were both non-working numbers. This just deepened the mystery for him. Who the hell was Patrice really?

Since Voncile handled all patient files, he wondered if she would know why Patrice had provided fake numbers. It didn't really matter, though, because it wasn't like he could call Voncile and ask her. After being in her creepy-ass house, he knew he wouldn't be able to have a normal conversation with her. He wouldn't be able to hold back from asking about Omar's phone, and the way she'd been acting lately, she just might call the cops on him for breaking into her house. The last thing Kasen needed was to be arrested on some bullshit charge while Raine was still missing and probably in need of help.

Kasen couldn't believe the brick walls he'd been running into. He paced the floor, racking his brain for an idea on how to proceed now that everywhere he'd turned wound up being a dead end.

When the doorbell rang, he felt a moment of relief, thinking maybe the fat cop had sent a detective over after all. Then again, what if they were sending someone over to charge him with breaking and entering? He headed to the door nervous, with his stomach in knots. What he saw when he opened the door nearly caused him to collapse from shock.

Raine was standing in front of him with tears rolling down her face, snot dripping from her nose. Her hair was wild and matted, her face appeared swollen, and her clothes were completely disheveled. Her bare feet were so ashy it looked like she had been dancing in flour. She could barely get her dry lips to open, but Kasen didn't care what she looked like or what she had to say. He snatched her into his arms and held her tightly.

"Oh my God. Baby, where have you been?"

Her body trembled as she sobbed against his chest, unable to speak. Kasen softly rubbed her back, comforting her and also feeling comforted himself by her presence. Until now, he had worried that he would never see her again.

He was so caught up in the moment that he hadn't noticed the white man parked in a truck in front of his house, watching the whole scene. Now as Kasen looked at him, the man hurried to brush away a tear. Kasen narrowed his eyes at the man as he lifted Raine away from his chest.

"Who is that man?" he asked, angrily recalling her letter that said she was leaving him for another man. Kasen felt totally confused. He loved Raine with all his heart, but he also hated her for leaving him the way she had.

Raine finally found her voice. "That man saved me. He found me on the side of the road outside the house where I was being held. A woman named Patrice—"

"Patrice?" Kasen shouted.

Raine nodded her head, looking at Kasen through wide, frightened eyes.

His anger scared her, but as Kasen started to put the pieces together, his anger wasn't directed at her. Somewhere in the back of his mind, he was starting to put the pieces together, and his subconscious mind told him that Raine had never left him for another man.

"Tell me how you know Patrice," he said.

"Your secretary Voncile brought me to her house," Raine explained. "Voncile kidnapped me."

Kasen's whole body felt weak, and he had to sit down on the front steps to keep from falling over. He reached out for Raine's hand, and she sat down next to him. With his chest heaving, his heart pounding, and tears in his eyes, he said, "Tell me everything."

As Raine launched into her tragic story about the day she had answered the door at their house to find Kasen's secretary standing there, the white man in the truck drove away. Now it was just Kasen and Raine alone, trying to make sense of the nightmare that had unfolded to disrupt their lives.

"Kidnapped," Kasen said incredulously when Raine finished telling him about how she had let Voncile in, was hit over the head, and later woke up to find herself in Voncile's house. Now he knew for sure who had scratched the word *HELP* into the wall. "I am so sorry this happened to you, baby. I had no idea Voncile was this kind of person."

Now it was Raine's turn to be angry. She looked at him with fire in her eyes. "Yeah, I guess you were too busy fucking her to notice what kind of a person she was."

Kasen opened his mouth to speak, but she shut him down before he even got started.

"Don't you dare try to deny it, Kasen. She set up a TV in the room where I was being held. I had to watch you having sex with her." Once the words left her mouth, she was sobbing again because the memory brought back the pain of the betrayal.

Kasen wiped away a tear as it rolled down his cheek. "You're right. I did it, and I am so sorry for that. I know I made the wrong choice, but I thought you were gone with another man, and I was hurting. I was devastated to think that you left me on the same day that I proposed to you."

"Why would you think that?" she asked.

"The letter that I found at the house," he answered. "You said there was another man."

She shook her head wildly. "There was no other man, and I didn't write any letter. I just told you what happened that day. Voncile was here."

As she said the words, everything suddenly made sense to him. "Oh my God. It's all my fault. She knew I was going to propose to you that day—I told her I was going to buy a ring—and that's why she kidnapped you. Now it's so obvious that Voncile wrote that letter. Why didn't I see all of the signs sooner?" he said, berating himself.

He reached out to hold Raine, feeling relieved when she didn't push him away. They had been through the worst possible nightmare, and he had betrayed her by sleeping with Voncile, but she wasn't rejecting him. Kasen had faith that their relationship could be healed.

"Come on," he said. "Let's get you inside and clean you up, and then you can tell me the rest of the story. We will have to decide what to do about Voncile, but first I want to make sure you're okay physically."

Raine leaned on Kasen as he helped her into the house and filled the bath with soothing jasmine-scented oils for her. As she sat in the tub and he washed her back, Raine started crying again.

"I thought you were never going to come for us, Kasen. I was so scared."

"Us? Who else was with you?" he asked, then deciding he knew what she meant, he added, "Was Omar there with you? I found his phone in Voncile's basement."

This caused Raine to sob loudly. Kasen didn't know what he'd said that upset her so much, until she finally calmed down enough to say, "Omar is dead. She killed him and threw his body down the basement stairs."

Kasen felt like someone had just punched him in the gut. His body started shaking as he came to the realization that if Voncile was capable of killing Omar, then she most likely would have killed Raine, too, if she hadn't escaped.

"Baby, we have to call the police," he said, certain that they would have to listen to him now.

She nodded sadly, still crying profusely.

"Come on. Let me help you out of the bath," he said.

As Raine stood up, she put a protective hand over her belly, and that was the first time Kasen noticed that her body had changed. Her once perfectly flat stomach now had a small bump growing.

He looked into Raine's eyes. "Baby, are you—"

His question was interrupted by the sound of someone pounding at the door.

Chapter 27

Kasen and Raine looked at each other, both of them knowing in their hearts that whoever was pounding on the door like that wasn't there for a friendly visit. Although neither one said it, they both had the same idea of who it might be.

"Stay right here," Kasen said, handing Raine a robe. "If anything happens, call the cops."

Raine put on the robe and nodded her head nervously. "Please be careful," she said.

Kasen walked to the door with every fiber of his being on high alert. Just as he had expected, he pulled open the door and saw Voncile, looking wild. Her clothes were dotted with specks of blood, her hair stuck out in twenty different directions, and her eyes were fire red.

There was no mistaking the anger in Kasen's expression, but she still tried to act as if everything was normal. "Hi, baby," she said with a crazy-looking smile. "We need to talk."

"The only things we need to talk about are you kidnapping Raine and killing Omar."

Her smile vanished as she eased her hand into her pocket. Before Kasen could react, she had pulled out a gun and was aiming at him. She spoke through gritted teeth. "I suspect that bitch told you all those lies about me, and that must mean her rusty ass is hiding in here. She couldn't wait to get back to you, could she?" She jabbed the gun in his direction and ordered, "Get inside."

Kasen hesitated for a second, not wanting to let her get near Raine with that weapon, but she waved the gun threateningly, screaming, "Now, Kasen, I mean it! I will kill you!"

She left him no choice, so he slowly backed away from the door and into the living room.

Voncile stepped inside, where she immediately spotted Raine standing on the bottom of the stairs in a bathrobe, with her arms folded over her belly. "You bitch," Voncile spat. "I see you already took your clothes off, huh? Just couldn't wait to get back here and fuck my man, could you? I ought to shoot you right now."

Kasen tried to divert her attention back to him. "You don't have to do this, Voncile. Put the gun away and we can sit down and talk. I can get you some help." Inside, he was praying that Raine had called the police before coming down the stairs, but he had no way of being sure. Besides, by the time the cops showed up, Voncile could have already killed both of them. He would have to do something to get them out of this situation.

Voncile screamed at him, waving the gun around wildly. "Shut the hell up! If you really want to help me, tell this ho to get out of here! She'd be dead already if she wasn't pregnant, but that baby is supposed to be for you and me! Everything would have been perfect for us if she had just stayed put at Patrice's house. I could have taken the baby, and then you and I could have raised the child as ours."

Kasen couldn't believe what he was hearing. All this time he thought Voncile was carrying a child he didn't want, and now he was learning that she wasn't pregnant at all, but Raine was. It was almost more than he could comprehend.

She whipped her head around and started yelling at Raine. "You dumb bitch, you done fucked things up for everybody. It's your fault I had to beat Patrice's ass the way I did. It's your fault she's dead, you know."

Raine's hand flew to her mouth in shock, which just made Voncile rant louder.

"Oh, please. Don't try to act all innocent like you cared about my friend," she yelled. "You just want to take away everything that's mine, don't you? First you take Kasen; then you force me to hurt Patrice."

Kasen noticed that the more Voncile was yelling, the more unsteady she seemed to be. Her eyelids were twitching and her hands were shaking. She looked like she was on the verge of totally losing control. If he was going to stop her, now was the time.

He charged at her like a raging bull, slamming his body against hers so that she fell to the ground. The gun flew out of her hands and slid across the floor.

Voncile was caught off guard, but she was no lightweight. She knew where to hurt Kasen— right between his legs. She lifted her leg, kneeing him in the groin.

"Aaaaargh!" he screeched, rolling onto his back as he held his throbbing sac. He had never felt pain so intense.

Voncile took advantage of the vulnerable position he was in, jumping on top of him and pounding his chest wildly with her fists. "How could you do me so wrong, Kasen? Don't you know I love you? That bitch could never love you like I do!"

"That's where you're wrong, bitch." Raine's voice was deadly calm as she stepped up to the two of them with the gun in her hands, steady as can be, pointed at Voncile's head. "I love him. He's mine, and you're about to be dead."

"Raine, no!" Kasen yelled, pushing Voncile off of him and getting up off the floor. He approached Raine carefully and put a hand on her shoulder, but she refused to lower the gun.

"Don't tell me no," Raine said. "She deserves to die for everything she's done."

Voncile sat on the floor, shaking and crying. "Don't let her hurt me, Kasen. Please don't let me die."

Kasen spoke calmly to Raine. "Baby, don't shoot. If you kill her, you will regret it for the rest of your life. You are not that person, Raine. You're not a killer." He was determined to keep talking until he convinced her to put down the gun. As a doctor, he knew what pulling the trigger would do to her. It might feel good in the moment, but she would live with guilt forever, and he wanted to protect her from that.

"I promise she can't hurt you anymore, Raine. Look," he said, stepping carefully over to the coffee table to pick up his cell phone, "I'm going to call the cops. We'll let them take care of her, okay? It's over, Raine. She can't hurt you anymore."

He dialed 911, and Raine listened to him report the incident to the emergency operator. "They're on the way," he said when he hung up.

Raine lowered her gun an inch or two but refused to put it down. She kept it steadily aimed at Voncile. "This bitch better hope they get here soon," she mumbled.

As they waited for the police to arrive, the only sound in the room was Voncile's uncontrollable sobbing.

Epilogue

Kasen was on his way to the hospital after receiving an urgent phone call. As he drove through the rainy night, he thought about how much his life had changed since that dreadful day at his house eight months earlier. If he hadn't acted when he did, Voncile would have killed Raine, and he would be in mourning now. Instead, he was a proud husband, and a loving father to the perfect, healthy baby boy that Raine had delivered. Now the outcome of this trip to the hospital might change their lives yet again.

Parking his car in front of the hospital, Kasen lifted his jacket over his head and rushed inside, heading up to the floor where he'd been told Dr. Whitmore would be waiting for him.

"Glad you came," Dr. Whitmore said when Kasen arrived.

"How is she?" Kasen asked. Ever since the police had arrested Voncile, he had felt like his family was safe. Now he was slightly nervous, knowing that she was not behind bars. What if she escaped from the hospital?

"She's pretty agitated," the doctor answered, which didn't help Kasen's nerves.

"Can't you give her something? She's a sick woman, Doctor. I'm sure you're aware of her history."

Dr. Whitmore looked slightly offended that Kasen was questioning his judgment. "Of course I do, Dr. Phillips. Don't worry. We have dealt with patients in custody before, and we've never had one escape," he joked. Kasen did not laugh, and Dr. Whitmore noticed it. He straightened up his demeanor.

"We'd like to give her stronger psychiatric drugs," he went on to explain, "but we can't do that just yet. As soon as she delivers the baby, we'll be able to give her the appropriate medications."

Kasen thought back to the day, shortly after Voncile's arrest, when he received the news that Voncile was in fact pregnant with his child. At first he didn't want to believe it, but he knew that the timeline added up. She was in the first few weeks of pregnancy, and given the date that Omar had been murdered, Kasen knew the baby couldn't be Omar's. This was no game, and Voncile had finally gotten her wish.

Kasen was devastated, and for a while, he couldn't find it in his heart to tell Raine. She had already been through enough, and he was afraid that the news would prompt her to leave him. When he finally gathered the nerve to tell her, however, she took the news much better than he'd expected. She cried her heart out at first, but several days later, she came to believe that it was a blessing in its own crazy way. After having their son, the doctor had confirmed that the possibility of Raine conceiving another child would be slim. She was crushed. When she found out that Voncile was pregnant, she came up with a solution that had shocked Kasen, but also convinced him once again of what a loving and caring person she truly was.

"It is not that baby's fault that it has a psycho for a mother," she had told him. "We can't let that child go into the system and be passed around from foster home to foster home for the rest of its life. That baby will come home with us, and be raised with our son."

There were still nights when Kasen would lay awake, worrying that the baby might inherit its mother's mental illness, but in the end, he had to come to terms with it. They were doing the right thing by taking the child, and as long as he and

Raine were together, they could handle anything that came their way. Of course, he would still do everything in his power to make sure that Voncile would never see a day outside of prison walls for the rest of her life, for everyone's safety.

"Do you mind if I go in and see her?" Kasen asked Dr. Whitmore.

"Sure. Go right in, but be prepared. She's not—"

"I know. I'll take it easy on her."

Kasen entered the cold room, where Voncile lay in labor, her arms and legs tied to the hospital bed. She had been moaning and groaning, but when she saw Kasen, her moans turned to harsh words.

"You finally decided to show your ass up, huh? I've been lying here for hours, going through all this pain, and you stroll through that door like you don't even give a damn!"

Kasen stood close to the door, keeping his distance. "At least I'm here," he said. "You should be glad about that."

The doctor and nurse in the room glanced at each other, but neither had much to say. They were trying to control Voncile. She kept yanking on the straps, trying to pull them away from the bed. Her legs were wide open, but a sheet covered her bottom half.

"Grrrrrrr," she growled while trying to lift herself from the bed. The doctor pressed her shoulder back, forcing her to lay flat on the bed. "Don't touch me!"

She turned her anger to Kasen. "I hate you. I hate your guts for ruining my life. This is all your fault. I don't know what I did to you to deserve this, but you'd better hope that I never, ever get out of this place—" She paused as another painful contraction hit her. "Ahhhhhhhhhh, shit! Damn, damn, damn! Why did I let him fuck meeeee? Somebody please help me! Please!"

Voncile was foaming at the mouth as she twisted her head from the doctor to the nurse, crying for some kind of relief. She was in enormous pain—pain that she wanted Kasen to feel too. She fixed her evil eyes on him, staring without blinking.

"I'm not intimidated by you, Voncile, and your harsh words mean nothing to me. So you need to relax and focus on your delivery. After you're done, I'm going to make sure you continue to get all the mental help you need. The baby will be just fine, and after I decide what to name her, I'll be sure to let you know." He was trying to remain as professional as possible, trying to think of her as just a sick patient in need of mental health treatment, but after all she had put them through, he couldn't resist adding the words that he knew would hurt her deeply: "I am quite sure that Raine will be a good mother to this child."

Voncile roared like a wild animal in captivity, and Kasen was satisfied that he had struck a nerve. He turned to Dr. Whitmore and said, "I'll be in the waiting room. Please let me know when I can see my baby."

He left the room, and Dr. Whitmore came rushing out behind him. "Dr. Phillips, she is in quite a fragile state. Are you sure you don't want to stay and help her through the delivery?"

Kasen stopped in his tracks and turned around to face the doctor. Without the slightest bit of hesitation, he said, "Nope. Her crazy ass is your problem now."

Also by Carl Weber

Man on the Run

Coming 2017

Kyle

1

"Oh my God! Oh my God!" Lisa moaned repeatedly as she squirmed around in the Jacuzzi. My wife was in the middle of a toe-curling orgasm, with her legs locked around my neck like a pair of vice grips, making sure I didn't go anywhere. Normally this would have had me beating my chest like King Kong, except this time, my head was submerged under water and I was on the verge of blacking out. If I didn't do something soon to stop her, she was going to have a whole lot of explaining to do, to both my kids and to the police. With the understanding that I was not going to break her death grip, I desperately made one last attempt to free myself by lifting her completely out of the water and onto the Jacuzzi's edge. She landed on her ass with a loud thump, her wobbly legs releasing me.

"What the—" I said after taking a moment to fill my lungs with air. But I couldn't be mad, because one look at her shuddering body told me my wife was completely oblivious to the fact that she'd almost drowned me. She blinked her eyes opened, a satisfied grin on her face as her feet dangled in the water.

"Fuck, that was amazing," she whimpered, staring at me as if I'd just performed a magic trick. Words could never express how much I loved to make her happy. "I didn't know you had that in you."

"I may not ever have it in me again," I joked half-seriously, giving her a mischievous grin. She didn't get the joke, so I moved on, pulling her in close. I kissed the wetness from around her neck, and despite the saltiness of her sweat, she tasted sweet to me.

I stared into her eyes and whispered, "I love you."

"I love you too," she murmured, running her hands gently up and down my back. "I can't believe we're in the backyard, in the middle of the day, making love. Do you know how long I've wanted to do something like this?"

I didn't reply, not verbally anyway. We rarely got moments like these, and I wasn't about to waste this one talking. I could show her how much I was enjoying this better than I could tell her, so that's what I did. I pulled her back in the water, spinning her around. Taking a fistful of her hair, I bent her over the Jacuzzi's edge, sliding my dick into her from the rear.

Lisa and I had a good life together. As a matter of fact, we were looking forward to the kids getting out on spring break so we could all go on a cruise to Jamaica. But that was a family thing, where once again we'd have to find stolen moments for ourselves. Right now it was all about us. With one in college around the corner at St. John's and the other a senior in high school, romantic moments like this between the two of us were few and far between. In fact, our sex life was starting to become somewhat uninspiring. It had boiled down to me waiting until the kids were in bed before rolling over and begging her, "Can I get some tonight?"

Finally, one night she sucked her teeth and told me how unromantic and predictable my actions were. Of course, that didn't stop her from giving me some. She knew she had to get it in where it fit in too, but I heard what she was saying loud and clear. Hell, I agreed with what she was saying. It was hard to get quality, unrushed time together for a little lovemaking.

Our time alone had to be strategically placed where we wouldn't get caught or interrupted by the kids. What better time than in the middle of the day when they were at school?

When I entered her, I was gentle at first, but my wife liked it rough when the kids weren't around, so that's exactly what I gave her. I plunged my dick into her hard and deep, and just to make it exciting, I pulled on her hair a little. She squealed with delight, encouraging me to pull it even harder. Lisa had this way of engulfing me with her soft, moist walls, then contracting her muscles into a hard grip that drove me crazy. I tried my best to remain in control, but when she started throwing them hips back at me, working her magic like only she could, I just went for broke, thrusting my dick in her like it might come out the other side.

"That's it, baby. Beat her up. Beat my pussy up! You know how I like it. Yeah, right there. Make her come! Oh, shit!" She encouraged my every thrust with her words.

The more she talked, the faster I stroked. I could tell by the way she tightened her walls around me that she was on the verge of orgasm, which was good, because I was too. I'm not sure why, but when we shared a climactic moment, it was always explosive.

"I love you," I said into her ear as I held her hips, pumping her against the side of the Jacuzzi. "And I damn sure love this pussy."

"You love it, huh? Show me how much you love it. Oh, yes, yes, make me come!" Lisa began moaning and shouting louder. I dipped in and out with finesse until I could feel the pressure of her walls squeezing and contracting like an out-of-control pump. "Oh, shit! Yeah, right there, baby. I'm 'bout to explode," she roared, her entire body shuddering, letting me know that the time was now. "Shit, I'm coming! I want you to come toooo."

In one deep stroke, my back stiffened up like a board, and I let loose inside my wife then collapsed right on top of her.

I'm not sure how long I lay on top of her with my eyes closed, not trying to break our connection, but it felt like eternity—until her body tightened up and I thought I heard applause. You know you've done your thing when your wife starts to applaud your performance.

"Kyle . . . Kyle . . . Kyle!" she repeated, louder each time.

"Yeah, babe." I figured I was probably getting heavy and she wanted me to move, but I did not want to break our connection. I just wanted to lie there and enjoy that feeling for the rest of my life.

"Ahhhhhh, we've got company!" She tried to lift herself and me up, but I was too heavy.

"Company?" I muttered. I still had my head on her shoulder with my eyes closed. "What are you talking about?"

"She's talking about us." The snickering male voice scared the shit out of me.

"What the fuck—" I blinked open my eyes only to come face to face with what looked like a small army of armed men. I felt like I was at the end of *Scarface*, when all those guys came over the wall after Tony Montana. I was just thankful my daughters weren't home.

"Anyone else in the house?" a tall white man asked with authority. He was the only one who wasn't pointing a gun at us, so I could only assume he was in charge. When Lisa and I didn't respond, he snapped, "I said is anyone else in the house?"

His voice rattled me, but it scared the shit out of my wife, who was now in tears. I positioned her behind me as I answered him. "No, no, we're the only ones here. Please, man, if this is about money, you got it. Just don't hurt us." I knew I probably sounded like a scared little bitch, but they had twenty guns, and all I had was a limp dick. At that moment, I would have admitted to being a scared little bitch if it could save the life of my wife and me.

"Nobody's going to hurt or rob you," the man in charge said, showing us a five-star badge. "My name is Deputy Donald Nugent, and we're with the U.S. Marshal Service."

"Marshal Service?" Lisa mustered the courage to speak up. I could feel her moving around behind me, trying to use my body to hide her nakedness.

"What do you want?" I looked around at all the men and noticed they were wearing black, with their bulletproof vests clearly marked U.S. Marshal or Police, which most likely meant he was telling the truth.

"Sorry. We didn't mean to scare you. We're just being cautious. First time we ever barged in on anyone in a Jacuzzi. Looks like fun." He chortled then reached down and picked up a towel, tossing it to my wife. "Why don't you folks get dressed?"

He didn't have to tell Lisa twice. She wrapped that towel around herself and scrambled out of the Jacuzzi to retrieve her clothes.

"What is this all about, Deputy?" I asked, angrier now that I knew I wasn't being robbed.

He reached inside his suit jacket and pulled out some official-looking papers. "I think this will explain it, Mr. Richmond. You are Kyle Richmond, aren't you?"

"Yeah, I'm Kyle Richmond." I stepped out of the Jacuzzi, picked up a towel, and wrapped it around myself as he handed me the papers. "What exactly is this?"

"That, Mr. Richmond, is an arrest warrant, along with a warrant to search these premises." His men started to disperse toward the house like they'd practiced his line and their response a thousand times.

"Arrest warrant?" Lisa, who was now half-dressed, squealed. "What are you saying? Are you here to arrest my husband?"

She had said what I was thinking, and I could feel butterflies taking flight in my stomach, despite the fact that I hadn't done anything wrong—other than be a rich black man with a white wife.

"No, Mrs. Richmond, we're actually looking for your husband's friend." Nugent stared at Lisa for a moment then turned his attention to me. "Fourteen hours ago, Jay Crawford escaped from Danbury Federal Correction Facility. You do know Jay Crawford, don't you?" He was asking a question I was sure he already had the answer to.

I looked up at the man, then over at Lisa, and back to him, swallowing hard. "Yes, deputy, I know Jay Crawford very well."

"Good, so why don't you tell me where the hell he is?" the deputy asked, staring at me, stone-faced. "So you and your wife can get back to what you were doing in the Jacuzzi."

Jay

2

I foraged around the outside of the quaint ranch-style house, lifting everything that wasn't nailed down. It had always been my experience, from hanging out with my well-off buddy Kyle, that one out of every five summer home owners left a key hidden somewhere on the property, just in case they had to send a repairman, had a friend coming by, or simply didn't want to take a chance of being locked out when they forgot the master key in their city house two and a half hours away. So far I'd come up empty. I'd been to multiple houses that didn't have an alarm sign in front, and I still hadn't found a key. Not that it mattered. I'd go through a hundred if I had to. You see, breaking out of prison was the easy part; it was staying free in the middle of a manhunt that would prove to be difficult.

Nevertheless, I'd done what most would have thought impossible: I'd escaped from a maximum security prison and was far enough away that I didn't have to worry about dogs being on my heels. Unfortunately, I hadn't slept or eaten in almost two days. I guess I should have thought this whole thing through just a little bit more. Escaping prison was something a man could do on his own. You don't really need anyone to plan an escape if you're truly motivated, which I was. But now that I was out, I realized that I definitely should have considered seeking a little assistance. I hadn't reached out for help because I really wasn't looking to put the few friends I had left in jeopardy—at least not yet, not until I started working on the bigger picture. Besides, it was less of a risk asking folks to help you when you were face to face. You know, when there was no one around to read your mail or eavesdrop on your phone calls and visiting room conversations.

I finally found what I was looking for under a flower pot at the sixth house I checked. Six had always been my favorite number.

"Come to Daddy," I said with a smile, bending over to pick up the dirt-covered key. Once it was in my hand, I headed straight for the front door.

"Fuck!" I exhaled, trying my best to keep it together. I can't even begin to explain my frustration when the key wouldn't fit into the lock. After managing to sneak onto one of the ferries from New London, Connecticut to Orient Point, New York and then finding my way to East Hampton without rousing any suspicion, I had finally found a key, but it didn't work. It was demoralizing.

With a shrug of my shoulders, I walked around to the back door. It was a longshot, but maybe my luck hadn't quite run out yet. When the key slid into the back door lock and I heard it click, my heart wanted to sing *Hallelujah*.

Taking a quick check of my surroundings, I pushed the door open, waiting a full minute to see if some sort of alarm was going to go off before I entered the house, locking the door behind me. The stale odor told me nobody had been there since the fall, which was a good sign, because it probably meant they wouldn't be back until late spring, and it was only March. I went straight for the fridge, where I found nothing of use, only some condiments and salad dressing. The freezer, however, was a different story. I found frozen vegetables, a whole pack of chicken parts, and a small box of Omaha steaks, all of which I removed. It was going to take them a few hours to thaw out, but I was going to eat good that night. Regrettably, I was hungry now, so I microwaved the vegetables, doctoring them with spices I found in the cabinets. I swear until you spend ten years in prison, you never know how good something as simple as Green Giant vegetables can be.

After my stomach was full, I located the master bedroom and went straight to the closet. To remind me that I was caught up in a real-life drama, the clothing belonged to a man who had to be at least half a foot shorter than me, about two sizes smaller, and his feet were just as small. I exited the closet and went for the dresser. I fished around in a couple of drawers until I found something that was workable.

"Well, Jay, old boy, you can't lose with a sweat suit," I said, pulling out the navy blue fleece. Then I went through each room, randomly looking through drawers, closets, and dressers for any loose cash or more appropriate clothing. The only thing I found that would be remotely helpful was an old mayonnaise jar full of change. Not exactly a windfall, but at least it was filled with mostly silver coins, and not all pennies.

By the time I finished ransacking the place, it was dark and I was tired as hell. I made it my business not to turn on any lights, because it would be just my luck someone would be passing by and call the homeowner. I did, however, turn on the TV in the bedroom. Not that it mattered. I'm sure I was asleep within ten minutes.

Wil

3

I let out a long, aggravated sigh as I watched two United States Deputy Marshals walk out of my office. They'd just drilled me for the past hour about my friend Jay, who had apparently escaped from prison. I eased my 290-pound frame back behind my desk and into my chair, waiting until both men disappeared onto the elevator before I picked up my phone. I dialed the only person who could possibly make sense of what the hell the deputies had just told me.

"Wil, what's up?" Kyle, my best friend of more than thirty-five years, answered. There was a tentativeness to his voice that made me think he'd been expecting my call.

"Jay escaped from prison," I told him. I was sitting on the edge of my seat, waiting to hear his reply. Kyle, Jay, our other friend Allen, and I had always been close, more like brothers than friends, but Kyle and Jay had a different kind of bond. I knew this news was going to hit him hard.

There was a slight pause on the line, which spoke volumes. Kyle wasn't normally one to hold back his opinion. "Yeah, I know," he finally responded. "The deputies raided my house about two hours ago. I'm still trying to calm Lisa down from the trauma of having all those men with guns seeing her naked."

"Raided your house? What the fuck is going on?" I shouted. His wife being naked registered, but I didn't want to touch that with a ten-foot pole. I did want to know why they felt the need to raid his house. I mean, couldn't they have stopped by his office like they'd done to me? Or did they know something I didn't?

"Jesus Christ, Kyle. You didn't help him escape, did you?"

"Come on, Wil," he growled angrily. "They raided my house because I'm the only one who has visited Jay regularly. I'm pretty sure I'm the prime suspect to have been his accomplice." There was a hint of annoyance in his tone, and I understood the reason for it. He was sending me on a little bit of a guilt trip.

Kyle had been on my ass for the last year to go see Jay more often, especially since he'd pulled some strings to have him transferred to Danbury, Connecticut, closer to us. I'd gone a few times, but the truth was I hated all the bullshit I had to go through. The guards treated us visitors like we were the damn inmates. I wasn't about to get into that "you don't visit him enough" argument with Kyle again, so I ignored his comment. Besides, we had a much more important issue to discuss at the moment.

"You didn't answer my question, and those deputies who left here made it very clear that they think he had help. So right now, I need to know it wasn't you."

"No, Wil, I didn't help him . . . but I'm not saying I wouldn't if he'd asked," he replied in a dead serious tone that quite frankly scared the shit out of me.

"What the fuck are you saying? That's aiding and abetting a fugitive! They lock people up for shit like that. You could lose your family, your business, and more importantly your freedom behind Jay's bullshit."

"Wil," he said in a low, calm voice. "He's been in prison for ten years, and we both know he's innocent."

"Do we?" I asked skeptically. I wanted to believe Jay was innocent, but I had my doubts.

"What do you mean, do we? Of course we do. He's our best friend, remember? He wouldn't do anything like that."

"Look, Kyle, I'm just saying, none of us know what went on behind those closed doors, but you've seen the evidence. That girl Ashlee was beaten up, there was evidence of vaginal injuries, and she had his semen inside her. Who are we to say she was lying?"

"I can't believe what I'm hearing. Wil, Jay didn't rape that woman. She set him up." His voice rose with his anger.

"If you say so, man." I really didn't want to continue the conversation, and thankfully, I was given an out when I spotted a dark-suited figure headed toward my office."Look, man, my director is headed this way. I'll give you a shout after work."

Malek Johnson, my boss of two years and fifteen years my junior, barely acknowledged my secretary as his short ass walked past her and into my office. Malek was one of those smooth-talking, brown-nosing Negroes who talked a good game to the white boys upstairs so that they thought he was a fucking genius, but he didn't know shit. If it weren't for me and the other department heads saving his ass all the time, he'd have been gone a long time ago.

"Everything all right, Wil? I heard you had a couple of cops come to see you." He lifted an eyebrow in a fake gesture of concern, which made my stomach turn a little. Guess he was on a fishing expedition.

"Yeah, two U.S. Marshals wanted to ask me a few questions about an old high school buddy who escaped from prison yesterday." I laughed, trying my best to keep the mood light, in spite of the seriousness of the situation. Just the fact that I knew someone who had escaped from prison was embarrassing as hell. I swear I could see Malek's smug ass suppressing a smirk. "But it's nothing," I told him. "They just wanted to know if he'd made contact with me."

"And has he?" Malek asked sternly as he settled into the chair across from my desk.

"No, and I don't think he will."

"Good." He nodded, folding his hands in front of him. "Have you taken a look at our stock price today?" I tried to read his facial expression and his body language, but he was impenetrable.

I shook my head. "Not since the merger rumors."

There were a few rumors floating around about a possible merger or a buyout, but I had tried not to pay attention to it. Some type of shift was definitely in the air at the pharmaceutical company, but whether the change would be for good or for worse, I wasn't sure. I just knew I couldn't get side-tracked from what I was supposed to be doing. The best thing for me to do, the best thing for any of us to do, was to just keep doing our jobs and doing them well. That way, if a merger did happen, there was a chance we could remain employed.

"It's no longer rumor," Malek said. "The VP told me about it a week ago, and CNBC reported it today. Stock's up almost ten bucks and climbing. A company guy like you probably made out well on your profit-sharing alone."

"I'm sure I've done all right." I smiled, because he was right. I'd held onto every share I'd been given or bought since the day I walked in the door twenty-five years ago.

"And I'm sure you'll continue to do all right, but there are a few people around here that won't." I wasn't sure what he meant by that, but I was relieved that it seemed the bad news wasn't directed at me. Either way, I didn't want to jinx my apparent good luck, so I kept my mouth shut.

Malek continued, "Wil, I need you to do something for me."

Even though I wanted him to think I was cool, calm, and collected, inside I was starting to become tense. Given the topic we were discussing, I could imagine several things he would ask me to do, and none of them were good.

"Sure, what's up?" I shrugged.

His eyes were cast downward. That was not a good sign. It's never a good thing when a man can't look another man in the eyes. Finally, he made eye contact.

"Like I told you before, the merger is going to happen. At least that's what they are calling it; but ultimately, we're being taken over. It's their CEO who's going to run things, which means his people. Upper management is going crazy trying to look lean so they keep their jobs." He looked out through my glass wall at several employees, the ones that I supervised, seated in their cubicles.

Dear Lord, if this man was in here to do what I thought he was about to do . . .

"What are you trying to say, Malek? Am I out of a job?"

He turned to me and shook his head. "No, but some of your people are going to have to go. I know you've been with the company a while. Some of your employees have been working with you just as long. Which is what makes this so difficult."

I swallowed hard, trying not to throw up. My stomach was doing so many flips.

"I need you to cut thirty percent of your staff."

"What?" I said in shock as I stood to my feet. I'll be honest and admit that a part of me was overjoyed it wasn't me being axed, but to have to deliver bad news to half of my employees—that was asking a lot.

"You can't be serious," I protested. "We barely get things done with the staff we have."

"Well, figure it out, 'cause I'm serious as hell," he replied, his tone all business and no sympathy.

"When do I have to do this?" I was beside myself.

"Tomorrow. Severance packages are being worked up as we speak, but we want all their IDs and computer passwords by tomorrow, end of day." He stood up from his chair. "I'm sorry, Wil. I know it's tough. Hell, it was tough for me just to come in here and ask you to do it, but our hands are tied."

I looked out at my employees. Some of those guys were like family. I'd been to their homes for barbecues, they'd been to mine; I'd gone to lunch with them, and they'd shared some of their personal problems. A couple of them even looked to me as a friend. I couldn't do this to them.

"Malek," I said to my boss as he was headed to the door. "I can't do this." I pointed to the window. "I can't do that to them."

He looked at me with not even a hint of compassion in his eyes. "It's part of your job, Wil, and if you can't do it, then we can find somebody who can, if you know what I mean."

The underlying threat did not go unnoticed. As much as I didn't want to see my team out of work, I had to look out for number one first, so I was quick to say, "If that's what you want me to do, then I'll do it."

The corners of his mouth raised, and then he said, "Thought so."

Allen

4

"I don't understand. I thought he was up for parole. Why would he do something stupid like this?" I asked Kyle, who'd picked me up from the subway and drove me home just to have this conversation. He informed me that one of my best friends, Jay Crawford, had escaped from prison and was on the run with a $20,000 bounty on his head.

"That seems to be the million-dollar question, Al," Kyle replied, pulling up in front of my house. His face was tense, like he was carrying the weight of the world. "I just hope he doesn't do anything stupid and get himself killed."

"Tell me about it." I sighed, genuinely concerned. Jay had always been a wild card, even as a kid. "You, Wil, and Jay are the only family I have left, other than Cassie."

Kyle and I sat in his car silently, each of us lost in thoughts of our fugitive friend, until I reached for the door handle and he grabbed my wrist.

"Hey, there's still a chance the marshals might be contacting you like they did to me and Wil. You be careful. These guys have orders to shoot first and ask questions later." He gave me the sternest of looks.

"I will, but I doubt I'm even on their radar," I told him, and he nodded his agreement. The only reason we could both be so confident was because, unlike him and Wil, I'd never gone to see Jay in prison or spoken to him on the phone. I'd wanted to. Hell, twice I even drove down to North Carolina, where he spent his first three years incarcerated, but I just couldn't bring myself to see the closest person I had to a brother locked up like that. I did, however, give Kyle money to put in his commissary every month and a gift package every holiday, but nothing was ever in my name or official.

"Oh, and Al, if by chance Jay tries to contact you, tell him to stay away from my house and my office if he doesn't want to get caught. Wil's too. They've got people watching us."

I nodded then stepped out of the car, heading up the walkway. I hadn't gone five feet before Kyle beeped his horn, rolling down his window with a goofy grin on his face. "Hey, on a happier note, how are things in paradise?"

"Everything's great. Couldn't be better." I was now grinning too. Kyle and Wil were always teasing me about my eight-month marriage. Cassie and I were the butt of every newlywed joke you could imagine. "Cassie's home. Why don't you come on in? I'll throw a couple of steaks on the grill and we can throw back some cold ones like the old days."

"Wish I could, but Lisa's been on the warpath ever since the marshals showed up at the house. I spend any time away from her and she'll think I'm conspiring with Jay. I'm going to take her and the girls out to the Melting Pot for dinner, see if I can get her off my back. Besides, don't nobody wanna be around you and Cassie with all that over-the-top kissy-face shit y'all be doing," He laughed, joking about how affectionate we were in public.

"What's the matter? You jealous?" I asked with a smirk.

"Damn right I'm jealous." He shook his head, looking disgusted. No man loved his wife more than Kyle loved Lisa, but my friend was an ass man, and no one had an ass like my wife. Fuck, nobody had a body like Cassie, period, that we knew personally. She was one of those women that had really big tits, a tiny waist, and shapely oversized hips that almost looked cartoonish, like Jessica Rabbit. Not to be bragging on the missus, but when she walked in the room, she turned heads—men and women.

"She's still sucking your dick without being prompted, isn't she?" he asked.

"Of course. She loves giving me head."

"Well, brother, you better enjoy that shit while you can, 'cause I'm here to tell you, it's not gonna last forever." There was no hiding the jealousy in his tone. "My wife ain't sucked my dick without being encouraged in fifteen years, unless it was my birthday, our anniversary, or she's pissed me the fuck off real bad."

"Stop hating, Kyle." I laughed.

"I'm not hating, Al. I've been married twenty years. I'm just predicting your future. You're no different than the rest of us, and neither is your wife."

I could hear him laughing as he pulled out of the driveway, and I made my way to the house feeling good about my current situation—at least the sexual part. The rest of it, well, that was something I needed to talk to my wife about.

"Cassie," I called out when I entered the house. I was home early, and I was actually a little surprised she wasn't laid out on the sofa watching

Maury, Steve Wilkos, or Jerry Springer. My wife loved herself some trash TV.

With no sign of her on the first floor, I went directly to our bedroom on the second floor. I entered just as the master bedroom shower stopped. The idea of Cassie being naked behind that door sent half the blood in my body straight to my groin.

I'd met Cassie a little less than four years ago, when she was working at the Library on Liberty Boulevard. She was this exotically beautiful biracial woman who really seemed to have her shit together, not just a pretty face with a dynamite body. I was so impressed that I'd gone to see her almost every day after work, and eventually we started going out for some very expensive dinners. Despite our sixteen-year age difference, she'd won my heart right away, and I pursued her like I'd done for no other woman. Not that she reciprocated my desire. For the first year, she made it very clear we weren't dating, although we did hook up a few times after a late night of partying. For the most part, it was more like we were hanging out and I had to pay. Not that I minded. Just being around her made me feel special; that is, until other guys started showing up and making their presence felt. Some of them were like me, hopelessly in love with the finest woman they'd ever seen, while others were just straight up players after her body.

After a year, I finally worked up the courage to ask her where things were going between us. That's when she gave me the "I love you like a brother" speech and dropped the bomb on my head that she was moving in with some thug from Hollis, Queens. Well, to say I was devastated is an understatement, but that didn't stop me from continuing to visit her at work. What stopped me from seeing her was when her boyfriend's jealousy got out of hand. I tried to ignore him, but eventually an altercation ensued. I would have loved to call it a fight, but he whipped my ass so bad it would have been unfair to him to call it anything other than a massacre. I didn't get in one punch.

Needless to say, that was the last time I saw Cassie, until she showed up at my doorstep two years later, beaten half to death. She wouldn't let me take her to the hospital or call the police. It took me almost two months to nurse her back to health, but she finally recovered, telling everyone she could that I had saved her life. On Valentine's Day of that year, she slipped into my bed, told me she loved me, and then asked me to marry her. I accepted, on one condition: that she stopped working at the Library and went back to school. She reluctantly agreed, and neither of us had regretted that decision—until today.

"Allen." The sound of Cassie's voice, along with the warm jasmine-scented steam flowing out of the bathroom and seducing my nostrils, snapped me out of my memories of our early years.

Cassie stepped out of the bathroom wrapped in an oversized white towel with her head wrapped in another towel. She reached up with her right hand and removed the towel covering her head, shaking out her dark, shoulder-length hair. At that moment, she looked like she could have been on a *Sports Illustrated* photo shoot. Every time I saw my wife, I was still stunned by her exotic beauty, as if I were seeing her for the first time.

"I wasn't expecting you home so early," she said.

"I'm sure you weren't, but I wanted to surprise you."

She took a step into my personal space, kissing me with those succulent lips of hers. She slid her tongue into my mouth, and I could taste mint. As much as I wanted to, I just couldn't resist. I kissed her back, enjoying the sensation for a minute before I pulled back to speak my mind.

"Yeah, I wanted to surprise you the same way I was surprised when I went to take my boss out to lunch this afternoon and my debit card didn't work."

"Oh, shit." Her eyes opened wide as she took a step back, her body language screaming her guilt.

I may have acted like everything was fine for Kyle, but I'd come home to deal with what was becoming a constant problem.

"Allen . . ." she started.

"Yes. *Oh, shit* is right. Pretty fucking embarrassing, huh?" I snapped sarcastically, raising my voice just enough to hold her attention.

If there was one thing I hated, it was confrontation, especially with Cassie because I really did love her. But this time she'd left me no choice.

"So I called the bank to see what the problem was. You know what they told me?" I studied her face, and her expression revealed that she definitely did know. "They told me that I didn't have any money on my card because my beautiful wife—oh, and they mentioned how beautiful you were continually—withdrew five thousand dollars from my checking account."

She started gushing desperately, "Don't be mad at me, baby. I'm sorry. I'm so sorry. I should have called you. Let me make it up to you, please."

Cassie took hold of my wrists, placing them on her hips so the towel she had wrapped around her fell to the ground. My eyes traveled up and down her nakedness, resting on her most distinctive feature.

My wife's smooth, almond-colored body was not just beautiful and sexy; it was a flawless canvas that had appeared on the covers of both *Maxim* and *Ink* magazines because of the bright green serpent tattoo that wrapped around her right leg then made its way up her thigh and across her ass and back, over her left shoulder, stopping on her left breast as the head of a cobra. Her right breast was tattooed with a bright red apple.

I'm not really a tattoo guy; it's just not my thing, but her snake was like nothing I'd ever seen before, and even when I was mad, the damn thing seemed to hypnotize me. I couldn't help but stare as she reached between my legs and began unbuckling my belt.

"No, no, no, I'm not going to let you do this. I know what you're trying to do, and we are not going to deal with this in the bedroom. I'm not going to allow it," I said, forcing myself to resist what my body wanted so badly.

"Not going to allow what?" She laughed, sliding to her knees as she held my erect penis in her soft hands.

"Stop. I mean it, Cassie," I protested weakly, placing my hand on her forehead. My palm barely made contact with her head, communicating just how conflicted I was about really wanting her to stop.

"So what are you saying? You're not going to allow me to suck your dick?" She shook her head at me pitifully, not giving me a chance to react before my penis was completely engulfed in her mouth. At that point, all I could do was let out a moan.

Less than five minutes later, I was laid out on the bed with my pants around my ankles, moaning like a little boy as my wife worked to bring me to orgasm. I opened my eyes and looked down. It just so happened to be the same time Cassie was looking up at me. The sensual look in her eyes as I watched her firecracker red lips molest the head of my dick sent electric shocks throughout my body. How had I ended up with such a stunningly beautiful, bright woman, who was great in bed and great at giving head? It was a question I'd asked myself a million times.

"Oh God." My chest was heaving as I threw my head back and looked up to the heavens. Call it blasphemy if you want, but I had to thank God as my body exploded in pleasure.

"Mmmm," Cassie moaned as she kissed and licked her way up my belly and to my chest. Once she made it past my neck and chin, she pressed her lips against mine, then pulled back and said, "You're not still mad at me, are you?"

Until she brought it up, I'd honestly forgotten that I'd come home to confront her. Cassie's head game was just that good. "I don't know what I am. Why would you take my money?"

"Allen, please, I'm sorry about your lunch, but I didn't take your money. I took our money." She tried to kiss me, but I resisted. "But if it will make things better between us, I'll put every nickel back in the account," she said sadly.

"No." I was so damn frustrated. She made me so weak with almost no effort on her part. "I want you to tell me why you stole my money."

"Stole? Is that what you call it when a wife takes money out of a joint account to try and better herself? Stealing?" She glared at me angrily. It was a look I almost never saw from her. She was usually a pretty agreeable person, which made for a peaceful home. But not now. Now she was pissed. She walked over to the dresser and brought back an envelope. "Here."

"What's this?" I asked, opening the envelope.

"It's a cashier's check for five thousand dollars made out to York College. They have a special program I got accepted to for people like me, who are misplaced in the workforce. I was trying to surprise you. I wasn't going to bring it up until tonight, because I wanted it to be a surprise. I wanted to make you proud. You did say you'd pay for me to go to school and further my education, didn't you?"

"Yeah, I did." My shoulders sagged with regret. I shouldn't have jumped to conclusions.

"Well, don't worry about it. I don't need you to pay for me to go to school. I can get my old job back anytime I want. I thought you were different, Allen." On that note, she walked out of the room, making me feel like a horse's ass. All I could do was jump up with the check in my hand, following after her, begging.

"Baby, baby, please, please! I'm sorry. You can have the money. You can have all my money."